THE GIRLS FROM SANDYCOVE

SIÂN O'GORMAN

Boldwood

First published in Great Britain in 2024 by Boldwood Books Ltd.

Copyright © Siân O'Gorman, 2024

Cover Design by Head Design Ltd

Cover Photography: Shutterstock

The moral right of Siân O'Gorman to be identified as the author of this work has been asserted in accordance with the Copyright, Designs and Patents Act 1988.

A CIP catalogue record for this book is available from the British Library.

Paperback ISBN 978-1-80483-006-2

Hardback ISBN 978-1-80483-005-5

Large Print ISBN 978-1-80483-007-9

Ebook ISBN 978-1-80483-008-6

Kindle ISBN 978-1-80483-009-3

Audio CD ISBN 978-1-80483-000-0

MP3 CD ISBN 978-1-80483-001-7

Digital audio download ISBN 978-1-80483-002-4

Boldwood Books Ltd
23 Bowerdean Street
London SW6 3TN
www.boldwoodbooks.com

All your dreams have led you here...
All those tales you wove...
But loss is just another name for love
Did you really think you'd had enough?
Oh no, because on you go
Don't even stop to breathe
Defiant, brave and free
For this time, it's your time, it's not just you anymore...
I'll bring you everywhere in my heart,
Because where there's you, there's me...

— WHERE THERE'S YOU THERE'S ME ©

O'HARE/FINNEGAN

1

FLORA

It was a beautiful early June morning and Flora had decided that, at thirty-two years old and after five years of marriage to Justin, it was time to talk about having a baby. He'd always said he needed time to establish his accountancy business before they could even think about starting a family, but as he was always going on about new clients or repeat businesses, surely they had reached that point by now?

Meanwhile, Flora had put her own career in the deep freeze while they settled down into his old family home, once his parents had both passed on, close to Sandycove, just outside Dublin, where Flora had also grown up.

When they had met, she had been a textile designer and was on the cusp of heading off to London to take up a master's at a major art college but she fell in love. Justin was so charismatic and fun to be around, so she stayed in Ireland and focused instead on making their life work. Her lovely weekend job as a sales assistant in the haberdashery in Sandycove became her full-time career.

But however much she loved Justin and wanted a child with him, she sometimes wondered if he was just an overgrown baby himself. There was a photograph of Justin as a toddler – the same overly ruffled hair, the same darting look in his eyes as though searching for hidden treats, his big cheeks puffed up, refusing to smile for the camera – which could have been taken last week. Even the clothes were similar – shorts and a polo top were his uniform then and now.

'I'll build the business, you keep us both alive,' he had told her when they had planned their wedding five years earlier. 'And then, when I'm up and running, I'll do the same for you.'

Flora had agreed happily. And as Justin's parents had both so recently deceased, it made sense to move into his old family home, while they established themselves.

'It's all falling into place,' Justin had assured her, 'and when the business is up and running, we'll extend the mortgage and do up the house.'

Once a baby was here, playing in the garden, things would be better, Flora told herself. A wonderful future was just on the horizon. Whatever frustrations she had about her stalled career and questions about how committed Justin actually was to their marriage, and if she was actually happy, could be dealt with once the baby was here.

She was sitting in the garden reading the weekend paper when Justin stood in front of her, blocking the sun with his body, a shadow falling over the table. He held up his phone. 'Five per cent chance of showers,' he said, giving his hair a ruffle with his spare hand. 'Five per cent in Irish weather terms means *alfresco tiempo*. Let's invite the guys for a barbecue.'

'The guys' meant Justin's old school friends and their partners.

Should she mention the baby now or should she wait until tomorrow, risking him being too hung-over to want to talk about starting a family?

He was smiling at her, happy of the promise of a late night, wine and fun. When he was happy, everyone was happy. 'You go and buy the food,' he said, already typing out a group text, 'I'll buy the wine after I've messaged…'

The guys, she mouthed.

'…the guys. Okay with you?'

Flora nodded. The baby would have to wait. She'd talk to him tomorrow.

* * *

On her way to the supermarket, Flora called in to her mother, Patsy, in Sandycove, just down the hill. It was the anniversary of her father's death – a day which meant little to Flora, being so young when he died, but meant everything to Patsy. There were still photographs of Jack, her one true love, on the wall.

Patsy opened the door, smiling when she saw it was Flora. 'Hello, darling,' she said. 'How lovely to see you!'

Patsy's face never failed to light up at the sight of Flora, it had always been just the two of them, and even now they were as close as they ever had been.

Flora put her arms around Patsy and hugged her tightly. 'How are *you*?'

'You remembered…' said her mother.

'Of course I did.' Flora pulled back and smiled. 'Did you go to the grave?'

Patsy nodded. 'Just tidied it up, planted some wildflowers. There were sea pinks and salvia at the garden centre and I thought he'd like them.' She smiled back at Flora and gave a little shrug. 'Time for a cup of tea?'

Flora nodded, following Patsy into the house, and sat down on the bench, at the kitchen table. 'And tell me… the other big news? Did you receive your result from the course?'

Patsy nodded, picking up an envelope from the dresser, and sat down across from Flora.

For more than a quarter of a century, Patsy had been the village's librarian and had also run a small curtain-making business from home, but last September, just as she had retired from the library, she'd embarked on an interior design course at the local further education college. After being permanently terrified for the first few weeks, she had ended up loving every single second of it. Each student was tasked with redesigning an interior of a room or a shop as part of their practical exam and so Patsy had tentatively approached Alison, the owner of a local café in Sandycove, and asked if she would like Patsy to renovate the space. Alison was delighted and even though the budget was minuscule, somehow Patsy had turned it from something unremarkable into a place full of warmth and character. She'd taken old rolls of wallpaper Flora had designed years ago, a light wash of blues and greys which gave the impression of being under the sea, and had papered the back wall. New crockery was handmade by a potter in Bray, new benches came from a Wexford woodturner, and the lights were a mix of fairy lights, paper lampshades and lanterns. She added in a neon pink for the long cushions on the benches and included two little nooks people, according to Alison, fought to sit in. 'Two women almost came to blows the other day because one was keeping a seat in the nook for her friend.'

'Go on,' Flora urged. 'Open it.'

Flora had more faith in Patsy than she had for herself. But that was the way things worked, it was so much easier to cheer on those you loved than apply the same encouragement to yourself.

Patsy pulled open the letter, her eyes squinting while she read. 'We're delighted to inform you...' She looked at Flora. 'Distinction,' she said.

'Distinction?' Flora grabbed Patsy and squeezed her. 'Distinction! My mother, the interior designer!'

'Not really... I mean, it was just a course...'

'What do you mean? The café looks amazing... you're now a *designer*!'

Patsy shook her head. 'I'm not,' she said. 'But *you* are. *You're* the designer.'

Flora pulled a face. 'Not any more,' she said. 'My mojo was lost years ago and anyway... I've got too much of everything else to do.' She glanced at the clock. 'Including the barbecue.'

And she was already reaching for her bag and rushing out the door before Patsy could even begin to ask her what was going on.

* * *

While she was in the supermarket, Flora's phone rang. It was Kate, calling from France. Flora wished she had time for a proper chat, a catch-up to see how life was at the vineyard and to work out a date when Flora could finally go and visit. 'Kate? I'm in the supermarket... we're having a barbecue... I'll call you back later, okay? I just have to pay for something. Everything all right?'

'Everything's fine,' said Kate. 'I'll talk to you soon. Love you.'

'Love you too,' said Flora, feeling that pang of regret she always did when she heard Kate's voice. If they lived in the same place, they wouldn't have to rely on snatched conversations or catch-ups on the phone. They could do all the casual, inconsequential things that friends did – walks, coffees, sharing each other's everyday lives. Kate was too far away, somewhere in rural south-west France, surrounded by vines and sunflower fields. It felt a long way from rainy, green Ireland.

* * *

As the ribs marinated, the wine chilled and the potato salad was liberally mayonnaised, Flora reflected on how proud she was of her mother and how it was now Patsy's moment to shine. Flora had only a vague recollection of her old self, the young woman who designed fabulous and exuberant wallpaper and fabric, the person who cycled to her local printers to order samples of her designs, the one who took on commissions from lovely restaurants in Dublin's city centre and papered whole sections in her beautiful and eye-catching prints, flowers and insects and sea creatures, neon and dark swirls of colour. She had felt invincible, thinking life would always look like this. But somehow, she had lost confidence, lost her way and was now wondering what had happed to that young woman so full of ideas, excitement and promise.

Later, beer cans were discarded, empty wine bottles were strewn on the edges of the patio, plates lay abandoned, cigarettes ground into the edges as though a bacchanalian feast had occurred, rather than a suburban barbecue. It looked more like a student party than a gathering of adults.

'So,' Joanna was saying to Anne-Marie as Flora topped up their wine, 'I told Ciaran I was in dire need of some me-time, and I was in danger of taking out my latent anger on him. All I'm demanding is time for nails, brows and a little hypodermic top-up. He cancelled his golf to let me go.'

Across the garden, beside the barbecue, the men stood holding beer cans and talking about the one topic which engaged them – rugby.

Flora moved along to Sandra and Pamela, married, respectively, to Robert and Fergus. Sandra was thin and tall, with shaggy, highlighted hair which hung around her shoulders and made her look not unlike an Afghan hound, especially with her long face. She always wore white jeans and gold jewellery, the bracelets jangling on her arms like she was a one-man band, and was always heavily fake-tanned.

'I'm surprised,' Sandra said to Flora, 'you still haven't put your stamp on the house. You know, changed the kitchen... it's like a 1980s museum in there. My grandmother had units like that. Nightmare on pine street.' She laughed too loudly as Pamela smiled slightly awkwardly. 'You're so lucky,' went on Sandra, 'getting a free house when the rest of us have mortgages...'

'It wasn't free,' said Flora, 'we *are* paying a mortgage...'

Naturally, being an accountant, Justin took care of their money, finances and investments, but Flora's salary from her job at the haberdashery went towards the mortgage and all their other outgoings. Justin paid a portion into her own account for anything she needed. Every month, she was surprised how little it was. But Justin knew better, didn't he?

'You could at least change the hideous kitchen,' said Sandra. 'And the fake mahogany fireplace in the living room.'

'We're just waiting for the right time to renovate,' said Flora, smiling at her. 'We need to get the business established first. Now, I'm just going to bring out the dessert. Back in a moment.'

In the pine kitchen – which *was* hideous, even though it pained her to agree with Sandra – Flora piled fruit and cream onto meringue and then placed it on a tray, along with plates and cake forks, and carried it to the garden.

She stood for a moment, bracing herself to re-enter the fray. Tomorrow she would talk to Justin. She felt thrilled at the thought. Kate would be godmother, obviously, and she would have to come home for the naming ceremony. Maybe she'd even stay for a while?

There was a shout from the garden. Justin? And then Robert's voice. To Flora's ears, it sounded as though they were arguing.

'Bastard!' That was Robert.

And then Justin: 'Don't touch me!'

The voices were becoming louder and Robert, normally mild-mannered to the point of near-invisibility, was now incomprehensibly ranting. Still holding the pavlova, Flora began speed-walking towards them. The cream was not quite stiff enough and the raspberries, like a landslide, were slowly slipping off the meringue edges as she powered along the path beside the lawn and towards the end of the garden.

And there, under the pergola, beside the smouldering barbecue, Robert was brandishing the barbecue tongs at Justin, shouting, while Justin held up a fork in defence. The guests, so recently animated with drink, now stood dumbfounded, their mouths and eyes wide with horror.

Like two prize fighters, Justin and Robert edged around each other, shouting and jabbing. What on earth had possessed laid-back Robert to start attacking one of his oldest friends?

Flora looked over at Sandra to offer her a smile of solidarity, of friendship, but instead of looking distraught, Sandra seemed entirely the opposite. There was something almost regal about her, like a triumphant queen surveying her army. Flora stared at her for a moment, confused, trying to work out what was going on. And then suddenly, as though drenched by an upturned bucket of iced water, Flora understood everything.

Robert and Justin were fighting over Sandra.

The ground underneath Flora's feet felt uncertain, as though she was unmoored. There was a feeling in her stomach which felt like poison spreading outwards. For a moment, she thought she was going to throw up. In an instant, life as she knew it was gone. The others in the group had also twigged and were darting glances at Flora and Sandra.

Robert now had his hands on the collar of Justin's polo shirt and the two danced for a moment until Robert loosened his grip to try to take a swing at Justin. In retaliation, Justin swung his arm towards Robert, narrowly missing Flora, who jumped backwards, stumbling into the rattan chairs, losing her grip on the pavlova, which leapt onto Sandra, instantly covering her white top and jeans, making one of the women laugh and then immediately stifle it into a shocked gasp.

Flora hovered for a moment, feeling as though she'd been sucked into a vacuum; time suddenly still, her thoughts clear. It was over. Everything. Justin. Her marriage. The house. Her life. The baby. And then, just as suddenly, she was back in that garden, heart pounding, chest thumping, legs weak.

Sandra was shrieking. 'My silk top! It's ruined. I only bought it this morning!'

Pamela was dabbing at Sandra with a napkin, and everyone was talking, pulling the two men apart, while Flora walked into the house and straight upstairs to their bedroom, the sounds of the chaos from the garden following her.

In the surrounds of the old-fashioned 1980s wallpaper with the rose and trellis pattern, the white and gilt beaded built-in wardrobes, the pink and cream swirly carpet, she wondered what to do. She could barely breathe as she tried to make sense of everything.

Outside, the guests were making swift departures. But hearing voices from the kitchen, she realised that Sandra and Robert were still here and she would have to go and face them. Hopefully, she had misunderstood and perhaps her marriage and her life were all salvageable?

In the kitchen, Justin was sitting at the pine table. But Sandra was beside him and her hand was placed on top of his. Flora looked at it for a moment and then realised that she hadn't misunderstood. Not only were Justin and Sandra having an affair, they weren't going to hide it. Facing them, glowering and scowling, was a defeated Robert and in the centre of the table was a bottle of Red Bush, Justin's most expensive whiskey, along with his crystal tumblers – a family heirloom only ever reserved for special occasions. Was this a special occasion?

'I'm so sorry, Flora,' Sandra said, her smile pitying and patronising. 'It shouldn't have happened this way. We wanted...' She glanced at Justin. 'We wanted you and Robert to find out in a less...' – she searched for the word – '...*public* way. Didn't we, babe?'

'Sandra didn't want to upset anyone... did you?' said Justin. 'It's not *ideal* to fall in love with someone else, but it happens. I thought we could all be mature about it.'

Robert had momentarily lifted his head out of his hands. 'Mature? You? That's a laugh. You're the one who painted his genitals blue for Jim's party and you couldn't wash it off. And what about the time you were so drunk you fell asleep in departures and missed my stag weekend?'

'We were younger then,' said Justin. 'I think we have all matured, which is why—'

'And what about when you did a wheelie on the moped in Portugal last summer and ended up in hospital?'

Flora hadn't been on that particular trip to Portugal, which had been sold as a 'guys' golfing week', but she had wondered about why Justin had returned with a broken arm. He'd told her it was a golfing injury. 'I have deeply knitted muscular triceps,' he'd explained, 'my swing is crazily strong. Tiger Woods has the same thing.'

At the time, Flora had found the story incredible but hadn't really investigated, because why would he lie? Perhaps Sandra had been on the trip and the wheelie was done to impress her?

'Come and sit down,' said Sandra, as Flora, feeling even more sick but numb with shock, took the chair next to Robert.

Justin poured her a glass of whiskey. 'Sandra and I have... well... we've fallen in love.'

Sandra nodded, a sad smile on her face, as though she really cared about Flora. 'Hopefully we can survive this and still all be friends...'

'How long?' Flora took a sip of whiskey just to keep her voice steady. It trickled down her throat, like a stream of boiling oil, settling in her stomach and setting fire to her insides. Her nausea immediately lifted. She could understand why people turned to drink at difficult times.

'About a year,' said Sandra, glancing at Justin.

'Last summer,' said Justin. 'In Quinta.'

They'd all gone to Portugal for another trip, to stay in Sandra and Robert's villa.

'We just felt something develop.' Sandra lowered her eyes, looking at Flora through her false lashes.

Beside Flora, Robert was hunched over, his head back in his hands.

'It had always been there,' said Justin. 'A connection. A *platonic* connection.'

'A meeting of minds,' added Sandra.

'And... well, *we've* drifted apart...' said Justin.

'We have?' Flora countered.

Justin nodded. 'Everyone knows homo sapiens are not meant to be with the same person for decades...'

'It hasn't even been one decade,' said Flora. 'It's only been half a decade...'

'My point exactly.'

'So, what are we going to do?' Flora asked, feeling stupid immediately, as though she was giving them all the power. She had to get angry, she knew that. But how?

'Well...' Justin looked at her. 'You can't stay here... it is *my* home, after all.'

'I thought it was *our* home,' said Flora. 'I thought...'

He shook his head, quickly.

'But I live here,' said Flora, incredulous. 'We're married...'

Justin gave a shrug, his face apologetic, but Flora realised trying to talk to drunk people was never a good idea.

'You could stay for tonight,' said Sandra, as though she was being kind and as though she *lived* there. 'I mean, it *is* late...'

Flora looked from Justin to Sandra and back to Justin. 'I think I'll go now,' she said. 'And I'll pick up the rest of my stuff later.'

It was after midnight when Flora cycled down the hill towards Sandycove, to her mother's house, the tears drying on her face in the breeze of the dark, moonlit night. She remembered a night, years ago, she and Kate coming home in the early hours after a school disco, a night just like this one. Except... it was a world away, just as Kate now was. *Wherever you are, Kate, I wish you were here.*

2

PATSY

Flora. It was the first thing she thought of when she heard the quiet, tentative knock. She checked the time on the small clock beside her bed: 12.43 a.m.

'I'm sorry, Mum,' said Flora, in a whisper, when she opened the front door. 'I forgot my key.' Her face was mascara-smudged and blotchy, her mouth quivering and her shoulders sagging. There was the smell of barbecue and complete defeat in the air.

'Oh, darling,' she said, holding out her arms and pulling Flora to her. 'What's happened?'

'Dustbins having gas and air,' Flora said, into her shoulder, crying and muffled.

'What?'

Flora looked up. 'Justin's having an affair...'

Of course he was. The ones who are so concerned with what the rest of the world think of them are the least likely to be concerned with the ones closest to them. Patsy felt anger rise within her, but she kept completely calm, for Flora's sake.

'Come on,' she said, sounding steadier than she felt. Anger wouldn't solve anything and this was a good thing, ultimately.

Flora could get on with her life again, away from that selfish, boring man. 'Let's get you inside...' Patsy closed the front door, the black of the night behind them.

'You don't look surprised,' said Flora.

'I suppose I'm not,' said Patsy. 'I mean there are some men – *most* men – who wouldn't do such a thing in a million years. And then there are others...' She tucked her hand through Flora's arm, guiding her into the kitchen and towards the chair.

As Flora sobbed and tried to explain what had happened, Patsy made them both a camomile tea and tried to piece the story together. As she'd said, she wasn't surprised Justin had done this. He was always going to love himself far more than he was ever going to love Flora and, unfortunately, Flora had to find out the hard way. As she boiled the kettle, Patsy felt complete and utter rage on the inside but remained calm and composed for Flora. The important thing was being there to pick up the pieces and help rebuild a broken heart. A mother's work, thought Patsy, was never done.

'My life has gone precisely nowhere. I've reached a dead end.' Flora teared up again, her mouth wobbling. 'And Justin was so *cold*. Baltic. Not only to me, to Robert too. And he's known Robert since they were *five*.'

Flora was too good for Justin, thought Patsy. But then she had never valued herself. She was the kind of person who thought everyone was so much better than she was. Kate was the more beautiful one, she used to say, whenever Patsy praised the two of them when they were dressed up as teenagers, and, yes, of course Kate was lovely, but Flora was gorgeous, with her dark hair and blue eyes. Or when she did so well in her Leaving Cert, she had just brushed it aside. 'I got lucky,' she'd said. And in the National College of Art and Design when she was chosen in her final year as best in class and then, as a result, got the scholarship for her master's at St Martin's College in London, she had shrugged her success off. No wonder she was so easily swept up in Justin's world, looking after his needs and becoming something of a glorified housekeeper. Patsy had watched Flora's confidence haemorrhage even further as he focused on his business, giving less and less time to their relationship. Flora had always seemed lonely in the marriage, as though waiting for things to change, and all through that time, Patsy had hoped her fears were merely borne from an overprotectiveness, but now she realised that she had been right all along. She longed to give Justin a piece of her mind, but she was also grateful that her daughter was finally free of that soul-crushing man.

'Could I stay with you?' Flora asked, and opened her mouth to say more, before beginning to cry.

'Of course you can.' Patsy put both arms around her and kissed her daughter's head. 'This is always your home.'

It was now nearly 2 a.m., and she knew she had to sleep, but her mind was busy, not just with worry for Flora but also about a meeting she had the following morning. She wasn't sure if she should be terrified or happy about it. Yesterday, after Flora had gone to prepare for the barbecue, her phone had rung.

'Hello,' a voice had said. 'I hope you don't mind me calling out of the blue...'

Double-glazing salesperson, Patsy had thought. Or scam, more likely. She had readied herself with a polite but firm 'no thank you', when the man continued speaking in a nice voice, not one you readily associated with scammers.

'I'm Killian Walsh,' he had gone on. 'The new owner of The Sandycove Arms, the hotel in the village. I don't know if you are aware of the work which has been going on for... well, far too long...'

The old coaching house had been part of the village for the

last two hundred or so years and had become shabbier and increasingly more desperate-looking, until finally, and ignominiously, it lay disused and dilapidated. But last summer, word had filtered out that it had been bought and was to be refurbished and then reopened as a new boutique hotel. Patsy had, of course, noticed the scaffolding outside, the vans parked on the pavement alongside it, and the cacophony of hammering and drilling. But why was he calling her?

'Alison Musgrave gave me your number,' he'd continued. 'From the café? She said you are the one responsible for its makeover.'

'Yes, that's right...' What on earth did he want? Did he need *curtains*?

'I *was* using my usual interior designer, but I was thinking he's not right for this job. He's done the bedrooms and the upper storeys in whites and creams. Maybe they need some touches such as blankets for the beds, lamps and lampshades...' He'd seemed to be talking to himself, as though thinking it all through. 'But the thing is, the more I looked at his designs for the ground floor – the reception, the bar, the public areas – and the more time I spent in Sandycove, I didn't think they worked. He likes a lot of gold and black... and it works in certain environments but definitely not in Sandycove.' He had paused, as though he wanted her to say something.

'Right, yes...' she'd obliged.

'So, I was having coffee at Alison's and I was looking around and I *loved* what I saw. And it's exactly the look I want, and what The Sandycove Arms needs. And deserves. It's eight weeks to opening... and so...' He'd paused. 'I wondered if you might consider replicating what you did there?'

'You want me?' Patsy had glanced at herself in the hall mirror. She saw an older woman, grey cropped hair, a red cardigan and a yellow scarf. The blue eyes which her long-departed husband, Jack, used to say were like sapphires – he was prone to hyperbole – were the only things which he would recognise now.

'It was the mix of the natural materials,' the man had explained, 'the artwork on the walls, the softness... it's very *Sandycovian*. I need you to recreate what you did in Alison's, in the hotel. Or at least make it the same... but different...'

'But that's...' Patsy had been lost for words. Impossible. In eight weeks? And, also, she wasn't a proper interior designer. She wasn't experienced. And she was sixty-two and her time for new experiences and challenges was over. She was just giving herself 'notions' – that old Irish sensibility of reaching too high and too far. She needed to return to making her curtains.

'I have a brilliant team of lads,' he had added. 'Carpenters, painters, decorators. And I need it to look welcoming, not intimidating. Warm, bright, beautiful. Different to all the other hotels around. Maybe some wallpaper as well? Nice fabric...'

She would go and meet him, she had decided, making a plan for Monday, but now, in the early hours of Sunday morning, she realised that after this evening's shocking revelations, Killian Walsh's proposals had become much more attractive. This was exactly what Flora needed. This rather overwhelming venture could be an opportunity to showcase those fabulous talents that had lain dormant for far too long. Now all Patsy had to work out was how to get Flora on board.

3

KATE

In the tiny hamlet of Saint-Sauveur, just outside the beautiful honey-hued town of Tournon in south-west France, Kate O'Hare was hiding something from her partner Jacques. She was twenty-six weeks pregnant – something neither he nor her had wanted, but after having the pregnancy confirmed, she knew she wanted to be a mother, and she fully accepted she would do it alone.

For the last two years, she had lived in a converted barn at the edge of a vineyard, loving the neat lines of the grapes crossing the rolling countryside, the sound of cicadas at night, the way the shadows were chased away by the rising sun in the morning. Her job was office administrator for the Aubert family who owned the acres of land and who produced some of the finest wines in the whole of the south of France. Kate organised shipments all over the world, liaised with buyers, facilitated seasonal workers and maintained the logs of the cellars. She had loved her time in France. Especially meeting handsome, kind and intelligent Jacques. They had talked very early on in their relationship about neither ever wanting children, both happy they had found someone else on the same page. There was a freedom, an ease, about not wanting a family, as though you could slow life down, make decisions to fit your own timescale, not be rushed by biological clocks, societal pressures or keeping up with your peers. You could make your own rules. But even with all their well-meaning, idealistic plans, Mother Nature had decided to throw them a curveball.

Jacques was a local journalist, but was just about to take a sabbatical to volunteer with refugees in Greece and now, however much she loved him, Kate couldn't wait for him to leave so she could work out her plans. He had spoken about volunteering for as long as she'd known him and there was no way she would get in between him and doing some good in the world. She had decided, after fourteen years travelling all over the world, she was going to go home, back to Ireland.

Being on her own hadn't been easy. There was a time in Nepal when the bus was stuck behind a landslide and they all had to sleep outside for three days until another bus managed to rescue them. In Mexico her rucksack had been stolen by a charming American who'd taught her how to play blackjack, and in India some men had tried to bundle her on to a tuk-tuk and – she still didn't know how she found the strength – she had kicked them and screamed her lungs out. A group of sari-clad women, a blur of jewel-coloured silks, had shouted at the men until they had left, Kate trembling, tears in her eyes.

It had been winter when Kate had arrived back in the northern hemisphere, feeling the need for Europe and wanting to find a home somewhere. In a small town in the south-west of France, a sign in the local supermarket had caught her eye: help needed at a local vineyard, someone to do admin, to manage the online orders, the visits. And another notice:

Camper van for sale. Needs cleaning and a good home.

So do I, she'd thought, before ringing both numbers and making an appointment to see the seller of the camper van first. It wasn't the world's most attractive camper van, being both too large and too small, as though it was about to topple over, but inside there was a neat kitchen, a seating area which was easily changed into a bed, and the headlights and the front bumper made it look like it was smiling. It was cheap, but there was something about a home on wheels, after just having a backpack for the previous decade, that made her feel secure. A home you could take anywhere. It was the best of both worlds. The van was a way of keeping her options open – you never knew when you might be on the road again.

Next, she called the second number, where she spoke to Elise Aubert, owner of an organic vineyard in Saint-Sauveur.

'We need someone to organise the sales of the wine,' said the voice at the end of the phone, 'to send things out, to arrange paying the staff. And we have a small barn where you can live, above the office.'

She met the Auberts and she took the job and for the first time in a long time, she had not just a job, but somewhere to call home.

She loved working for the Auberts, in their beautiful vineyard, with the gloriously sunny days and the stark winters, but even though she wondered if perhaps France might be where she would make her forever home, with the pregnancy everything had changed.

She had told Elise Aubert that she was thinking of leaving, hoping that she wouldn't be leaving them in the lurch, but Elise had always been so kind, taking Kate into her heart, sensing she was a young woman who was yet to find her place in the world. 'Don't worry about us,' she had said. 'You worry about you. Just let me know when you decide.' Perhaps Elise guessed that it was

something more than wanderlust or itchy feet, but if she did, she
didn't let on.

Kate never spoke about home or her past and, if Elise had
asked, Kate might have told her about her rather unconventional
upbringing: raised by her loving, talented but fundamentally
flawed mother, Lola, in Sandycove, until the age of sixteen, when
Lola had left to go on tour with her band, The Islanders. It had
been a tough choice for Lola and she had wanted to take Kate
with her, but Kate had refused to go, wanting to finish school and
not leave Sandycove – and hoping Lola would stay at home with
her. But Lola chose music. Kate had moved in with her best
friend, Flora, and her mother, Patsy, and pretended to everyone
she wasn't hurt and didn't feel abandoned. However, the truth was
clear – her mother had chosen fame and fans over her. And that
was when the distance between them began.

She and Lola had kept in touch – emails, the odd phone call –
but what had started out as regular contact was now sporadic, an
emotional distance now as well as one of geography, and Lola
knew little to nothing of Kate's life. Lola now lived in California
and had become another person entirely – a life of success,
money and private planes had changed her.

Despite learning the piano to Grade Eight, singing in the
school choir, even once wanting to be a singer herself, over the
years Kate had left even *that* behind, another legacy from her
mother she felt hurt by. She knew she was silly and she wanted to
grow up and get over it, but the feelings lingered. And as the years
passed, it was almost as if they'd got out of the habit of each other.
They were now pretty much estranged, as though they were old
acquaintances, figments of each other's past. After all this time, it
hurt less and less, but Kate guessed their relationship would never
be the same again.

It was early June and Jacques' last night before he was leaving for two months in Greece. He and Kate sat in the evening sun, their backs against the wall of the barn. She was feeling emotional about saying goodbye to him, knowing she would never see him again. She wished she could tell him what she was planning on doing. He wouldn't stop her, she was sure of it. Jacques would understand that if she had decided to keep the baby and return to Ireland, then that was her decision. He might be disappointed that their relationship was over, but he would more than survive. He believed in people fulfilling their own destinies, following your dreams and not being controlled by others. He, after all, was disappearing to Greece, where there would only be sporadic Wi-Fi.

'Two months is a long time,' he said, lightly brushing her hair back from her face.

'It'll be grand,' she said, smiling at him. 'It's going to fly by...'

He laughed. 'Fly by. I like it.' He always loved the phrases she used and seemed to find so much of what she said and how she said it to be as charming as she found his way of speaking. 'Like a bird,' he said. 'Time flies like a bird. Unless it's a flightless bird. A penguin...'

Now, she laughed. 'I need to record you saying "penguin" and I'll play it every day, to cheer me up.'

He frowned, as though suddenly worried about her. 'I thought you said you were looking forward to me going away...'

'Oh, I am!' she replied, her usual cool and confident self. She hated being dependent on anyone and now, more than ever, she had to be strong for herself and the baby. She stood up. 'I'm going to make dinner...'

'*I'll* make dinner, you open the wine...'

She shook her head. 'Not for me. Too tired. I'll fall asleep. Don't want to miss your last night, do I? I'll do it...'

She was going to miss him. But he was so adamant about not

having children. He'd never thought of himself as being a father, and when he and Kate had first discussed it, in the early days of their relationship, both had beamed to discover another person on the same no-kids page.

It had begun with one missed period... and then a second and when she went to the health centre in Tournon, she'd had the news confirmed. Jacques hadn't suspected a thing. Now, she was more than six months... she needed to get herself organised and sorted. A hospital, a place to live, somewhere to think straight and seriously. She had the overriding sense she could only do it in Sandycove. There, she knew, she would be able to gather herself and plan what she and the baby were going to do. And she missed her best friend Flora, and wanted to have her by her side. Flora always made everything seem better.

* * *

The following morning, Kate watched Jacques' little orange 2CV car as it wound its way along the vineyard's drive to the main road, his arm waving out the window. Blinking back the tears, her heart crumpled.

Hormones, she thought, *have a lot to answer for*.

Jacques would be fine. He always said he never saw friend-ships or relationships as long-term things. 'Transience, is it not?' he'd said, one evening when they were sitting in the square, at their usual table, drinking wine. 'We are all nomads. Our essential nature, no?'

His brown eyes used to change colour, Kate would think. Lighter in the day when he was working and thinking, a darker tone at night. When it was just the two of them, they glittered and shone. She'd miss those eyes, she thought.

At Flaubert's café, in Tournon's main square, under the early-summer blue sky, Kate sat in the shade of the linden trees, contemplating her options. Beside her, on the ground, birds pecked at croissant crumbs and customers at the morning market chatted to each other at the stalls selling cheese and olives and sweetcorn straight from the farm, rows of sweet melons, bottles of the best olive oil Kate had ever tasted.

She finished her coffee and called Flora. The thought of being with her again, even if it meant having to put up with that self-obsessed husband of her, was reassuring. Could she live in the van on their drive? Or perhaps there was somewhere else she could park it?

'Kate?' Flora's voice, her Irish accent, hundreds of miles away, was enough to make Kate feel stronger. 'I'm in the supermarket... we're having a barbecue... I'll call you back later, okay? I just have to pay for something. Everything all right?'

'Everything's fine. I'll talk to you soon. Love you.'

'Love you too.'

Kate checked her phone for emails. Nothing from Jacques. Obviously. But there was one from her mother.

Kate, darling, how are you?

Kate could hear Lola's voice now, all the way from Newport Beach, California.

I've been sorting through a box of Paulie's things which were sent to me and it's funny how much stuff he kept from the early days. I can't believe some of the rubbish he held on to. There was even a flyer from a gig we did in Sandycove. Probably one of our first. We could only have been seventeen or something. Anyway, hope all is well... love, as always, Lola.

Lola's messages were always strangely impersonal, as though they were just random thoughts, sent to a random person. What *was* important to Lola was the band, her music, and Paulie, the co-founder of the band and best friend. Paulie had died six months earlier and Kate had heard the news on local radio and wondered how Lola was going to deal with his loss.

Kate had been part of the band in the early days, sitting between Lola and Paulie in the van, seat belt-less, on their way to wherever they were playing that night. By the time they performed, she was normally asleep on a few chairs pushed together behind the stage, her mother's voice singing her to sleep. But with Paulie now gone, Lola would be lost without him. He'd died in his huge house in Nashville, far from home.

Even though she loved Paulie, Kate had decided not to go to the funeral and instead had gone to the church in Tournon and lit a candle for him. He'd always loved old and dusty churches and lit candles wherever he went. 'For St Paul,' he'd once told her, as they held the taper towards the jumble of night lights. 'He was the best-looking apostle. A total ride.' He'd winked at her, making her laugh.

Now Kate wished she'd gone to the funeral. Forget Lola. She should have gone for Paulie.

She reread her mother's email, and then quickly wrote back.

I've decided to head back to Ireland. Probably Sandycove. Just to see people. I've missed Ireland, I suppose. Will send on my address when I know what I'm doing.

Kate packed up her belongings, her books, her few clothes, presents for Flora and Patsy and Jacques' old sweater, the one he had given her to wear last winter when the icy wind had whistled around the barn and nothing, other than the jumper, was able to warm her.

Elise Aubert looked devastated. 'So, you are finally going? We will miss you with all our hearts,' she said, hugging Kate. 'Your Irish spirit.'

Kate laughed. Elise was always mentioning Kate's Irishness and she had never felt less Irish after all these years living away. Even Ireland felt foreign to her.

'And you will come back and see us, yes?'

Kate nodded. 'Of course...' She didn't tell Elise about the baby because what if it got back to Jacques? He had nieces and nephews he loved, but when he returned to Tournon, after a weekend of playing hide-and-seek with them and taking them for ice creams, he said how much he valued his peace and quiet. 'And sleep,' he said, smiling at Kate. 'We can sleep while those parents can't...'

'And what about Jacques?' Elise asked her, as she helped Kate put the last of her boxes in the van.

'We're not together any more...' Kate shrugged, hoping the gesture would communicate that these things happen and that she was fine, and so was he... and life went on. Which it did. Life could change in an instant and here she was, at that point where her entire world had been shaken upside down, and she was hoping that when everything settled, it would all make sense. At the moment, she couldn't even think straight.

On her last birthday, Jacques had booked a table at a special restaurant. Elise had looked concerned. 'What will you be wearing?'

Kate hadn't given it much thought and Elise, very gently, had suggested she could borrow something of hers.

'My Dior,' she'd said, 'will be perfect. It's magnificent.'

It *was* magnificent but had made Kate feel like a child let loose in the dressing-up box. The silk was so stiff, the collar stood up like a neck brace and even Elise had to admit it didn't work. In the end, Elise had brought out a beautiful, beaded dress which trailed on the ground, the sleeves falling around her wrist.

'Now, *this* is magnificent. We have found the one,' Elise had gushed, finally satisfied. 'My work, as you say, is done.'

Kate and Jacques had a table in the courtyard of the restaurant, surrounded by vineyards, listening to the cicadas, the farmhouses in the valley like little fairy lights. It had been like being in a dream, sitting under the stars, the murmuring voices, the ridiculously exquisite food, Jacques pouring the champagne, the two of them couldn't stop smiling at how over the top it all was and how perfect.

Afterwards, Elise had insisted she keep the dress, refusing to accept it when Kate returned it shrouded in the dry-cleaning wrapper. 'It's not mine any longer,' Elise had said, hands up, in surrender. 'It found a new owner.'

Kate couldn't think about Jacques any more. For one thing, she couldn't explain her U-turn on having children or why she wanted to return to Ireland. It wasn't because she wanted the baby to play hurling or to speak Irish or play the tin whistle, she wanted it to feel Irish, deeply, properly, incontrovertibly so. If nothing else, she wanted it to have an identity, a tribe.

Elise's husband, Gilles, placed two cases of their very best wine under the back seats of the van, and he, Elise and their four children waved Kate off. As she headed in the direction of Cherbourg and the ferry to Rosslare, she felt like bursting into tears. She was starting all over again, and this time, it was terrifying. It wasn't just her any more. It was her and her baby. An *Irish* baby.

I'm bringing you home, sweetheart. We're going home.

4

_____

LOLA

Ten thousand miles away, Lola O'Hare – lead singer and surviving member of The Islanders, Grammy winner, recent inductee into the American Music Hall of Fame, songwriter, producer and global superstar – stood on the deck of her Newport Beach house overlooking the Pacific Ocean. She was musing on a question for which she currently had no answer.

What the hell was she going to do now?

With Paulie gone, she wasn't quite sure what life looked like or where she existed within it. Instead, her entire existence had taken on an amorphous shape, and her career seemed to be practically over. There had been a few solo projects over the years, the song which had been on a film's soundtrack, the recent recordings she'd done over the last few months of Paulie's life... but what did it add up to? Without Paulie, there was no band, and without the band, there was no real point to her. If she wasn't Lola O'Hare of The Islanders any more, then who was she?

For the last six months, since Paulie had gone, she'd existed in a state of shock, barely able to speak, or smile. It was as though part of her had been removed, and she couldn't acclimatise to the feeling of a lost limb. Poor Richie – her boyfriend, guitar and mandolin player and the sweetest-hearted bearded giant there ever was – was doing his best to support her, giving her space as well as trying to persuade her to eat. But he was in the way, really. She needed time to grieve, time to think, and time to work out where and how she'd gone so badly wrong. Because she had, really.

Despite the success, she felt empty and she was desperate to know if that was because of Paulie, or something else? She missed Kate, her daughter. Had missed her for the last fourteen years, and probably because of what Lola had done, but also because of distance, they'd grown apart, so far apart that Lola didn't even know what to say any more in her emails, as though she couldn't quite picture who she was contacting. And that broke her heart.

Now, with so much time on her hands and lacking direction, Lola reflected on her life, wishing she had done so much differently. The worst was a decision she'd once made, which was probably the biggest mistake of her life. At the time, it had seemed not to have been such a big deal. The Islanders had been offered an eighteen-month world tour and it was either stay at home or follow the dream she and Paulie had been pursuing all their lives. She had hoped Kate would come with them. There could be tutors and they could visit Ireland occasionally. But even then, she had known she was asking too much of her sixteen-year-old daughter and, of course, Kate had refused to come and instead moved in with her friend Flora.

To be honest, it had suited Lola because it meant she got to go on the tour which had changed all their lives and ushered The Islanders into a whole new stratosphere of success and it meant financial freedom for all of them, including Kate. Except Kate had never accepted a penny and Lola now realised that she had left Kate behind. Not just physically but in every way. She had hoped little would change, that being a mother was such a tight bond that nothing could break it, but when Lola came to, when she was able to focus on life beyond the next date, the next flight, the next soundcheck, Kate had already moved on. All they had now were sporadic emails, which contained little to no information.

Lola missed Kate and however much she tried to explain to Richie, he would shrug and say, 'So go and see her then. Call her.' And she couldn't explain that it wasn't that easy. But she was running out of excuses.

She could hear Richie in the kitchen, making dinner. He'd been living with her for the last three years. Tall, sexy and – this was uncommon for the men in Lola's life – a good person. Too good for Lola. Usually, the men in her life were the ones who didn't call, who put her down when she was the one paying for everything, or refused to remember her birthday. Richie was the opposite. He minded her, cooked for her, worried about her, filled her car with petrol, made sure he cleaned up the bathroom and never left his clothes in a heap. Lola was suspicious. Was he for real? What did he *want*? Nothing, it seemed. And he liked to talk, which made a change. Most of the losers she'd clung to in the past were the quiet, moody types. Richie was a talker – to anyone: people in shops and restaurants, the homeless man who sat outside Target, the girls in their local coffee shop. His voice, with those low, Southern tones, was like swimming in the Mississippi Delta or being coated in molasses.

Richie had also become the neighbourhood's fix-it man. If he heard Maria who worked for the Bergmans next door calling his name, he would jump up and run out to assist in putting out the trash or opening a jar or, randomly, hanging a door.

'Where have you been?' Lola had asked him once.

'Oh, hanging a door for Maria,' he'd said, as though it was an entirely natural and ordinary thing to do.

'So that's what you call it,' she'd said, and he'd grinned, grabbing her, kissing her neck.

'You're even more beautiful when you are jealous,' he'd said.

And he was a listener – another revelation. Whenever Lola opened her mouth to speak, he'd look up, alert like a collie, ready to take it all in. It was almost disconcerting. She'd have to let him go soon, she knew. Someone like Richie deserved someone less selfish and much kinder. Someone younger, of childbearing age. Richie would make an amazing father. And she was no use to anyone these days; being alone with her thoughts was all she craved. Paulie's death had left her feeling as though she'd been sliced apart from some demon surgeon and she was left exposed and vulnerable.

Ten years younger than Lola, Richie had the body of a man who had spent his youth in rodeos and hauling bales of hay. He deserved someone better, not some washed-up singer who drank green juices in the glittering sunlight of California but longed for pints of Guinness in an old, dark pub in Dublin, the kind with a fire crackling in the corner. But these days, she couldn't even listen to music because she had Paulie's voice in her head, telling her what he thought of it. 'Jesus Christ,' he would have said, 'he sounds like his testicles are in a vice.' Or, 'Why is he dressed like he's going on a play date? And his face looks like he's found a slug in his kale sandwich.' He was in her ear all the time, which was both reassuring but also disorientating because she had to keep reminding herself he was gone. Growing up, he'd been more family to her than her own mother and it was Paulie who'd encouraged her to dream big and strive for more. Sometimes she thought that it was those aspirations which had helped her survive.

Years ago, when she had watched her own mother – dead now, thank God – giving out about something, as she always did, nastiness and unhappiness filling the air like a noxious cloud, Lola would imagine herself on stage, performing, living her future *extraordinary* life, well away from her caustic mother and her small-town attitudes. Yet, when Lola and The Islanders had played a huge homecoming concert at Landsdowne Road, Lola had swallowed her pride, rung her mother and said she would put some VIP tickets aside for her.

'No, thank you,' her mother had said. 'It's the novena at the church. Nine days of praying. The novena is far more important than...' – she had paused as though trying to find the right word – '...*music*.'

Feck you, Lola had wanted to say to her mother. Not for the first or the last time.

Lola's whole childhood had been spent in a grey gloom until Sundays, when her mother fizzed about fervently. But even Lola liked Sundays because of the church choir. She didn't mind that the songs were about God, as her voice soared above all those small-minded people in the pews, their heads bent over their Bibles, the priest waggling his bony finger about unmarried mothers and sin. Being stubborn was worn as a badge of honour, an armour against the world. Her mother used to shout, scream and threaten, and Lola – then plain Lorraine O'Hare – still wouldn't change her mind. No, she wasn't going to go to Mass any longer; yes, she was now in a band; yes, she *was* going to keep the baby; and no, the father was unimportant, a man who wasn't interested in raising a baby and had already disappeared to wherever he had come from. Lola had long regretted the encounter but she didn't regret the baby. '*Je ne regrette* nothing,' as Paulie used to say.

Lola and Paulie had grown up together, two streets apart in Sandycove, him at the local Jesuit school and her at St Mary's. They were both in the Sunday school choir, and because few of the other children could keep a note in their heads, she and Paulie would look at each other, their voices swooping around the other's like a double helix of harmonic sound. He was the one who had insisted they start a band and the rest was well-documented history – from pub gigs and tiny festivals, to their big break of four nights in the Olympia, and then the TV performances, bigger deals, longer tours and a life of private jets, handmade suits (him) and designer dresses (her). It was the kind of life where everyone was pleased to see you, the world populated by smiling faces, the best tables in restaurants and treated with ridiculous reverence.

She was the person to whom he had come out aged fifteen. 'You think I didn't already know?' she'd said, pretending not to notice the tremble in his hands. 'Now, let's go and get some chips.'

'Let's go and get some chips' entered their permanent lexicon. For years, through everything, it was their leveller. Once, in Tokyo, they had a problem with one of their visual panels and there was a transport issue which meant difficulties getting their trucks in, and their melodeon player hadn't returned from a full moon party in Bali. Paulie had turned white with the stress.

'Come on, Paulie,' Lola had said, 'let's go and get some chips.' And suddenly he'd laughed, making everyone around them – the crew, the roadies, the backing singers, the Japanese team who were putting everything together – look at them in wonder as she and Paulie cracked up, tears rolling down their faces, now on their knees howling with laughter, these two mad Irish people.

Another time, in Miami, when they were preparing for a huge concert, Hurricane Louise was rapidly changing course, forcing everyone to remain in the hotel. They were all running out of cigarettes, food, drink and the will to live. Lola had stared out of the window, wondering where in the world Kate was, and if she was safe from this storm, or another one. Paulie had tapped her on the shoulder. 'You know what we need to do? We need to go and get some chips.' And she'd smiled at him, knowing he knew what she'd been thinking. *I wouldn't have done this with anyone else,* she had thought. *I* couldn't *have done this with anyone else.* She and Paulie had gone down to the hotel's kitchens, which were empty of staff, and made ham, cheese and pickle sandwiches. They'd also procured a case of wine because the locked walk-in fridge was wide open. She'd felt invincible. She'd stalked the stages of stadia and auditoria, feeling like a queen, hewn from Irish granite, willed into being by sheer determination.

But it all came at a cost – a personal one for Lola and a cost to Paulie's health. As he lay dying, he had taken her hand and said, 'I'm jealous about all the adventures you're going to have without me.' Not that she was having any these days, and maybe never would again. But, oh my God, the adventures they'd had, the career in music which she still had to pinch herself about, the awards, the plaudits, the fans, the money... all of it. And even though they had made a lot of money – too much money, Paulie used to say, as he bought another painting or another car he didn't need, as well as buying his mother a holiday home in Spain – Lola gave a lot of hers away, to women's refuges, to the rape crisis centre back in Dublin, food banks, individuals who wrote to her, and she also banked money for Kate, hoping one day she might forgive her long enough to accept even some of it. And through all those years of obscurity and then fame, fortune, Paulie had been her rock, her platonic other half. He had helped her discover all she was capable of. Without him, she would have been incomplete, a dreamer, someone who never made it. He had encouraged her to become what she always knew she was meant to be. Except... it was only now, now the dust had settled on everything, that Lola wondered perhaps if it had really been worth it? At the time, success was everything. Getting to the top of that mountain, selling all those records, playing to all those crowds, writing all those songs, was only possible because she had left Ireland, and left Kate. She had thought she was building a life for the two of them. In reality, what it had meant was she was rich and successful but she didn't have much of a relationship with her daughter. They barely communicated, rarely saw each other, and the bond they had once shared seemed forever broken. Kate hadn't even come to Paulie's funeral. *She probably won't even come to mine*, thought Lola.

5

FLORA

Lying in her old single bed in her childhood bedroom, Flora didn't need any further reminders of quite how much of a failure she was. She thought of Justin and Sandra and the way they had spoken of being 'in love'. How easily it had happened for them, and how cruelly they had dispatched both her and Robert. She'd always known Justin had a selfish streak, but she had never thought she'd be on the wrong side of it, or quite how single-minded and selfish he actually was. She had thought of him as ambitious, determined, but it seemed that once he was tired of her, he was determined to move on. As fast as possible.

But how was she meant to move on after this horrible humiliation? How could she show her face around the village, knowing how much everyone liked to gossip? She thought again of Kate, who was far more practical and clear-sighted, and would soldier on and push through, but then Kate was always braver than Flora. Flora had always wished she was a lot more like Kate.

The two girls had become friends aged eleven – their first year at secondary school. Flora had seen Kate around, a black hoodie over her school uniform and a tattoo of a butterfly on her wrist.

Flora had kept staring at it in French, where they had been placed together, wondering if it was real and, if it was, what eleven-year-old was allowed to have a tattoo? But she had heard Kate's mother was in a band who were about to play at the Olympia in Dublin's city centre. A singer's daughter would have a tattoo, reasoned Flora, wishing she too had a singer for a parent instead of a boring librarian.

Kate had caught her staring. 'It's not real,' she'd whispered, so Madame O'Keefe wouldn't hear.

'It looks real,' Flora had said.

'My mum was in New York and there was a shop selling really good fake ones. She didn't want to buy it for me, though. Paulie, he's Mum's best friend...'

'He's in a band with her, isn't he?' Flora had seen them perform on *The Late Late Show* the other week and the singer – in a white dress, half-bride, half-banshee – had looked as though she had come from another world entirely. And then there was the guitarist, small and scowling in a pale blue suit and turquoise eyeliner.

Patsy had glanced up from her sewing. 'They're from Sandycove,' she'd said. 'She was in my school. Lorraine, she used to be called. Goes by Lola now. And there's Paulie. The two of them, like brother and sister, always were.'

Flora had watched the television, incredulous that these two unearthly figures were from Sandycove. The music was different, a rock-Celtic fusion, a pinch of punk, a touch of disco. Flora had no idea how to categorise them, but whatever it was, she had liked it. And now, she was sitting next to the banshee's daughter.

In class, Kate had grinned – the fun and brilliant girl hidden behind the hoodie and the back-brushed hair, was suddenly revealed. 'Anyway, I like your ring.'

'It's opal,' Flora had said. 'My birthstone.'

For some reason, this cool girl looked as impressed as Flora had been with her fake tattoo. 'It's beautiful,' she had remarked. 'Like a mood ring.'

'What's a mood ring?'

'A ring that can tell you what mood you are in. It's useful when you wake up and you don't know how you feel, you know?'

Flora nodded, but really she always knew how she felt. Moods weren't that difficult to work out, but Kate hinted at a more complicated life beyond school and cereal for breakfast and a mother who worked in a library and made curtains to make extra money. Flora's father was dead, *that* was complicated, she supposed. But she didn't remember him and couldn't imagine life with him, and anyway, she liked just her and Patsy. And Kate didn't have a dad around either – he was some musician, apparently, that lived a bohemian life in County Clare – and she seemed fine about it.

The two of them began sitting next to each other in every class, spending every break time together, and were soon inseparable.

'Do you want to come on a march on Saturday?' Kate had asked one day. 'Supporting the workers. Looking for an increase in the minimum wage.'

Flora had never heard of the minimum wage, nor had she given much thought to workers before, so she had willingly and gratefully entered Kate's world, a place where they went on marches and saw subtitled films and ate vegetarian food. It was as though she had met another part of her, a part she hadn't acknowledged, or even known existed, and yet, here she was, in the form of Kate. And even while marching, fists in the air, chanting slogans, they had laughed, the two of them regularly falling to their knees in fits of giggles. Being with Kate had given

Flora the impression she'd always be laughing, always be happy. And now? Life stretched ahead of her, a wilderness, devoid of laughter, fun and a husband.

On Monday morning, Flora cried in the shower, cried getting dressed, cried brushing her teeth, all the time trying to do it as silently as possible so her mother wouldn't worry. She'd already been in with a cup of tea, wondering if Flora was going to go to work, and she'd quickly wiped her eyes and mumbled that she was and would be down soon. In truth, Flora was devastated. She'd never really grasped what the word had meant before now, but she felt as the world looked after a hurricane, when everything you knew was swept away and there was nothing left.

She skipped breakfast and cycled to the village, her legs mechanically pumping up and down, her heart half the size it had been a mere two days before when she was so full of excited anticipation. Perhaps, she thought, she should go back to the house to try to talk to Justin? Maybe once they talked, away from Sandra, sense would prevail. Okay, their marriage wasn't quite the perfect union she had hoped it was, but they'd been going through a bad patch. He had been busy with work. And with Sandra, it turned out. But people did have their heads turned, they did have affairs, and they got over it. One day, perhaps Sandra would be a footnote in their lives, and they would look back, over the curly, tousled heads of their grandchildren, and barely remember this crisis. She just had to talk to him.

Unfortunately, she had no choice but to get on with her day. Flora parked her bike in the rack in the middle of the village, beside the outdoor seating of Alison's café, where there were the usual early birds, the sea swimmers gathered in their dryrobes, coffees and teas in front of them, talking in loud voices about currents and tides.

Unlocking the front door of Waters & Co haberdashery, Flora flicked on the lights and stepped inside. The shop's owner, Edith Waters, lived in the flat upstairs and relied on Flora to carry out the day-to-day running, assisting customers, ordering stock, designing the windows. Flora loved her job and adored Edith. She had begun working there while in college, as a weekend job. If she didn't like this little shop, with the ribbons and buttons, the old wooden shelves filled with rolls of the most beautiful fabric, the silks, cottons and tana lawns, the heavy velvets, the braid and the tassels, then she might have been more inclined to leave and forge her career. If it was any other kind of shop, she couldn't have stayed so long, but it was a place where creative people gathered, where sewing and knitting projects were discussed as seriously as politics and a space where people left feeling even more inspired and excited.

She couldn't even blame Justin for having settled into her lot. *She'd* made the choice not to go to London and stay with him, and she'd listened when he'd told her she was better off working at the shop so she'd be around in the evenings when he finished his work. She'd believed him when he said he would make his business a success, then it would be his turn to support her. Looking back, she had been blindsided.

She opened the post – mainly bills or catalogues from interiors companies – and quickly tidied up, before switching the closed sign to open. Flora served three customers, sorted the remnants basket, packaged up a cushion-making kit, dealt with phone orders and wrapped them up, ready to be taken to the post office. She then sold fifteen metres of champagne silk to a woman who was going to make her daughter's wedding dress. And there was a lovely young designer who came in with samples of fabric she'd created herself. She had just graduated from college, she said. Industrial textile design. Flora didn't tell her it had been her course too. She wanted to say to the young woman, not to give up. Don't let *anything* stop you, but she didn't want to come across as a mad, unhinged person, so she kept quiet and, when the young woman left, Flora was busy in the shop all morning, until her boss, Edith, arrived.

Edith had taken over the shop when her father had died, and had meant to sell it but had never quite managed to do so. Having Flora in charge meant Edith could remain hands-off and appear only fleetingly. Lately, however, she'd been arriving every morning with a paper bag with cakes inside for them to share.

'Morning, Flora!' she said, loudly, trademark silk scarf draped around her shoulders. 'Macaroon or currant slice?' Edith was in her late sixties, perhaps, with short, bobbed grey hair, a brisk voice, didn't suffer fools *at all*, and had something of the Lady of the Manor about her, as though at any moment she would find something for you to do.

As Flora rewound some loose ribbon, she realised she was going to find it hard to hide what had happened from Edith. Yet, she didn't want to cry in front of her. They didn't have that kind of relationship.

'Flora?' Edith peered up at her. 'Everything all right?'

Flora managed to nod. 'Yes, fine,' she croaked.

'Really?' Edith stepped closer. 'You don't look fine. You look like death. White as a ghost. My departed mother had the same pallor on the funeral home slab. They asked me if they should apply blusher to brighten her up a little. Brighten her up? She's dead, I told the man. You could electrocute her and she would remain unanimated. But then, she wasn't the most animated when she was stalking this good earth of ours. But you, my dear, are very much alive with the pallor of someone...'

'On an undertaker's slab,' said Flora, as a tear rolled down her cheek.

'What's wrong?'

'I've moved out,' Flora admitted.

Edith stepped closer, her bright eyes narrowing. 'Of where?'

Flora swallowed. 'Of my home. With Justin. He's been... well, he's met someone else and so I'm back with my mother.'

Edith frowned. 'Why did *you* move out? Surely he...? Wouldn't it have been more...?'

Flora shook her head. 'It's his parents' house. So... well, I have no right... I mean, I don't think we own it. Well, there's a mortgage and... well... I didn't really have any... any legal reason to remain. Obviously. And so... well...' She wilted under the laser glare of Edith.

'Are you sure there is a mortgage?'

Flora nodded. 'He used to tell me there was... I never gave it a second thought. He wouldn't lie to me, would he?'

Edith's eyes narrowed further. 'You do know he's a gurrier, don't you? And you do know it won't work out with... whoever this eejit of a woman is? And you do know you have *rights*?'

Don't cry, Flora told herself. *Just have the macaroon and you and Edith can return to only talking about the shop and what is selling and what isn't.* 'Shall we...' she tried, '...have a cup of...?'

But the tears began rolling again and then, before she knew it, she had collapsed on top of Edith, like a sack of potatoes, but Edith braced herself and held her up.

'I failed,' managed Flora, self-respect utterly out the window, floodgates well and truly opened. 'I'm a failure.' She managed to peel herself off Edith and clamber onto the stool behind the service desk.

Edith gave her a gentle smile. 'Failure? Hardly.'

'But I am... My marriage. I don't have a career... I mean, I love working here but...'

Edith nodded. 'I know, I know, it's not the dream. I understand.'

'But it's not a *bad* dream,' Flora gabbled on, 'it just wasn't, isn't... Oh, I don't know. It's just I gave up everything for him... and I've nothing to show. Except failure.'

'You're not a failure,' said Edith. 'Far from it. I always admire anyone who even tries to have a relationship. I didn't. But you did. And that's brave.'

'But what do I do next? How do I live?' went on Flora, snuffling. 'My head is so full of him, I feel half-mad. I don't know how I managed to cycle here this morning without crashing. And I just want to be left alone to cry. I just don't know what to do.'

'Take it one day at a time,' said Edith, standing back and leaning against the counter. 'It's amazing what happens when you let time do its thing.' She put her two hands together, steepling her fingers. 'I was in love once. A most passionate and wonderful attachment. We were so happy... until... well, until we realised it wasn't to be. Parents, you see. Didn't approve. On either side. We were, you might say, a little ahead of our time. My love interest went off to Paris to be a pastry chef. And I became aimless. Tried to write a book. Became an academic. Women's Studies. Hated it. Ironically, the head of department was a misogynist. And then, my parents died, and I had a choice to make, either sell the shop or take it over and keep it going. And you came along, with your wonderful way with customers, and you've been such a success. You've meant this business has survived. So, the very last thing you are is a failure...'

In the decade she'd known Edith, Flora had no idea about this forbidden love or the parents' disapproval, or even her academic career and the ironically misogynist head of department. 'What happened to your partner? The pastry chef?'

'They stayed in Paris... and well... made their own life...' Edith shrugged. 'We had all moved on. I knew I would never be attached to anyone ever again, so I admire you for giving it a go, and it's not your fault you married a nefarious ne'er-do-well. You took a chance.' She paused. 'Now, cake? I'll put the kettle on and we'll have one of these. Cakes cure all ills and you can tell me more about what happened and we can try to decide what you're going to do.'

6

PATSY

The Sandycove Arms was a chaotic mess of piles of wood, copper piping, paint pots and mysterious packages tied to pallets. Builders, plumbers and carpenters heading in and out of the front door, the sound of drilling and hammering, the smell of sawn wood, fresh paint and old dust in the air. Patsy felt a chill run down her spine.

I'm doing this for Flora, she told herself. *I have to be brave for Flora.*

She hadn't managed to tell Flora about her plan to involve her in this potential job, but she needed to know quite how much they were taking on, before presenting it to Flora. She hoped she could manage it.

In all her life, Patsy had never been asked to do something so *visible*. The café had been one thing, but it was small and manageable and very local. A hotel was something else entirely. She had convinced herself that the café was just helping out a friend, but this was a professional job. She felt terrified at the thought.

I am sixty-two years old, she thought, *and I am still scared of life.*

What exactly was wrong with her? She thought of her friends

who were busy getting on with things, confidence only increasing
as they gave fewer fecks about people's opinions. Everyone went
on about your sixties being a time when you find yourself, *know*
yourself and fly through life. But all Patsy could think about were
the mistakes in the café, the fact she'd hung the pictures too high
and the benches were a little too narrow. And... well, she could
go on.

'Patsy Fox?' A young man, maybe around Flora's age, handsome with a broad smile and short, sandy hair, had his hand
outstretched. 'Killian Walsh.' He shook her hand, hard. 'Thank
you for coming.'

Patsy listened as he chatted about the hotel and the other ones
he owned, one in Dún Laoghaire and another in Howth, two in
Dublin's city centre.

Killian handed her a hard hat. 'After you...' He ushered her
through the main door, stepping over the oak floorboards which
were being hammered into place and ducking around two of the
electricians who were reeling in a large cable coil.

She tried to hear him over a soundtrack of drilling, banging
and the tinny sound of music playing from a radio.

'It's always like this at this stage.' Killian raised his voice. 'Total
chaos.' He grinned as though he enjoyed it. 'Our opening is eight
weeks away – August the third. So, this is the foyer, which is the
area I would like you to concentrate on...'

It was a large space, bright because of the two large windows
on either side of the door, summer sunlight pouring through the
front door. It was at least six times the size of the café, and that
was easier because it had a defined purpose – for eating and
drinking. A hotel reception was so many things – meeting area,
checking in, people stopping for a coffee... It was too much for
Patsy.

But Flora, she thought. *Flora needs to start up again.*

She cleared her throat. 'You know,' she said, 'I'm not really an interior designer. I did a course...' She had to manage his expectations. 'But my daughter...'

He looked at her, smiling pleasantly while Patsy urged herself on. This was a perfect opportunity to get Flora back on her feet. It made her heart weep to think of how she had been treated by that pompous Justin Moriarty, but she had to keep reminding herself that he had done her a favour, even though, judging by Flora's red eyes this morning, she herself was a long way from seeing it.

'My daughter, she's... well, she's a textile designer and I thought she could design some bespoke wallpaper, fabric for cushions...' She looked around. Seating there. Rug there. A book nook, like the one she'd made at Alison's. And over at the window, two armchairs, plants on the low windowsills, and heavy curtains. Slowly, she realised that she was seeing beyond the chaos, the room was taking shape in her mind. The colours would be soft, peaches, pinks, moss greens. The reception area at the back, with a feature wall of Flora's wallpaper. And the pattern could be repeated on some of the cushions. Maybe a neon fringe? Her eyes darted around the space, mapping and planning. Although the fear was still there, there was something else which felt as though it was sprouting like a green shoot in spring. Adrenaline. Excitement.

'If your daughter would like to be involved, then absolutely.' Killian was smiling at her. 'I want what you did in Alison's. Something beautiful. No clichés, nothing heavy. A kind of quiet femininity. I mean...' He laughed. 'I like *loud* femininity as well. But a place not just for visitors, locals dropping in... A place like a home, but better. No clutter, for one thing, dust or cat hair...' He paused. 'Dog hair I don't mind. It's part of a happy home.' He smiled. 'I'm a dog person,' he explained. 'Hence the random dog reference. I've even got it in my dating profile. I thought that was an important thing to state. What do you think?'

'Well,' she said, 'if you want to meet a fellow dog person, I suppose.'

He nodded. 'Well, yes, yes, I do. Thanks for the advice. My profile will remain.' He was still smiling, as though he enjoyed his life and even online dating. Patsy liked him immensely. 'Well, then,' he said. 'We're already on the same page. And we should talk budget and your fee...'

She hadn't thought of her fee yet, though it had been drummed into them at the college that they must never undersell themselves. For Alison's café, there'd been a tiny budget. This, obviously, would be many times that. 'Why don't you tell me what you're thinking of and we can go from there?' she said. 'And thank you,' she said. 'We're really looking forward to the project.'

She hoped she sounded more confident than she felt.

* * *

That night, Patsy sat up in bed with a cup of tea and turned to the photograph of Jack on her bedside table. 'What do you think, Jack?' she said. 'Do you think I'm mad saying yes to the hotel? What if I make a mess of it?' But Patsy owed it to her daughter to lead by example and work outside her own comfort zone. She turned to Jack again. 'Wish me luck. I'm going in...'

7

FLORA

Flora was crouched down, browsing the lower shelves in the Sandycove Stores, a posh supermarket which didn't sell much in the way of baked beans but specialised in sourdough bread, expensive coffee and health supplements. She had decided she needed some kind of energy-giving, life-imbuing substance, the chlorellas, the spirulinas of the world. Something which would stop her from being on the verge of tears and make her feel a little bit less fragile. She couldn't subject Edith to another crying session. But then, just as she was reaching for something called a 'bliss ball', she heard the voices of two women above her, standing on the other side of the out-of-date chocolate basket.

'Sandra *says* they are in love,' said one. 'She *says* she and Robert were *never* a meeting of minds. Not even bodies...'

Flora froze as the two women giggled.

'But to do it like *that*,' said the other voice. 'In front of *everyone*.'

Flora hoped perhaps by remaining crouched, she was somehow invisible.

'Robert suspected something for some time,' said the first

woman. 'And then, apparently, Sandra *showed* him that she and Justin were more than friends.'

'How exactly did she show him?' asked the other.

Flora's thighs were really beginning to burn from crouching down for so long, and she clutched at the lower shelf, trying to keep herself upright.

'Justin wanted to take a photograph of the sausages he was cooking on the barbecue...'

'As you do...'

They giggled again.

'And Sandra offered to take it for him, and she opened his phone.'

'What do you mean?'

'She knew his passcode!'

'Ah!'

'Exactly!'

'Very intimate!'

'Indeed... and it was all the evidence Robert needed. So he snatches up a sword...'

'A sword? How did he get his hands on a sword?'

'I don't know if it was exactly a sword... maybe a knife, a cutlass...'

Barbecue tongs, Flora wanted to tell them. Did people actually think they had swords and cutlasses to hand? She could never even find the big scissors.

'Anyway, he challenged Justin to a duel.'

They both laughed again. 'How hilarious. Like an episode of *Fair City*.'

'Or a costume drama!'

'What about Florence, or whatever her name is?'

'Flora, like the margarine...'

'You mean Marge!' They laughed again.

'Her own *husband* having an affair and she's the last one to know!'

Flora's fingers lost their grip on the shelf and her thighs finally gave way, causing her to fall and sprawl at the feet of the two women. They both stared down at her.

'Hello,' she said. 'Just looking for some spirulina... it's very good for...' She couldn't remember what it was good for or why on earth she needed it for this great crisis in her life. A crisis which she had single-handedly made so much worse for herself.

'Flora!' They had the grace to look horrified. 'Fancy seeing you here!' One of them reached out and pulled her up. 'The floors in this place are so slippery,' she said.

'They really are,' said the other one.

Now on her feet, Flora's face burned with embarrassment, fury and hatred... and any other emotion which she knew was not conducive to a happy and peaceful existence. She needed more than spirulina to feel better. She needed a miracle.

She staggered out of the shop and cycled home, her legs wobbly, her head down. What if she met someone else she knew? Would the Sandycove whisperers already be out in force, every hedge tingling with gossip, every curtain being twitched, every wall reverberating with her great shame? She began to cry again, the tears drying on her face in the evening breeze. She missed Justin. She missed her old life. Now, she was anchor-less, home-less and completely out of ideas.

As she arrived at her mother's house, the living room light was on, which meant Patsy was working. *At least one of us has something going on*, Flora thought, as she opened the front door.

'Flora?'

She quickly wiped her eyes with the heels of her hands, and cleared her throat. 'Yes?'

'I have a proposition for you!' Patsy sounded happy.

'What is it?' Flora pushed open the door of the front room.

'Right, I've got you a commission!' Patsy was sitting at the old dining table, her two sewing machines at either end, an A4 sketchbook open in front of her. Flora could see a drawing of a room plan and scribbles. Patsy's large book of colour swatches was also on display. Flora had seen her working like this over the last year, while designing for the course.

'What kind of commission?' she asked warily.

'It's all sorted and I've said you'll do it,' said Patsy, quickly. 'You're designing the new wallpaper and fabric for the hotel in the village, The Sandycove Arms. It's got to be done in two months, so there's no time to waste.'

Flora blinked at her. 'No way. I'm not doing it.' Didn't she have enough to deal with? Yet here was her own mother, piling on more pressure.

Patsy remained calm as though she had expected this reaction. 'You used to *design* wallpaper,' she said. 'And fabric. Remember?'

'*Of course* I remember,' muttered Flora. 'But that was the old me, she's dead... and gone.'

Patsy acted as though she hadn't spoken. 'Stunning they were. The wallpaper was sublime. I'd never seen anything like it before. You were amazing... so talented.'

'Past tense.' Flora glowered, feeling like a teenage version of herself. But Patsy was right. She had been good at it all those years ago. She had done well. Which made it all even more unbearable, the idea she'd allowed her life and talent to slip through her fingers and she'd given up her future for Justin, just as he'd now given up on her.

'De Courcey's in the city centre is still exactly the same as the day you papered it and upholstered the seating,' went on Patsy. 'Every time I walk past, I pop in to have a look. It's beautiful. The pinks and the reds and the yellows... and the other design, the one with the green fields... what was the theme?'

'High days and holidays...' Flora was practically inaudible. 'No,' she went on. 'I can't. I have no idea where to even begin. I've been too long away.'

'You're not a tennis player who needs to be match fit,' said Patsy. 'All you need is decide to do it and you're back, right where you left off.'

'No...'

'Flora,' said Patsy, 'I need you. I can't do this on my own.' She sounded anxious, even vulnerable. 'I'm going to design the space,' she continued. 'And all I want from you is a fabric design, a wall-paper for behind the reception area. And it has to be *Sandycovian*.' She gave a shrug. 'Which I take could mean anything. So will you?' Patsy looked at her hopefully.

'No...' Flora hesitated. She knew she was letting her mother down but her own fear – much to her shame – overrode everything.

'Why not?'

'I'm... scared.'

She and Patsy looked at each other, and then Patsy spoke. 'So am I.'

'Are you?'

Patsy nodded. 'Hugely. I feel sick...'

'So do I!'

'I feel worse...'

'No, I'm worse. I feel really sick... as though I am about to throw up at any moment.'

Patsy laughed. 'I promise you, I am far more scared than you could ever be.'

'I doubt it...' But they were smiling at each other. Oh God, if only her mother hadn't said she was scared. But the thought of letting her go into battle on her own was unthinkable. 'Okay then...'

'Okay?'

'Yes, okay...' She gave Patsy a look. 'Just wallpaper and fabric?'

'Two colourways,' added Patsy quickly.

'Just this, and you will never ask me to do anything ever again?'

'Promise,' said Patsy.

'And if it's awful, you won't use it out of pity, I couldn't bear everyone judging it...'

'Promise. Cross my heart.' Patsy's eyes were shining. 'So you will?'

Flora nodded from under her hood. 'Okay then...'

Patsy rushed towards her, flinging her arms around Flora. 'I am so relieved,' she said. 'This is wonderful, thank you...' She looked at Flora. 'We both need to be more confident, okay?'

Flora nodded. *For Mum*, she thought, *I'm doing it for Mum.*

8

KATE

As Kate peered through the front window of the camper van, edging her way on to the Cherbourg–Rosslare ferry, she could see the ship's name. *Inish Beag*, small island. A memory from another lifetime popped up. There was a small island off the coast of Sandycove. Years ago, the summer when they were still in school and Lola hadn't been home for eight months, she and Flora had taken the boat across. She had lain in the long, spiky grass, soaking up the sun, her arm across her eyes. Beside her, Flora had been drawing some of the sea holly and a lichen-covered rock, the colour of an egg yolk.

Just that morning, Kate had received a hastily written card from Lola in Nashville, where The Islanders were recording their second album. She missed Lola more than she thought was possible. She was nearly eighteen and meant to be grown-up, but it had been much harder than she thought it would be. Her person, the one human who was there only for you, was gone, and Kate felt adrift. Determined she wouldn't live in Lola's shadow, she planned to make her own life, one that didn't involve Lola or The Islanders. She was one of the few people who didn't buy *Finally*

Free, but it followed her everywhere; even in Tibet, she'd once heard that bloody album, her mother's voice, coming out of a small CD player at the back of a rug shop.

Lola hadn't had the best maternal role model herself. There was no way Kate could have gone to live with her grandmother, Lola's mother, with the Bible-bashing and pursed lips, the utter disgust of anyone who wasn't going to Mass at least once a day. God knows how Lola had survived a mother like her. In fact, the last time Kate had been in Ireland was for her grandmother's funeral and she hadn't stayed long enough for Lola to trap her in any conversations. The only person she had talked to was Paulie, who had kept a place up at the top of the church for her.

In Cherbourg, all these years later, Kate kept her eyes on the bumper of the large Range Rover with the Dublin registration plate as she manoeuvred the van onto the ramp, willing the engine not to splutter to a stop and keep going up into the belly of the ship.

Later, she stood on the deck and watched the whooshing as the engines of the ferry swirled up the sea. The water bubbled and boiled below, as the ferry slowly pulled away from land, heading straight for Ireland. *Goodbye France,* she thought. *Thanks for everything.*

* * *

Finally, dry land and the tyres of the camper van bumped off the ferry and onto the smooth tarmac. Ireland. For the first time in a long time, Kate felt a little emotional being back on home soil. She was going to start singing 'The Fields of Athenry' if she wasn't careful. There was a catch in her throat.

Jesus Christ, she thought. *I've gone all soppy.*

It was the baby's fault. Things she would have barely noticed were now making her cry. A couple of weeks earlier, in the market at Tournon, she had seen a woman walking her equally elderly Jack Russell and for some reason Kate had welled up. It was the way they looked so happy together, life partners, a perfect relationship. Also, saying goodbye to Elise and Gilles and the children had been much harder than she had thought it would be. Just thinking of practical, unsentimental Jacques was making her emotional. But she'd moved on. Her old phone was already in the box under the seats at the back of the van, beside the cases of wine given by Gilles, the opening of which would have to wait until after the baby was born. Perhaps Jacques would try to call her on her French number, but then he might not; they were both, after all, free spirits.

She followed the line of cars and lorries in their slow passage across the terminal, peering over the roofs of the cars to see green fields, hedges, wind-battered hazel trees, a rowan in full colour. A particular green, unique to the landscape of Ireland, a bright, fresh, yellow-green grass, which glowed and shone with radiant good health. This was Ireland. This was home. This was the place she had left, as a naive eighteen-year-old on her quest to find herself. She hadn't quite succeeded yet.

Again, a lump in her throat, which she swallowed away, but there was definitely something about this incredibly green countryside, the small fields, the gorgeously higgledy hedges, the cowslips in the ditch beside the road, the yellow of the rape fields. Look, she wanted to say to the baby, look at how lovely everything is.

Sandycove was two hours away along the coast. At a petrol station, just outside Rosslare, Kate stopped and filled up the van, before heading towards the small shop to pay. Bales of briquettes and firewood were stacked outside, along with buckets and spades and a sign for the ice creams of Kate's youth.

A woman with grey straight hair and an oversized checked shirt stood behind the counter. 'Lovely day,' she said, smiling, 'just the petrol, is it? Would you be wanting anything else?'

'Chocolate?' Kate hadn't had Irish chocolate for years. Mainland Europeans may have thought theirs was the best, but they were very wrong. 'Dairy Milk,' she said. 'And a cup of tea, please.'

'Just off the ferry, are you?'

Kate nodded but suddenly she felt dizzy, the long drive, the adrenaline of getting herself through France, onto the ferry and now back on Irish soil had made her light-headed. She steadied herself by holding on to the counter.

'You sit here,' said the woman, rushing out and unfolding a camping chair in one move. 'I'll make you a nice cup of tea and you don't move a muscle. Frank! *FRANK!*' She suddenly shouted with the force of a foreman. 'Move the camper van out front, will ye?' She turned back to Kate. 'Frank will just pull in your van, so you can rest awhile. Keys in ignition?'

Kate nodded, sinking into the chair, as the woman disappeared behind the crisps and the sweets into a back room and she heard the hapless Frank start the engine of the van and rev it furiously before swinging it around the forecourt at top speed and, in an almost handbrake turn, skidded right outside the glass windows. Kate was too wobbly to react.

The woman returned with a cup of tea. 'There you go, loveen. How are you feeling now? You poor divil. A bit better, are you?'

Kate nodded. 'I think so.'

'You eat the Dairy Milk now, all of it, and drink your tea. You'll have another before you're on the road again.' She smiled again at Kate. 'I'm Marie, by the way.'

'Kate.'

Marie gave her a quick rub on her shoulder. 'You're carrying a little one?'

Kate nodded, nearly crying again. 'How can you tell?'

'What else makes a young woman such as yourself suddenly go white as a sheet? I was the same with all four of mine. Legs would go from under me. No notice at all. I'd be grand as you like and then, next minute, like a newborn lamb trying to stand up. Long drive ahead of ye?'

'Dublin,' said Kate, sitting on the chair. 'Sandycove. I grew up there.'

'Your mam's looking forward to seeing you, I would say. Mine are all in Dubai, Melbourne, Perth and Boston. Wouldn't mind one of them coming home sometime, I can tell you.' She smiled again.

'My mum doesn't live there,' said Kate. Again, the tears began to pool. What was wrong with her? Hormones. But also it was the fact she had come back with no plan, nowhere to stay, and had given up a perfectly good life in France to return to a country she hadn't lived in since she was a teenager. She'd been hasty and stupid. Why hadn't she rung ahead and told Patsy and Flora she was on her way? She hadn't planned any of this at all well.

'You must have *someone* belonging to you,' said Marie.

'I have friends,' replied Kate, wanting to reassure Marie, who was now nodding, relieved, there was at least a hint of *someone*. 'Flora. And her mother, Patsy. They're like family. She's married to this man,' she told Marie. 'But I don't think he *approves* of me. But they seem happy.'

Marie tutted as though she didn't approve of Justin, and handed Kate another bar of Dairy Milk and another cup of tea. 'Vitamins,' she said, 'are all very well. But there are times in a woman's life when chocolate is the only necessity.' She peered at Kate. 'Don't set off quite yet,' she said. 'Stay a night, and then see how ye are in the morning. I always say if ye don't rush the journey, the arriving is all the sweeter. Now, what do you say? I'll make you some dinner. And you take your time. Looks like you've got a lot going on. Potatoes all right for ye? Bit of mash and a few sausages?'

Kate found herself nodding, grateful to be told what to do for a moment, happy to relinquish decision-making and control for one night. She slept in the van, parked in the driveway of Marie's house, just beside the filling station, and in the morning Frank tinkered away in the engine, retuning it, changing the oil and doing all those little jobs that hadn't even crossed Kate's mind.

When Kate finally felt able to set off again, Marie hugged her goodbye.

'Now, remember us. Rosslare Filling Station. You've got friends for life here, you hear me? And let us know how you and the baby are, will you?'

Kate drove off, waving out of the window to Marie. Even Frank made an appearance, hovering behind Marie and raising his hand in a goodbye.

Next stop Sandycove.

9

LOLA

Lola read Kate's email again. Sandycove. It would do her good to get out of California for a while. She was having the same conversations about the weather here with the girls in the juice bar and the women in the nail bar. And her neighbours always wanted to talk about this storm here, or the political problems, or the fact their new Tesla was making some kind of rattling sound. It was getting harder and harder to nod as though she cared. Before, she liked people, loved hearing what someone was up to, or listening to the life story of a stranger. These days, she had no patience for anyone. It was as though all her past mistakes were now festering and roosting inside her.

Poor Richie, he didn't deserve to live with such a misery. But, really, there was little joy to be had anywhere. No fun, nothing to look forward to. Nothing. She'd made mistakes. *Many* mistakes. Leaving Kate was the biggest one, and the only one which mattered now. The thing about mistakes was once they were made, they could never be undone. You had to live with the consequences, knowing forgiveness was something you could never assume. Richie's advice was to give it a try. 'Suck it and see,' he

said, as Lola agonised. 'You'll never know anything by just
guessing.'

This was probably her last chance to see if Kate would find
room in her heart for her, but going back to Ireland was also a
chance to walk along the coast like she used to do, the rain on her
face, the wind in her hair, buttoned into coats and layers and
jumpers. There was nothing like it. In California, everything was
the same. No wonder people over-exercised on their Power Plates
or Pelotons or consumed their own placentas, seeking a kind of
rebirth, but all they really needed was a pint in a pub, a bag of
cheese and onion crisps and a chat with a stranger. Lola could still
taste those pints, even when she was trying not to gag while
drinking her green juice. Made with actual grass, would you
believe? Actual fecking grass. Paulie had loved the trappings of
the high life, but even he drew the line at what he put in his
mouth. Proper food, he always insisted on. Their chef, Mikey, was
from Dungarvan and knew exactly what Paulie wanted.

Lola started to laugh.

'What are you laughing about?' Richie stood in the doorway.
'Gotta say, it's good to hear.'

'I was remembering the time Paulie had a shot of wheatgrass,'
she said, beginning to laugh again. '"Grass?" he said. "Would
anyone tell these Californians that humans don't eat grass, cows
eat grass. Come to Ireland," he said. "Eat our butter. Best in the
world *because* of the grass. Jaysus. Next they'll be milking
humans."' She smiled at Richie. 'It's probably not funny now,' she
said. 'But it was at the time. His face when he drank it down, a
sight to be seen. He only did it because Antonio said he was a
coward.'

Antonio was Paulie's on-off-on-off thing. At the funeral,
dressed in a black satin suit, mopping his eyes with a ginormous
handkerchief, making wailing sounds as though he and Paulie

were love's great dream. Well, they were, when Paulie wasn't also with Mikey. 'I'm going straight to hell, darling,' Paulie used to say, whenever he reappeared from a one-, or two-, or three-night stand.

'I'm more of a bourbon man than green juice. Or grass,' said Richie, stretching his arms over his head, his T-shirt riding up, exposing his lower stomach. He was wasted on her, he really was. He smiled at her. 'Need more alone time?'

She nodded. She had too much going on in her head and couldn't calm it all down for long enough. Writing songs had always helped to soothe and sort out her feelings, but now songwriting made her think of Paulie too much.

'I'll put the coffee on,' Richie said, slipping back inside the screen door. 'You tell me when you're finished communing with the Buddha or whatever it is you are doing.'

She picked up her phone and read again Kate's email.

I've decided to head back to Ireland. Probably Sandycove. Just to see people. I've missed Ireland, I suppose. Will send on my address when I know what I'm doing.

No Buddha, thought Lola. *Sandycove*. She closed her eyes. *And a pint*, she thought. *My beach house for a pint. But most of all my daughter. One more chance to be a mother. Which is more than I deserve... a lot more than I deserve.*

Lola O'Hare was going home too.

10

FLORA

In the haberdashery, Flora was unpacking a delivery from the new fabric designer. She laid the rolls on the cutting table, feeling the smooth cotton, examining the pattern. The collection was called 'Spraoi', the Irish for play, and the designer, whom Flora had met the other day, was experimenting in colour clashing, oranges and purples, greens and pinks, in tiny dots and dashes which up close were distinct and vibrant and from afar gave a shimmering, hazy feeling, as though the colour was bouncing on the folds of the fabric. She felt a lurch of jealousy, not the kind she felt when she thought of Justin and Sandra, but something else, as though someone was living the life meant for her and there was nothing she could do about it. Jealousy was an awful emotion, but she felt so envious of this designer, this woman who had her whole life and career stretching out in front of her and who wasn't stupid enough to make the kind of mistakes Flora had.

The bell above the shop's door rang and she looked up to see Patsy, dressed in her blue trouser suit.

'How are you doing?' She came over and gave her a hug. 'All right?'

'Fine,' Flora lied.

'Ready? We're meeting Killian Walsh at the new hotel, remember?'

'I haven't forgotten,' said Flora, re-rolling the fabric.

'Oh, it's lovely...' Patsy reached over and felt the material, rubbing it between her fingers. 'So unusual, the colours...'

'It's new,' said Flora. 'We're trying it out, see if people like it. She's a young designer...' Flora pretended not to notice the look Patsy gave her and placed the roll on the shelf.

'Well, you're a designer too,' said Patsy, 'and who knows what might come of it?'

Flora thought she was going to start crying again, and for a moment turned her face away, hoping Patsy wouldn't notice. 'Come on,' she said, as she locked the shop behind them, 'let's go and meet that man who thinks Sandycovian is an adjective.'

Patsy slipped her arm through Flora's, and as they walked past the posh supermarket, the scene of her great undoing, Flora shuddered.

Patsy seemed to sense something. 'You'll be okay,' she said, insistently. 'All of us face... challenging times... and we all, mostly, survive...'

'I know...' Flora began, remembering a time, in another life, in another desperate need of solace when she'd been teased at school because she had an old khaki bag rather than some trendy sports brand. She'd come home tearful and disappeared into her room. Patsy had knocked on her door, carrying a tray with tea and a Wagon Wheel on. 'School is hard,' she had said, sitting on the edge of the bed, 'especially for lovely, sensitive girls like you. You'll meet a friend, just like you.' Flora had wished she wasn't lovely or sensitive. It would have been far easier to have been like the super-confident girls, with their glossy hair and loud voices and trendy sports bags.

And here she was now, nearly twenty years later, still being soothed by her mother.

Flora checked her phone again. Nothing from Justin. He'd dropped in a suitcase of some of her clothes which he'd left outside Patsy's front door, but there was still so much of hers in the house. Flora half-hoped that they could get over this and she wouldn't need to move out, she could be moving back in instead. Just imagining there was hope, forgiving Justin – 'No harm done!' – was so much easier than accepting that you were not loved and were surplus to requirements.

'Are you listening, Flora?'

'What? Sorry... what were you saying?'

'I was saying life is a succession of starting-overs,' Patsy continued in an urgent way. 'You have to gather yourself, find your strength. Life isn't just one journey, it's a series of interlocking loops...'

'Like a pattern on wallpaper,' said Flora. But she was thinking she didn't want to start over...

Patsy laughed. 'Exactly. Like wallpaper. Which you're about to design...'

But Flora's brain was empty of all inspiration. Years ago, she would spot something small which would trigger an idea – a crack in a wall, ivy trickling down, even a spider she had once spotted in the corner of the art room had made an appearance on to one of her designs.

'I'm looking forward to meeting this Killian Walsh,' she said, not wanting to think too much. 'I bet he's the kind of man in loafers without socks and wears sunglasses indoors.'

'He's the very last person to commit such a crime,' said Patsy, confidently.

They stood in front of The Sandycove Arms. On the stone flagstones in front of the hotel, tradespeople had set up HQs – the carpenter was sawing wood, a team of electricians, laden with tool belts, were working, coils of cables stacked beside them. And the painters who were daubing the exterior wall in a dark grey, the windows a bright white, had their paint organised on an old cloth.

'The exterior colour is nice,' said Patsy. 'Very smart.'

'I suppose it's an improvement,' said Flora. 'The old colour was a dirty yellow. Or forlorn daffodil, as I always thought of it.'

Patsy laughed. 'What is the name of that grey, do you think?'

'Abandoned house grey? Trying too hard grey?' Flora smiled, as they walked inside.

The size of the foyer was good, she thought. Very nice proportions, big without being cavernous, and the windows were full-length, ideal for a window seat and people-watching. And for a moment, she felt something, a fizzle of synapse, a sizzle of an idea. She could see the window, finished, the curtains long, the colour blue... tweed... or something else?

Beside her, Patsy was talking, almost to herself, as though she too was imagining the future life of the building. 'Curtains there,' she was saying, 'seating there – maybe two low sofas facing each other. Upholstered, cushions. Bookcase...'

This was how it worked, Flora remembered, you had to have imagination strong enough to place it into the here and now. Years ago, it used to come so easily to her, but her mother, she was pleased to see, was already a natural. Flora found herself smiling at her.

'Let's measure up,' said Patsy, taking out her retractable tape and notepad. 'And then we can start thinking.'

There was a man's voice behind them. 'Hello, Patsy. Lovely to see you again.'

Flora turned around to see who was speaking. He didn't look like your usual hotelier; no dark glasses or cigar. Thankfully, no visible chest hair. He was tall, slim and wearing a pair of navy chinos and a pale blue shirt. Attractive but low-key, unlike Justin, a golden-haired man who turned heads when he walked into a room, his shirts unbuttoned, his huge, charming smile. She'd seen women – and men – blinking in his sunlight. Once upon a time, she had been one of them. Now, it was Sandra's turn.

'Killian, this is Flora, my daughter,' said Patsy. 'She's agreed to work on the project with me.'

Killian shook Flora's hand, smiling. 'So, design runs in the family?'

'Well, I'm not a designer... not any more,' she said, feeling shifty. 'I'm just helping Mum out...'

'Right...' Killian glanced at Patsy, curiously, as though she had misled him, or he was trying to work them out.

'I mean, I *was* one,' Flora tried to explain. 'College and everything but... well, I never really took off...'

'She was *meant* to take up a master's in London,' said Patsy, stepping forward. 'But she gave it up.'

'I *was* going to set up my own company,' added Flora.

'And did you?' asked Killian.

Flora shook her head. 'I kept meaning to, but I never got around to it.' She suddenly realised she was doing neither herself nor Patsy any favours. 'But I have been keeping my hand in and I work in Waters & Co.' She looked at him, expecting to see pity in his eyes or condescension, but he nodded briskly, as though he understood.

'You know, you can't do everything at the same time. You were too busy living,' he said, 'doing other things.'

'Too busy minding that husband of hers,' said Patsy. 'Waste of time, that was...'

'Mum!' Flora was appalled.

'You've nothing to be ashamed of,' said Patsy. '*He* has.' She turned back to Killian. 'Affair.'

Killian looked at Flora. 'Me too. Join the club.'

Patsy looked at him. '*You*?'

He laughed. 'No, not me. I was the adulter*ee*... is that a word?' He shrugged. 'Water under the bridge now. We've all moved on. She is currently about to be married to husband number three... and adopt her fifth schnauzer. We didn't have children. Fortunately. Or unfortunately. But we're good friends. Well, *good enough* friends. Actually, not really friends. We uncoupled consciously and are quite happy never to set eyes on each other ever again.' He laughed again. Flora found herself smiling at him, impressed that he carried his situation so lightly, someone who had regained control over his life again. People who were able to deal with the knocks and blocks of life, and come back stronger – even *happier* – were impressive.

'How did you find out?' asked Patsy. 'About being adulterated?'

'Oh, he was married and his wife heard them talking on the baby monitor and went full Sherlock, looking for further evidence and found deleted text messages, credit card receipts, the whole lot.' He pulled a face. 'She'd just given birth to their second child, and we were all at the christening when she stood up and said she wanted to make a speech. Started presenting her evidence and we were all... well... gobsmacked. Me more than anyone. Didn't suspect a thing. It was quite the christening. He was a friend of mine...'

'Same as me,' said Flora. 'My adulterating husband was best friends with Sandra's – she's the woman – husband.' She wondered if she would ever reach a point where she would be able to talk about it with the casual disregard, even humour, like Killian could.

'How did *you* move on?' Patsy persisted.

'Ah, you know... took a fair bit of soul-searching, counselling, the works – yoga, even – to get me feeling in any way good about myself.'

'Flora, you should try yoga,' said Patsy. 'Might help with *everything*.'

'I can't do yoga,' said Flora. 'And I don't do "soul-searching"...' She made squiggly marks in the air with her fingers.

Patsy gave her a furious look, but Killian laughed. 'I know I'm a cliché, but it got me through.'

'I'm going to remain single for the rest of my life,' vowed Flora. 'The thought of ever going through this ever again is horrible.' Although, she hoped, she and Justin would soon be back together, having put this all behind them, and the question about being single forever would remain irrelevant.

Killian glanced at her sympathetically. 'I was telling your mother I'm actually in the throes of online dating. It's quite the eye-opener...' He laughed. 'But I'll save my fascinating stories for another day.' He smiled at them both. 'Right, let's return to more important matters – the hotel...'

11

PATSY

Later, she and Flora were sitting at the kitchen table discussing the hotel when the sound of an engine rattling along the road made them both look up.

'Sounds like a tractor,' said Flora. 'Lost its way. Or Cyril Kidney's Morris Minor.'

'More like a van.' Patsy was brought straight back to the time, a lifetime ago, when Jack had taken her off in his battered HiAce to a folk festival on Inishbofin, off the west coast. Those four days had felt like weeks, as they slept in the back of the van, the open door revealing swirling sea views, and spent the evenings in pubs listening to music, holding hands under the table and falling in love. That weekend on Bofin, they had lain on a moth-eaten rug listening to Christy Moore, drinking warm cider and picking wild-flowers. Patsy hasn't listened to Christy Moore since, and even now, if she heard a note of 'Lisdoonvarna' or any of his other songs, she had to leave immediately. Flora was named after the flowers Patsy had picked on the trip and brought back to Dublin, pressing them in the pages of the map of Ireland found in the van's glove compartment. It was Jack who chose the name. 'Flora,' he'd said, 'how could she not be beautiful with such a name?' Patsy could still see him in the armchair in the front room, holding Flora.

And then it was all over. He'd been coming back late at night from a delivery to Belfast. Driving rain, no visibility. Someone said later they had seen a motorbike skidding in front of the van. Jack had swerved and went straight into a wall. Patsy had been up most of the night with Flora, only half-wondering where Jack had got to when the Guards knocked on the door to tell her.

Resilience. Strength. Starting over. She had tried to say some of this to Flora earlier, but it had come out so badly. You *do* survive, she wanted to tell her. You think you never will but you do. Scars, yes. Wounds, of course. But you're alive.

Outside, the rattling van had come to a spluttering stop. And then, a moment later, the doorbell rang.

'Are you expecting anyone?' she asked Flora, who was already standing.

Please don't let it be Justin begging forgiveness, thought Patsy, remaining at the kitchen table while Flora went into the hall. *Let it be over and allow Flora to reclaim her life.*

But there was a scream from Flora and, as Patsy dashed into the hall, she saw someone's arms around Flora, the two of them jumping up and down, their hair entangled, both squealing.

Flora turned around, her eyes shining. 'It's Kate!' she said. 'She's come home!'

Kate rushed over to Patsy and hugged her. 'I hope you don't mind,' she was saying breathlessly. 'It was a spur-of-the-moment thing, just to come and see you all...'

'Of course not,' Patsy said, kissing her. 'It's so lovely to see you. This is your second home, remember?'

Kate's eyes filled with tears. 'Thank you... Oh, it's so lovely to see you both.'

For the two years Kate had lived with them, Patsy had done everything she could to make Kate feel loved and wanted but she'd watched as she had become increasingly determined to leave Ireland, to do her own thing, to prove she didn't need anyone. Whenever she did come home, Patsy always wondered if she was finally ready to stay.

Kate looked as beautiful as she always did and well and healthy; her long hair hung loosely over her shoulders and was sun-flecked and golden-toned.

'I'll start dinner,' said Patsy. 'And maybe Flora can set up your old bed?'

'I've got my van,' said Kate. 'I can sleep in there. If you don't mind me parking in the drive?'

12

KATE

Kate and Flora stayed up talking until long after midnight, sitting on either end of the sofa, facing each other, their legs parallel, just the way they used to when they were teenagers. Then, it was Kate who needed the counselling, the talking-to, the pep talks, the propping up. Now, it was Flora.

Kate had been planning to tell her about being pregnant. The only people in the world who knew about the baby were the nurse in Tournon's medical centre and Marie from the Rosslare filling station. She barely had a bump and her usual uniform of loose linen shirt and linen trousers, both bought in the market in Tournon, weren't exactly revealing. She had opened her mouth to blurt it all out to Flora, all about Jacques, Elise and the vineyard, her life in the little apartment above the barn... and about the baby. But then Flora had told her about Justin.

I knew it, thought Kate. *From the first moment I met him, I knew there was something wrong about him.* 'I drove to your home,' said Kate, 'and a woman answered and said you didn't live there any more...'

'Sandra,' explained Flora. 'Robert's wife...'

'I couldn't take my eyes off her streaky fake tan,' said Kate. 'What did she apply it with? A fly swatter?'

Flora laughed, which made Kate feel relieved. If she hadn't come home, she thought, she wouldn't have heard all this about Justin and she wouldn't have had the opportunity to be there for her friend. She was suddenly so glad to have come back.

'She's inordinately keen on her fake tan,' added Flora.

'Too keen,' remarked Kate, 'obviously.'

It was good to see Flora laughing again, despite being so obviously upset.

Kate took her hand as Flora told her more about what had happened.

'It's like I hung around for all those years thinking there was a point to it all,' said Flora, 'we were getting somewhere... to a family. I wanted a child... *children*...'

Now was not the time to share her news, thought Kate. She would just have to find the right moment.

* * *

Later, Flora returned from the kitchen with two hot mugs of tea and a packet of chocolate digestives. 'Are you sure you don't want wine? Or has living on a vineyard meant that you can only drink the best kind?'

'Something like that...'

'So,' said Flora, happily, sitting down on the sofa, and tucking her legs underneath her, 'tell me about Saint-Sauveur and the Auberts... it all sounds glorious.'

Kate nodded. 'It was. It's such a beautiful area... I loved the market on Saturdays. Everyone from the surrounding area would come into town with their fruit to sell or flowers. There was a little café I loved, Flaubert's, and I would sit and have my coffee. I always thought how much you would love it. I wish you'd come and stayed...'

'I would have done,' said Flora. 'I should have done...' She sighed. 'And I wish I'd met Jacques. How is he?'

'Well...' Kate looked at her. 'I'm... I mean... I'm having a... I'm...' She hoped Flora would be okay about this. She didn't know if she could do it, without Flora's support. She had to tell her. 'I'm twenty-six weeks pregnant.' Kate reached out her hand and took Flora's. 'I didn't *want* to... I mean...'

But Flora was smiling. 'That's amazing! A baby!' She leaned across, flinging her arms around Kate. 'Now I understand why you are on the *tea*...'

'You're not upset?'

Flora was shaking her head. 'Of course not. If you're worried that I am upset just because you're pregnant, I'm not. If you are happy about being pregnant, then I am too... of course I am. The idea that I wouldn't be pleased for you...'

'I'm scared more than anything,' admitted Kate. 'It just happened. I didn't plan it or prepare for it and then I discover that I'm going to have a baby.'

Flora nodded, taking it all in. 'And what about Jacques?'

'We've gone our separate ways, you know how these things go,' said Kate. 'Currently volunteering in Greece.' She shrugged. 'Exactly the kind of thing he'd do. He's been planning it for the last couple of years and eventually was able to take a sabbatical. But he always said he didn't want to have a child because he wanted to be able to do things like go off and volunteer. I thought I'd just come home for a bit, see everyone and then decide on my next move.' Whatever the hell *that* was going to be, she thought.

Stubborn, that's what Lola had called her the last time they'd met. It was at Gran's funeral and Kate wouldn't take the money Lola tried to give her. 'I'll buy you a house,' Lola had said, 'something nice.' She'd turned to Paulie. 'You talk sense to her, Paulie,' but he'd raised his hands in surrender, turning towards Kate, the leather of his cowboy boots squeaking.

Paulie had earlier said that they were the worst things to wear to a funeral. 'People will either think I'm farting all the way to the front pew,' he'd whispered to Kate while they stood outside the church, Lola looking rigid, as the undertakers hoisted the coffin from the hearse, 'or they'll think I've bought myself cheap leather boots.' He'd paused. 'I'd prefer it if they thought I was farting.'

Flora looked worried for Kate, as though taking on the momentousness of Kate's predicament. 'And you're going to sleep in the van...'

'It's comfortable. I have a ridiculous amount of pillows and... well, it's mine.' Kate had been trying to make a plan in her head. Being back in Sandycove felt good but there was a bittersweetness to it all as her mind wandered back to the vineyard. Had she done the right thing by leaving? Had Jacques tried to call her disconnected mobile phone? Several times she had thought about calling Elise and Gilles, to see how they were, but also to wonder, casually, if they'd heard from Jacques. Tears welled up again. *More self-pity*, she thought, as she wiped them away.

'What's wrong?' asked Flora, leaning towards her, concerned.

'A combination of hormones and feeling sorry for myself,' she said. 'But I'll be fine.'

Flora smiled at Kate. 'I'm glad you're home.'

Kate felt furious when she thought of Justin and the woman with the fake tan, Sandra. Kate had been so surprised when she had answered the door that she hadn't reacted properly. If she'd known, she would have told Justin and Sandra exactly what she thought of them. 'And you can share my van, whenever you want,' said Kate. 'And I'm going to find a job and then plan for the birth.'

'So, you're staying?' Flora looked delighted. 'For a *while*?'

Kate nodded. 'As long as Patsy doesn't mind me cluttering up the drive...'

'She doesn't mind in the slightest.' Flora grinned at her. 'You can stay as long as you like, you're home now.'

* * *

Later, under the diamond stars in the night sky, Kate drew the curtains in the van. Here in Sandycove, surrounded by sleeping, suburban life, the odd fox stalking or hedgehog scuttling, and a few hundred metres away the soft sweep of the sea, she felt safe.

Tomorrow, she would go to hospital and sign herself into the Irish health system and get herself at least officially pregnant. She put her hands on her belly and thought she felt a flicker of her baby moving. *Whatever happens*, she thought, *I'm not going to let my baby down. We're in this together.*

13

LOLA

Her bags packed, passport in her hand, Lola stood in the door of the living room. Richie looked up. 'I'm going to Ireland,' she said. 'For an indefinite period of time.'

He looked shocked, shaking his head, as though he couldn't quite find the words.

'You told me to suck it and see,' she said. 'You *wanted* me to go.'

He still couldn't speak, which was so unlike him, so she carried on.

'I'm getting older. You're still a spring chicken. Or rooster. You need to go and flap your wings and squawk at some chicks... I've got unfinished business,' she said in what she thought of as her brisk voice, one which she'd used over the years when she needed to get things done. 'A few loose ends which need to be tied up... bridges built, that kind of thing...'

He found his voice, finally. 'I can help you build bridges,' he said. 'I'm strong...'

She shook her head. 'It's better this way, believe me. What did Englebert once say? I'm releasing you and letting you go...'

He was still looking at her, bemused. Why could he not see

this was good for him? This was his chance to meet someone nice. 'But I don't want to be...'

'You do,' she said. 'You really do. Now, I know of several nice women who would be very happy if you called them up. Maria from next door for one. Promise me? You'll go and be happy?'

For a moment, she thought he was going to cry. *Please don't. Just make this easy for me.* Over the years, she'd left men behind in houses and hotel rooms, moving on, feeling determined this was the right thing. And, of course, leaving Richie *was* the right thing to do.

'You'll be grand,' she said, firmly. 'Now, let's have a bourbon to toast the lovely time we've had.'

They sat on the porch, singing together, while Richie played his guitar.

'It's been good, hasn't it, Richie?'

He nodded. 'It's been quite a ride...'

'And promise me you will find someone nice, someone who deserves you...'

'I'll put the ad in the Lonely Hearts column in the morning,' he said. '*Woman wanted. Must be more interesting than the last one... but doesn't need to build bridges or even space to build bridges.*' He winked at her. 'Reckon it'll work?'

'They'll be flocking to you,' she said. 'All those chicks.'

'Can I come too?' he asked, those brown eyes taking her in.

'No,' she said quickly, looking straight ahead. It was dangerous to look in those eyes, she might say yes. 'Anyway, you'd only be in the way.'

'I'll miss you, babe,' he said.

Ah, he'd be grand. Fine man like Richie would be snapped up.

'Well, why don't you write a song?' she said. 'You're always saying you're too happy to write songs.'

Ouch. He looked away. Once, they'd been walking along the

waterfront, and he'd grabbed her and said he could never write another song because when you're happy you don't produce the songwriting hormones. No one wanted to hear about happiness, they wanted to sing along with your heartbreak. And no one knew that better than Lola O'Hare. She and Paulie had won a Grammy for *Corners of the Room*, which one critic had described as the 'greatest sublimation of lost love ever created'.

* * *

Lola arrived at LAX and remembered why she always thought of it as the world's worst airport. As she hadn't bothered with VIP, she was wearing dark glasses and a Hermès headscarf. Long ago, she and Paulie had worked out how to get around unfollowed and unbothered. It was a matter of charisma, Paulie reckoned, you could turn it on, off or up... you just chose your charisma setting. Paulie *loved* being recognised and usually would take off his cap to show off his red hair – '*Golden blond*, darling.' But there were times when it was overwhelming even for him. Of course, that was back when The Islanders had three singles in the US Billboard chart top ten, as well as their album, *Finally Free* – the one which featured Lola totally naked on the cover, her long blonde hair which was wrapped around her body. Some US congressman had wanted the album banned and one crazy man had gone into Walmart and set fire to one of the covers. She could laugh now at the zeal and passion of some folk. But at least they were passionate about something. Lola worried sometimes that she was losing everything she ever cared about. Kate felt like one of the few things worth caring about.

Spurred on by knowing her daughter was returning to Sandycove, Lola had booked herself into a flat above a shop on the main street for a month. And wherever Kate was staying, she would find her. She'd go to Patsy Fox's house first, because surely she would know, but anyway, no one could stay hidden in Sandycove because everyone knew everyone else's business. The valley of the twitching windows, Paulie called it. Lola used to think of it like being dropped in a barrel of squirming eels, everyone slipping and sliding all over you and you couldn't breathe. In Ireland, people didn't go in for celebrity and if they knew you were famous, they actively avoided you or pretended they'd never heard of you just so your ego didn't explode. 'Doesn't he think well of himself,' was what her mother used to say whenever there was someone on television merely trying to present the best of themselves. *She'll be saying the same thing about me*, Lola used to think before any big interview. *Well, guess what, Mam? I do think well of myself. No thanks to you.* Paulie always thought well of himself, he never had a moment's self-doubt and would look in the mirror and actually smile at his reflection. He was born confident, like all babies, but no one ever stamped it out of him. Born lucky as well.

Paulie used to miss Ireland more than anything, becoming misty-eyed as he misquoted Yeats or raised a glass of whiskey on Paddy's Day. Didn't miss it enough to give up his orange grove in his Nashville compound, Lola would tease. On his trips home for gigs, he fired around, seeing all his aunties, his mother, being full-on charming Paulie, and as they flew back – private, of course – to the States, he would dive under his cashmere blanket, a Barry's tea in his hand. 'Don't make me go back there, Lola,' he would say. 'I'm not myself when I'm there.' He did go home, for good. His body flown over the Atlantic, taken from Dublin Airport and brought to the funeral home in Sandycove, his mother standing vigil over his coffin as friends, family, hangers-on, fans all trooped in. Lola was relegated to just a guest, like anyone else... peering around in the church, hoping Kate would be there.

It had gone on for long enough, it was time to talk. It was unforgivable of Lola to have allowed any of this to happen and she'd been selfish, she really had.

Once, years ago, Lola had rung Patsy, trying to track Kate down. 'Nepal?'

'I think so,' Patsy had said, 'and then overland to Ladakh...' Her voice had faltered as though she was aware of the ridiculousness of one woman telling another about her daughter's plans. To think of Kate out there somewhere in the world with just her rucksack was heartbreaking.

'Ms O'Hare,' said the shiny-faced Irish stewardess, when she got on board the Aer Lingus LAX–DUB flight, 'if there is anything I can help with, please do not hesitate to ask.'

'Champagne please,' said Lola. '*Two* glasses. One for each hand.'

14

KATE

The National Maternity Hospital at Holles Street in Dublin's city centre was a grim Victorian building which had seen better days. Outside, there were heavily pregnant women in dressing gowns and fluffy slippers, taking last breaths of air before heading back inside. Some looked already exhausted as though dreading the days and weeks ahead, while the earth mothers glided about with beatific expressions on their faces.

Kate was in the former group – daunted and scared – when a phrase came back to her. *Be brave. Feel the power within.* It was something Lola used to say when she headed off to gigs.

When Kate was small, she'd watch Lola dress for her gigs. She'd brush her hair, dab glitter on her eyes and cheekbones, and zip herself into one of her long, shimmery dresses. Lola would turn around. 'Right, how do I look?'

'Like a princess,' Kate would say.

'A *Celtic* princess?'

'Definitely.'

And then, Lola would look in the mirror. 'Be brave,' she used to say every time. 'Feel the power within.' And Kate would shut her eyes tightly, hoping her mother did indeed feel the power within. And the spell worked, because, in just a few years, The Islanders were offered their first US tour and the rest... well, everything changed at that moment. But before all that, they had loved and adored each other, before that pivotal moment when they both went their separate ways. She remembered Lola kissing her before leaving for a gig. 'Wish me luck, little girl,' she would say.

'*Your* little girl,' Kate would correct her.

'*My* little girl.' Lola smiled at her. 'The best girl any mother ever had...'

They were happy in those early years and Lola had done her best to give them a better future, but their bond was broken.

'Are you one of our new ladies?' said the nurse behind the reception desk.

'Yes,' said Kate. She hadn't asked anyone to come with her, thinking it was just like any other doctor's appointment, but it wasn't until she stood in reception, surrounded by pregnant women, busy-looking nurses and the sense of history of all the babies who had been born her, all the women who had laboured, all that *life* and love, did she wish there was someone to hold her hand.

'Take a ticket and a seat,' said the nurse, pointing to a machine, the kind of which Kate had last used at the deli counter in the large Carrefour in Tournon. She sat on a hard plastic seat, attached to the wall. Next to her were two women.

'What are you?' said one woman to the other.

'I'm thirty-six and a half,' said the woman. 'You?'

'I'm thirty-three and three-quarters...' The first woman turned to Kate. 'What about you?'

'I'm thirty-two and...' Kate tried to work it out. Was this a thing now to be so exact about your age? 'Two-thirds.' She smiled. 'Or thereabouts. I was thirty-two in September.'

The two women looked at each other and laughed. 'No, the dates of the *baby*,' one said.

'Oh... well, I'm not sure exactly,' Kate said hastily.

'My fella wanted to be here,' said the second woman. 'Hasn't missed a scan, an appointment, he's googling everything... but he's been struck down with man flu and I said to him, he's not bringing his snivels and germs into the hospital.'

'Mine is at work,' said the other one. 'He's got the kind of boss who doesn't believe in men being around for all the appointments.' She turned to Kate. 'Where's your partner?'

Kate didn't know how to respond. 'He's... well, he doesn't...' Kate tried to explain her situation. She'd forgotten how much Irish people asked the kind of questions French women wouldn't dream of asking. Small talk didn't exist, you'd begin by talking about the weather and then end with telling each other the deepest, darkest family secrets. 'He's not around. He's... gone.' She hoped it sounded mysterious enough to ensure they didn't ask any further questions.

The woman cleared her throat, one hand on Kate's, her eyes filled with tears. 'When did he pass?'

'Pass?' And then Kate nearly laughed. 'He's not *dead*. Or at least I don't think he is. He could be. But I don't think he is... unless...'

'Right...' The woman looked a little perplexed. 'Does he know you're here?'

Kate shook her head. 'He doesn't even know *it's* here,' she said, gesturing to her stomach, and just as she was going to try to explain, or rather not explain, any further, a doctor came out and called out 'Eighty-four!' and the woman gathered up her folder of notes and her bag, and rushed to follow her.

* * *

Finally, it was Kate's turn and there was a large and terrifying crucifix over the door.

The doctor noticed Kate's upward glance. 'Don't mind that, it's one of those hangovers which insist on lingering. I'm Sinéad O'Leary.' She glanced down at Kate's stomach which was well covered with her linen shirt again and her worker's jacket and scarf. 'Date of conception?'

'I'm not actually sure,' said Kate. 'I wasn't really... I didn't think... I wasn't planning...'

Sinéad nodded. 'Best if you lie down and I have a poke around. Okay with you?'

Uncertain quite what she meant, Kate was relieved when all it involved was Sinéad pressing very firmly and carefully all over her stomach, eyes squinting in concentration. 'Right,' she said, 'let's go for the ultrasound... Now, is there any reason why you haven't presented to us before now?'

'I've been living in France,' explained Kate, feeling wretched and worried. The baby, oh God, she hoped the baby was all right. 'On a vineyard... and so... well...'

'Okay, no need to show off...' Sinéad smiled at her. 'As stories go about why a woman hasn't presented nice and early to us, yours wins. I don't think I'd bother getting myself into the Irish health service if it meant leaving a French vineyard. Now, do you want the good news or the bad news?'

'The bad news.' Get it over quickly. Kate's fingers clutched at the side of the bed.

'Well, the bad news is, you have a very lively baby. And the good news is, she or he is doing very well indeed.'

Kate felt a relief so deep, she wouldn't have thought it possible. She hadn't realised how worried she had been that the baby was doing okay. Now, it was becoming almost real. She fought back tears.

'Now,' went on Sinéad. 'I want you to go straight for a scan. I want to see the baby doing his or her gymnastics. I think we might have a future Olympian on our hands. And we'll be able to tell its sex, if you want to know, and then we can check your bloods and everything else and just get you fully into our system.' She smiled at Kate. 'Okay with you?'

Kate nodded.

'I'll walk you down to ultrasound now. I wouldn't mind having a look myself and see this wonder baby who is doing it all by herself. Or himself.'

Outside the room, she offered Kate a wheelchair.

'There's no shame in it, you know,' she said. 'We want our ladies to feel as though when they step through our doors, they are here to be looked after.'

'No, I'm fine,' said Kate. Suddenly, she was feeling totally over-whelmed again, something happening to her which was bigger than anything she could have imagined. When she'd been talking to her baby, she hadn't really thought of it as a *baby*, but here in this hospital, the enormity and reality of what was happening was really sinking in.

And then the ultrasound. The cold jelly, the terrible wait and then... 'Oh my God... oh my God...' There it was. Her baby. Looking exactly like a baby. She could see its profile, its nose, it even waved – kind of.

'Hello, baby,' said the nurse.

'Looks fine to me,' said Sinéad, staring at the screen. 'I think this little person has done really well, getting to twenty-six weeks all by itself.' She smiled at Kate. 'Now, we'll take your bloods and a few more tests and you're to come back to me in two weeks' time. And then once a week. I wouldn't mind keeping an eye on you, okay?'

'Okay.' She nodded. And lay back again, and then suddenly she tried to sit up. 'Is it a boy or a girl?'

The nurse smiled. 'A girl,' she said.

A boy would be easier, less complicated. Girls and their mothers were always destined for difficulties, look at her and Lola, and Lola and her own mother. With a son, she might have a hope of not repeating her mother's mistakes.

The nurse was looking at her, waiting for some kind of reaction.

'I have three of them myself,' she said, taking Kate's hand in both of hers. 'Don't know what I'd do without my girls.'

But Patsy and Flora weren't complicated. They loved each other, no drama, no questions. Neither had ever spent more than a moment wondering about the other's motivations or reasons. And anyway, wasn't Kate being a bit of a narcissist already introducing drama into her child's life, before it had even been born? She was having a baby girl, and this was her chance to do *everything* differently to the way Lola had managed being a mother.

'I love her already,' she said to the nurse, who visibly relaxed and patted Kate's hand.

'How could you not?' she said. 'All babies want to do is love you, so why wouldn't you love them even more?'

Kate nodded, slipping off the bed. 'Am I too small?' she asked the nurse. 'My bump... shouldn't I be bigger?'

The nurse shook her head. 'Bumps come in all shapes and

sizes, just like women. Your baby is growing fine, that's all that matters. Do you have bump envy?'

Kate laughed. 'A bit...' In a matter of months she would be giving birth, all being well. *Be brave*, she told herself. *Feel the power within.*

After the blood tests and a myriad other tests, Kate gathered herself up and walked back to the bus stop back to Sandycove, where the woman behind the newsagents' counter looked familiar but Kate couldn't quite place her.

'Kate?' The woman stared at her, her face smiling. 'It's me, Aisling. Aisling Byrne. From *school*. French? Remember? We used to—'

'Aisling! God, it's been a while. How are you?'

'Grand, grand, not a bother... how are you? Haven't seen you in years... Back visiting, are you? Heard you were away. Somewhere nice, I hope. I've been here all this time, bored out of my mind...' She smiled back at Kate. 'You look the same though.'

'I'm here for a few months. Or longer. And I need a job,' she said. 'Do you know of any?'

Aisling thought. 'Haven't heard of anything... except for... you probably wouldn't want it. Honeysuckle Lodge. The nursing home. My aunt Abigail is the manager. They need someone to make tea for some of the residents, play cards with them and whatnot. Abigail would talk the hind leg off a mule, but it's a lovely atmosphere up there. Why don't you walk up there and meet her?'

It didn't take Kate long to walk through the village to where Honeysuckle Lodge was situated. Hidden behind large gates, a tangle of honeysuckle twisting over the arch, the house was a once fine private home. Now, it was painted a slightly depressing shade of cream and there was a mat in front of the large oak doors which said 'Fáilte'.

Kate rang the doorbell and she heard footsteps and then a woman with pink lipstick and a leopard-skin blouse and matching elasticated waist trousers appeared.

'Good morning!' she said, in a loud voice, as though she was used to talking to people who were slightly hard of hearing. It was strange being back in Sandycove but over the last decade, moving to a new place, finding work and getting on with things, was practically second nature. Sometimes Kate wondered if she would ever settle down, find a home which was hers forever.

'I heard you needed help,' said Kate. 'I need work for the next few months... and, well...' She felt a bit foolish all of a sudden as the woman looked surprised.

'News travels like lightning these days,' she said. 'You must have heard by telepathy.'

'Aisling told me,' Kate explained. 'We were in French together, years ago...'

The woman smiled. 'Ah, well, that explains it.' She peered at Kate, as though she was trying to place her. 'Why don't you come in for a cup of tea? I'm Abigail Duffy, manager of Honeysuckle Lodge.'

'Kate O'Hare,' said Kate, holding out her hand and shaking Abigail's.

'Kate O'Hare, you say? Daughter of Lola?'

'That's right...' You couldn't move in Ireland without people being able to pin you to either a place or a family within seconds.

'Well, why didn't you just say? Come on in...'

Inside, there was a beautiful tiled hall with dark-panelled walls and a noticeboard with a list of 'meals for the week', 'outings and events', and even a 'bird of the week', which was the woodpecker. They walked past a large sitting room, where Kate glimpsed a woman reading a newspaper and another knitting. Abigail ushered her into a small office.

'Now,' she said, sitting across the desk from Kate, 'maybe you could tell me about yourself and leave nothing out.' She smiled. 'By the way, I went to school with Lorraine. Lola. I never got used to the change. The Islanders did us proud around the world. All those Japanese and Korean children playing the tin whistle because of them? Amazing, isn't it? So, you've come home?'

'Not sure,' admitted Kate. 'I don't even know where home is any more.'

'Home is here,' said Abigail, emphatically. 'Of course it is! You can leave Sandycove, but Sandycove doesn't leave you!' Her red face was suddenly a shade darker with passion. 'The very idea of losing your home, just because you leave. It doesn't work like that. Talk to the diaspora, those who left starving and hungry, the ones who went in search of jobs and ways to feed their families. Are you telling me Ireland is no longer their home?'

Kate managed to shake her head, but it seemed Abigail was just getting started.

'My great-great-grandmother left Ireland for the mills of Lancashire. My brother has been in Canada for the last twenty-five years, I have American cousins, Liverpudlian ones, and do you know? They are as Irish as me.' She clutched at her chest for emphasis. 'Home is where the heart is.' She turned to Kate. 'So, now what do you say? Where is *home*?'

'Sandycove?' Kate said meekly. Abigail was right, though, émigrés really did create pockets of Ireland around the world. But when she'd met fellow Irish travellers, she hadn't gravitated towards them and talked longingly about who was winning the All-Ireland or would Ireland qualify for the Eurovision. She had avoided them, wanting to meet people from other countries, *expand* her horizons, shake off all the cultural nonsense which bound people to a national ideal.

'Exactly.' Abigail looked triumphant. 'Now, to tea. You take milk, I presume, none of this black nonsense.' Abigail went over to a drinks trolley where there was a kettle, an old-fashioned cream-and-blue striped milk jug and cups and saucers. 'And you'll have a biscuit. Tea and a biscuit is like Ant and Dec, you can't imagine one without the other, wouldn't you say?'

This woman was a little manic, thought Kate, wondering how to make her excuses and leave. It was probably best if she found something a little less intense. She'd have the tea, absorb any more passionate postulations and then leave. There had to be *other* jobs.

Abigail stirred the cup and handed it to Kate. 'Now, custard cream, Bourbon or digestive? I favour one of each. Keeps energy and spirits up.'

'Digestive,' said Kate, taking one from the saucer.

'Right,' said Abigail, sitting down. 'Back to the job... or perhaps Aisling told you the job description already? No? Well, among our residents, we have six elderly ladies who have all requested a little bit more stimulation. We have the normal morning events, such as the book club and the Irish lessons and the what have yous. But these particular ladies say they need something else for the afternoons. They have gone on strike about the television, saying they have no interest in home improvement programmes or buying houses in the sun.' Abigail shrugged. 'I have to agree they have a point. I had thought that a little bit of television would be a nice thing, but they have said no, they are bored. I need to come up with something else to keep them busy. They know their own minds.' Abigail paused for a moment. 'And anyway, we work flat out, night shifts and day shifts, three meals a day, plus afternoon treat, usually a slice of fruit cake. But we need someone who will spend a couple of hours every morning organising a few activities. I'm thinking Scrabble, bridge, whatever that is exactly. A quiz. Six days a week, 12 p.m. to 4 p.m. Would it suit you?'

Maybe it was what Abigail had said about Sandycove being her home, or maybe it was the way Abigail just accepted her, or maybe it was the thought of these elderly women who needed someone to play Scrabble with, but Kate thought she was going to cry. The teacup rattled on the saucer as her hand trembled and the first tear welled up and splashed into her tea. And then the second and then the third. In a fleeting and surprisingly energetic move, Abigail was on her knees beside her, taking the cup from her, patting her back and making soothing sounds.

'I'm sorry,' Kate managed to say, between gulps.

'Hush-shh-shh,' Abigail said soothingly, 'Let it all out. That's it. Don't you worry.'

'It's...' Kate tried to focus. 'I haven't been home for so long. Just for quick visits. My grandmother's funeral. But not much. And... well... I'm *pregnant*.'

Abigail didn't react. 'Well, no wonder you're so emotional,' she said. 'Coming home would bring a lot of those feelings to the surface. And now you have a little one to think of...'

'I'm just trying to find my feet again. The baby was quite a shock.'

'They can be,' Abigail acknowledged. 'Undoubtedly a seismic event. And where are you living?'

'In my camper van on Patsy Fox's drive?'

Abigail nodded. 'I heard Flora's back in with her mam. I know all about Justin Moriarty and that Sandra Boyle. Carrying on with each other for the last year. And talking of babies, I would not be surprised to discover he has a low sperm count. I've seen him in cycling shorts. Had to avert my eyes.'

Kate laughed. 'Glad I missed out on that,' she said.

'It was an eyeful,' Abigail said. 'Not in a good way.' She gazed at Kate. 'Now, you've got some decisions to make...'

Kate nodded. 'I've never been very good at decisions but I'm trying to get better. I always make the wrong ones but for the first time in my life, I'm trying to think of someone other than me. My partner – my *ex*-partner, I suppose – doesn't want a child and neither did I, until I was having one, and now I love her already. And she's not even born. But I didn't know what to do.'

'So, you came home,' said Abigail, still on her knees, patting her hand. 'You did exactly the right thing, sounds like you made a very good decision.'

'You think so?' asked Kate, looking up, wiping her eyes.

'I do,' replied Abigail, getting to her feet and then pulling over a chair and sitting beside Kate. 'I do indeed. I think you've been making very good decisions all your life.'

'But running away, refusing to come home, being stubborn? They don't sound like very good decisions.'

'The best decisions are the ones you make at the time. All those decisions make up a life, and you're here, healthy, alive, carrying a baby. I think you're doing really well, I really do.'

'Thank you.' Kate wiped her tears with her hands. She needed someone to say she was doing okay.

'So, if it suits you, you can work here for the next few weeks. Light duties, of course. And then you can decide what you want to do. What do you think?'

Why not? It wasn't as though she was weighed down with options, so Kate nodded. 'Thank you.'

'We have a caretaker's house. In the grounds. We did have one, you see, and he lived there, but he's gone to Longford to live with his sister. But... I was wondering what to do with it. If you want it, we can have it cleaned and painted. One bedroom, small kitchen, no mod cons, but it's at the end of the orchard and I sometimes think I wouldn't mind moving in there myself.' She smiled. 'No pressure. Why don't you see where you are, what you're at and whether you're coming or going. All right with you?'

Kate nodded.

'Right.' Abigail stood up and smiled. 'Let's go and introduce you to everyone. It's nearly lunchtime so the day room should be full. You can start properly tomorrow.'

15

PATSY

Just before dawn and unable to sleep, Patsy had gone to her sewing room, trying to get her thoughts together, hoping her ideas and plans would magically find a way of working themselves out. There was the balance of colours and shapes and proportion to determine. She was thinking of a grey-blue, pink, cream, and she needed something else, just to balance. A navy? A deep green? She also wanted ruffles on the cushions, but the hems left raw so it looked more contemporary. And what kind of books for the reading nook? Books on trawlers and the local fleet, she thought, and on wild swimming, local walks and a copy of *Dubliners* for good measure. What about blankets, and then log baskets for beside the wood stove? She quickly made a few more notes. *Flowers?* she wrote. Or plants? Or both?

There was a knock on the front door and she glanced at the clock on the mantelpiece. Not even 6 a.m. Flora was coming down the stairs and they opened the front door together. 'Must be Kate,' she said.

But there – long white hair streaming down her back, in a long white dress and ancient denim jacket, bare feet, red varnish on

her toenails, silver Birkenstocks and huge Chanel sunglasses –
was Lola O'Hare. A small suitcase was at her feet and a beautiful
leather tote bag on her shoulder. Patsy had last seen Lola on television at this year's Oscars ceremony performing her song 'What
The Heart Doesn't Know', which was used in one of the big films.
She'd been accompanied by a big, beardy bear of a man on a
mandolin in a tight black T-shirt, and at the end Lola had spoken
breathlessly into the microphone. 'This is for Paulie and for
everyone who has lost someone special this year. Love you,
Paulie.' There had been tears on her face.

When Patsy hugged her, she detected something about her
which was different, as though she'd lost something of herself,
changed in some way. Lola had always been brighter than
everyone else, even in school, she had an energy about her, but it
was as if her lights had dimmed. Yes, no one was full of beans just
off the red-eye from America, but Patsy knew Lola had lost her
best friend and collaborator. Once magnificent, she now looked a
little defeated. *I know that look*, thought Patsy. *I've been there too*,
she thought. Grief consumed and smothered you like Virginia
creeper.

'I'm so sorry to barge in on you at this unearthly hour,' Lola
was saying. 'I thought you might be up, that's all. In California
6 a.m. isn't remotely early. It's actually considered quite a late
start.'

Lola was a few years younger than Patsy, but once, in a school
show, the first time Lorraine O'Hare had become Lola O'Hare,
she'd performed 'I Don't Like Mondays', much to the nuns'
horror. Even at the age of thirteen, she had commanded the stage,
stalking around like a disaffected teenage goddess. When all the
girls clapped, cheered and lost their minds, Lola soaked it all up.
Later, Patsy heard Lola and Paulie Finnegan had formed a band.

'I heard my daughter might be in town,' said Lola. 'I just

thought I'd drop in to say...' Lola shrugged, dismissively. 'I don't know... hello, *ciao*, *buenos dias*... whatever...' She gave an awkward laugh, as though embarrassed. 'I was becoming a bit bored with life in California. I even missed the rain.'

'Well, the forecast is for sun,' Patsy said. 'I think you may have brought the Californian weather with you.'

Lola wasn't really listening. 'So, have you seen Kate? I thought you might know...' And then Lola turned back to the camper van, her eyes falling on the French number plate, just as the side door of the van opened and Kate appeared, her coat on over her pyjamas, her hair tied up, looking shocked.

'Mum? What are *you* doing here?'

They stared at each other.

'My flight landed an hour ago,' said Lola.

'Okay...' Kate looked in shock. 'You should have said you were coming... it's really early...'

'It's not that early,' said Lola. 'It's 6 a.m.'

'But this isn't California,' remarked Kate. 'It's Dublin, and here it is early. Poor Patsy... you can't just do this.'

'I've already apologised,' said Lola. 'But the birds are singing and the sky is bright... and, well, where would I go?'

'Why don't we go inside and have a cup of tea and a bit of breakfast?' Patsy suggested.

Lola turned back to her. 'Tea would be most welcome. You can't make a decent cup anywhere in the States. Sewage in the water, apparently. Shall we go in?'

And Patsy had the strange sensation of being led into her own house.

16

LOLA

Patsy's kitchen was cosy, thought Lola. Early-morning light streaming into the window, shimmering on the walls. The kitchen units were painted sunflower yellow and there were open shelves with a rather lovely collection of coloured vases and jugs. A large painting of a harbour was on the wall. 'That's very nice,' said Lola, approvingly, studying it. 'Where is it?'

'Inishbofin,' said Patsy, who was making the tea in the pot, while Flora gathered cups and was pouring milk into a jug. 'I was there on holiday once... and every time I look at it, I think of it.'

Kate was sitting rather stiffly and although Lola hadn't expected her to run into her arms, perhaps their estrangement was deeper than Lola had thought it might be. As they drank their tea, Kate played with her hair, staring at the split ends, and then twisting it around and around. Maybe something was wrong? Why was she living in a camper van? Didn't she have any money? Lola wished Kate would just accept the money she'd been putting aside for her. She could make Kate's life so much more comfort-able, and if she did insist on living in a van, then Lola could buy her a really good one. One day, she might accept the money she had been saving for her, you never knew. 'Guilt money,' as Paulie had once referred to it. If Lola's mother ever had a spare coin, it went straight into the collection basket at church.

'So,' said Lola, 'how are you?'

'Grand... you?' said Kate.

'Not too bad... so... it's been a while since we saw each other... your grandmother's funeral...'

Kate nodded. 'How long are you staying?'

'Well, as long as I need to... it's nice to be home.' Flora and Patsy were taking their time to make the tea, as though to give Kate and Lola a chance to talk. 'I missed you at Paulie's funeral...'

'How did it go?'

'It was a funeral,' said Lola. 'Not much fun to be had.'

'No... I lit a candle in a church for him,' said Kate.

'He'd have liked that,' replied Lola. 'You know he always said the abundance of candles was the only good thing about Catholicism. Anyway, it was a beautiful service...' She paused. 'Pity he missed it.'

For a moment, Kate looked up, a half-smile on her face, both of them knowing it was a joke Paulie would have appreciated, but the conversation in Patsy's kitchen then began to flag and Lola felt an obligation to keep it flowing. Richie would have been invaluable here, she thought, always being so good at small talk. He loved hearing the minutiae of people's lives – how they liked their coffee, how they rated their electric car, who they were going to vote for. She wondered if he'd been purloined by Maria yet.

'I was really sorry to hear about Paulie,' said Patsy. 'It must have been a shock.'

Lola felt her face freeze for a moment and wondered if she would be able to talk. It was six months now and grief was this amorphous, dark creature which wrapped around her so tightly sometimes she couldn't breathe, and then at other times it hovered above her, like a black cloud, threatening at any time to burst and rain over her. And she hated all the condolences, the sorrys and the pity glances. Each time, she would have to say a few words about Paulie and each time she had to keep her voice steady.

'Yes,' she said, but her voice had lost all its strength. 'It was something of a shock.'

Kate looked up. 'I can't believe he's gone. He was like an uncle to me. He was such a good person.'

Lola nodded. 'He was a good person. He was my best friend, really. My better half.' She hoped her smile expressed resilience and strength, rather than looking pathetic, which was how she felt. 'I mean, we'd been through everything together. He was my rock.' She glanced at Kate, who was looking back at her. She loved Paulie too.

Kate nodded. 'I remember at Christmas he would dress up as Santa and bring over my presents.'

Lola smiled. 'He used to borrow the costume from the man who ran the Sailor's Kitchen in Dún Laoghaire.'

'And he came in,' went on Kate. 'Big beard, stuff his stomach with a cushion...'

'He was always a tiny stripling of a thing,' said Lola.

'And I was so excited,' said Kate. 'But then I looked into his eyes. "Paulie?" I whispered. "Is that you?" And he winked. "Santa's asked me to help him out," he said. "Will you keep the secret?"' Kate laughed. 'And until this very moment, I haven't told anyone.'

'And you used to play the piano,' said Lola. 'And I'd sing, and Paulie on guitar... we gave quite a twist to "Jingle Bells" and "O Come All Ye Faithful", I can tell you... you were always such a talented piano player...' She smiled at Kate.

'I haven't played in years,' Kate admitted. 'Think I've forgotten everything.'

'But you got to Grade Eight,' said Lola.

'There's more to life than music, Mum,' said Kate.

Lola drank her tea, her hand trembling as she held the tiny handle on the cup. Delicious. If Californians knew about it, they would go crazy, ship the water over, call it a health drink and charge a fortune. She glanced over at Kate who had returned to biting her nails. She'd seen a glimmer of reconciliation when they spoke of Paulie. Maybe Paulie would bring them back together? But how, exactly, she couldn't possibly imagine. 'Would you like to come and see his grave sometime?' Lola asked her. 'We could take some flowers.'

'Peonies,' said Kate.

'His favourites.' Lola smiled at her. 'So would you?'

'Yes...' But Kate didn't look that keen.

'More tea, Kate?' Patsy was holding up the pot.

'I'm fine,' she said.

'I couldn't live without my coffee,' said Lola. 'I drink cups and cups of it every day. If I go without one for half an hour, I can feel a raging headache coming on. Before he died, Paulie gave everything up. Caffeine, animal products, dairy. I said to Paulie, "Cheese? Really? You're going to live without *cheese*?" He was eating this thing called nutritional yeast. Anyway, he still died.' She blinked away the tears in her eyes. 'So, I say bring on the coffee, bring on the cheese. Let's party while we're still here.' Lola stood up. 'Thank you for the tea. I'll go and find out where I'm staying and check in...' She looked over at Kate. 'I'll catch up with you later?'

But Kate seemed to have temporarily lost her hearing and was busy collecting the cups and taking them to the sink, almost as though Lola hadn't spoken at all.

'Would you like to come with me? Just for a walk? I could buy you breakfast...'

Kate half-nodded and half-shook her head. 'I've got a few things to do.'

'Ah, go on. Quick walk... see the sights of Sandycove?'

'I've got to get ready for work...'

'What kind of work?'

'In the local nursing home,' said Kate. 'Keeping the residents entertained.'

'Well!' said Lola, lighting up, her arms held out. 'If someone knows about entertaining people, I'm the one!' She could have kicked herself, showing off, being the big star, the 'entertainer'.

Kate smiled. 'Yeah... but... I just... I'm...'

Lola nodded. 'You want to do it alone.'

'Well, yes...'

'Well then, I will see you later,' said Lola. 'And we'll do that walk soon. When you're ready.'

It was too early to check in to the flat she had rented, so she found a café in the village, thinking of Paulie and how he always loved a Full Irish for breakfast. But mainly she thought of Kate, who was so close and so far. *I love you*, she thought. *More than you will ever know. Just please forgive me, I want you so much in my life.*

17

KATE

It had been quite a shock to hear the knock on Patsy's house and then hear Lola's voice. Kate had pulled open the corner of one of the curtains in the van and saw Lola looking like the white witch from Narnia. And what was her accent? Traces of Irish, but there was some kind of Californian in there. Lola had almost taken on an unreal quality, almost as though she wasn't her mother any more, she was a big star to Kate, just like she was to everyone else. But then she had spotted the look on her face when they had talked about Paulie, and Kate had felt that twisting sadness for her mother. That was the problem with Lola, she was either the big star who inhabited another plane entirely, or she was this vulnerable woman who had been constantly criticised by her own mother. There was no middle ground with her.

Lola looked tired, but her ethereal quality, the pale skin, the silver hair like a Connemara pony's tail, those famous blue eyes, were still all there. But something about her was lost. Kate felt, once again, on the brink of tears. What was wrong with her? She thought she'd arrived at some kind of peace regarding her mother and she'd been proud of managing to keep a civilised contact. But, *of course*, Lola would come back at the very worst time. Kate loved Lola, she just couldn't deal with her, especially now.

'Kate?' There was a knock on the door of the van. It was Flora. She poked her head in. 'I was just wondering how you feel?'

'Like I need to leave,' said Kate.

'Ah, don't say that,' soothed Flora. 'She's not going to be here long...'

'She always complicates everything...'

'It doesn't have to be complicated,' said Flora, carefully.

'It's so hard to explain.' Kate had felt independent from Lola since she was sixteen, but she had not realised then that they would never spend significant time together ever again, and that Lola choosing that tour meant that she was calling a halt on her responsibilities as a mother. It was as though Kate just wasn't important enough. Over the years, Flora had tried to understand but when your relationship with your mother wasn't complicated, how could you really ever comprehend something that was so far from your own experience? And, yes, now Kate was an adult herself, it mattered less and less, but there was a sense that she wasn't ready to just pretend nothing had happened. Happy families weren't ones you picked up and put down on a whim, they were something you worked at. 'I thought I was over it,' she told Flora. 'I thought I had got on with my life and she couldn't affect me any more. And there she is, exactly the same and all she can talk about is herself... My God. She's not remotely in interested anyone else.'

But Lola's face when Patsy had mentioned Paulie... she had looked... *broken*. After all this time, Kate didn't *want* to feel sorry for Lola, not when she needed to focus on the next few months, getting her life together for her and her baby. When Lola had chosen music over Kate all those years ago, it had been hurtful and it had felt like a very personal rejection, as though she really hadn't mattered that much to her mother. Even now, when she knew she should have been able to get over it, to move on, to see the bigger picture, part of her still held on to her younger self, the one who had told Lola to go on tour, and not to worry about her, but the one who had hoped her mother wouldn't go.

'I don't know why I still feel hurt, too much time has passed. I love her... but I don't *know* her.'

'Well, Mum and I love you as well,' said Flora. 'And this is your home.' She stood up and hugged Kate. 'I've got to go to work, but you know where I am, okay?'

* * *

On her walk to Honeysuckle Lodge, Kate knew she was still trapped in this ridiculously childish loop regarding her mother. Of course Lola should have gone on that tour, of course she should have followed her dreams, but it broke their relationship and they had never found that closeness again. Kate had felt adrift for all those years, rudderless, anchorless, moving on and away. But now, hadn't she made her own life? And yet... she was still hurt.

In front of her was Honeysuckle Lodge. *Come on, Kate*, she told herself. *Focus. And smile. You're meant to be entertaining the ladies.* They deserved someone bright and happy, not some misery guts.

She took a deep breath and knocked on the door.

In the day room, she and Abigail faced the six ladies who were sitting on two low sofas which had been pushed together to make one long row. Some looked up at her, pleasantly and with interest. One had her head buried in a crossword. Another woman had a small chihuahua tucked inside her cardigan and she was sneaking it what looked like, to Kate's eye, Mint Imperials.

'Kate's moved back to Sandycove from France,' said Abigail.

'She's got a lot to sort out and so has taken on this most important job while she decides what next to do.' She gave Kate a quick smile. 'Now, ladies... has everyone had a think about the kind of things you'd like to do with Kate? I made a few suggestions which didn't go down too well, remember?'

'You suggested a Lego competition,' said one woman in a pink cardigan. She raised her eyes, witheringly.

'Not one of my best ideas, admittedly,' agreed Abigail. 'I just thought it might be an unusual activity.'

'I have arthritis,' said one of the ladies. 'I can't even pick up a book, never mind a brick the size of a fingernail.'

'Maybe some of you have some ideas of things we could do?' suggested Kate. 'I was thinking of a creative writing project...'

The ladies barely flickered.

'Or...' she went on, 'perhaps some crafts. Maybe candle-making...'

'Candle-making,' said one woman. 'Why would we want to make candles? For our own funerals?'

'Or...'

'A choir,' said a voice. It was the woman who had been poring over the crossword. She was now looking up. 'You can sing, can't you?'

Kate was about to shake her head. Lola had well and truly put her off singing, but she'd spent her childhood singing along with Paulie and Lola, as well as years of piano lessons. 'Yes...' she admitted.

'What a fabulous idea, Marjorie,' said Abigail, turning to Kate, eyes shining, clasping her hands. 'A choir!'

'I'm not sure if I can...' began Kate.

'Can you play the piano?' It was the woman again.

Kate nodded again. 'I'm a bit rusty though...'

'You're talking to a group of women with a combined age of 468,' said Marjorie. 'I think we might be the rusty ones.'

Everyone laughed, including Kate.

'Our piano hasn't been played in years,' said Abigail. 'I'll have it tuned. Well... what does everyone think? Is Marjorie's choir idea better than my Lego one?'

'Oh yes,' said one woman, in a mauve cardigan and large diamanté brooch. 'Sounds very invigorating.'

'It does, doesn't it, Kitty?' agreed Abigail.

'Perfect,' declared the woman with the small chihuahua tucked in beside her. 'I've always wanted to be in a choir.'

'Well, now is your chance, Dorothy,' said Abigail.

There was an old upright piano at the side of the room and Abigail began to tug it closer to the women, waving Kate away from helping.

'Don't you even think about lugging this heavy thing,' she ordered, 'you go and stand there...'

Kate stood, rather nervously, in front of the women. 'Okay, then,' she said. 'Shall we start?' She tried to think of a song, and then she remembered one they used to do in school. 'Who knows "When The Saints Go Marching In"?'

There was nodding and a murmur of assent, as Kate sat at the piano, which Abigail had angled so she could play and see the ladies at the same time.

'Wait,' said Marjorie. 'What are we called?'

'Voices Of Experience,' suggested the woman with the chihuahua, making everyone laugh.

'What about the Honeysuckle Warblers?' offered Kitty.

'I like that,' said Abigail. 'What does everyone think?'

There was a general murmur of agreement, as Kate played a few notes. It didn't sound too bad.

'Okay, then, Honeysuckle Warblers.' She played the opening

bars of 'When The Saints Go Marching In'. 'Everybody join in... one... two... a one, two, three...'

And the Honeysuckle Warblers began to sing, their voices a mixture of shrill and thin, some sounded faint, others hesitant, but there was something there.

A choir! Of all things. But the ladies looked so happy at the end of the session, filled with all those good hormones only singing induces. She'd turned her back on music over the last decade. But it was so satisfying knowing you were doing something good. Just seeing the faces of the ladies as they sipped their post-choir cup of tea and fruit cake made her feel good.

18

FLORA

Edith arrived in the haberdashery, placing a white paper bag on the counter in front of Flora, along with two takeaway cups of tea.

'Cream doughnuts today,' she said. 'I know we shouldn't, but sometimes, I find, a cream doughnut is the solution to life's vagaries.' She smiled at Flora. 'Especially Sally-Anne's. The woman is a veritable alchemist. Now, *how* are you doing?'

Every morning, Flora was waking up with a nauseous feeling in her stomach and she had to tell herself all over again why she was in her old childhood bed. And then, there were moments when she had to remind herself she'd been married, and she started sorting through memories. The holiday in Portugal. The first few amazing months with Justin. How committed he was to his job. How sometimes she felt on the edge of things, as though he didn't consider her important to his goals. Or the baby she had wanted.

'Fine...' She smiled back at Edith. 'Kate's home for a while... and Mum's making me do some designs for the new hotel. I think she was worried about me.'

'Well, of course she was,' said Edith. 'And I heard she had been asked to design the new foyer. He seems a nice sort, does that Killian Walsh. He was in the café the other day chatting to everyone, telling them about the plans. So, two months to go? Doesn't give you much time.'

Flora shook her head. 'Such a tight turnaround might actually be better.' If she had too long she would agonise and procrastinate. She had no choice but to get going. But it was the getting-going bit that was proving a little difficult. 'Mum has been drawing and redrawing plans all week.'

'And what about you?'

'I'm working on an idea,' said Flora. 'But it's been a long time since I've done anything like that...'

Edith surveyed her. 'Can you ride a bicycle?'

'Yes... of course. Mine's outside,' Flora replied, nonplussed.

'And if you didn't cycle for one year, ten years, would you remember how to do it?'

'Of course...'

'And what about swimming? Or reading... or speaking Japanese...'

'I don't speak...'

Edith held up her hand. 'You take my point? You'd be rusty, perhaps, a little wobbly... your Japanese – for illustrative purposes – a little slow... yes? But it would come back to you? With practice? You don't want to waste another moment in the past,' said Edith. 'Press on. Move forwards. What else is out there? The hotel sounds like a very nice challenge. I think everyone needs a period to grieve over what's happened, come to terms with the loss, eat cakes, cry or whatever you need to do, and then decide that it's time to carry on. I think six weeks is enough time. How long has it been now?'

'Two weeks.'

'Well, then, you have a month left... and then... no more,

okay?' She picked up a cream doughnut and they sat on the sofa at the back of the shop, drinking their tea and eating their cakes.

A month left. By then, the hotel *and* heartbreak would be finished, or well on their way. Both seemed an impossibility.

'I saw Lola the other morning in the café. I think she might be having what is known as a midlife reappraisal. It's like a midlife crisis – which is what men succumb to, the sports cars, the cycling obsessions – but for women. It's less reactionary and more reflective.'

'How can you tell she's having one?'

'It's the look we get in our eyes once we're past the age of fifty... we sift through all the memories, as though we're making a scrapbook of our life, and then we realise we have too much of something and not enough of the other things. And the other things are normally the events that would have made us happier...'

'Are you doing it? Making a scrapbook?'

'Oh yes,' she said. 'And it's shocking how many empty pages there are, where there might have been so many wonderful things. I'm determined not to let it happen for the next however many decades I have left.' She gave Flora a look. 'I would say that Lola O'Hare is at the beginning of her reappraisal crisis.'

'Maybe...' Flora's phone flashed. A message from Justin.

Flora, wld u like 2 arrnge 2 cm & pck up rst o' ur thngs? Hppy to drop em down 2 u. We cn b out of the hse this eve, as gng 4 dinner.

She stared at the message for a while and then texted a reply. Deleted it. Tried again. Delete. She texted and deleted and texted and deleted.

She looked up to see Edith squinting at her.

'Everything tickety-boo?'

'I'm not sure. It was Justin. Asking me to collect the rest of my things... but maybe it's not the end... maybe...' Flora knew she sounded ridiculous but what if it wasn't? He wasn't the most emotionally intelligent man on the planet. In fact, he could be in the bottom percentile... but that was okay. She'd always done the emotional labour for the two of them, and never minded when he didn't buy Christmas presents because he was too busy or forgot one year to buy her a birthday present. 'Maybe he's sorry,' she said. 'Maybe it was just a thing?' She knew she sounded pathetic and desperate, but Edith's face didn't change, except for the tiniest movement of one of her eyebrows.

'I never had you down as a fool, Flora,' she said. 'Don't be that person. Take your life and your being and everything you have, and hold it close and run for your life. And shout "thank you" over your shoulder for him saving you from one more day with him.'

Flora had no idea Edith felt so strongly about Justin. But Edith hadn't finished.

'Life is precious. Don't waste it, especially not on such a shiftless wastrel. Learn your lessons and learn them so well you never make the same mistake twice, and believe you me, he's a mistake. That boy was raised to always be on a pedestal, but I remember once seeing him walk past Marjorie Byrne who had tripped up. I was rushing from the other side of the road, and Justin Moriarty just stepped over her. When I shouted at him to help her, he said he was catching a train into town and he was late for a meeting. I thought to myself, how can Flora Fox be married to such a selfish article...'

'That's horrible,' said Flora, shocked. But she could imagine it happening. Nothing stopped Justin, not even elderly ladies who had fallen over.

Edith gave a nod. 'He was a mistake. But that's fine. We learn and grow from mistakes. And move on...'

It was so easy for Edith, Flora thought, who had never been married, even if there had been that pastry chef.

She texted Justin back.

I can be there at 7 p.m.

The answer came back immediately.

Gr8.

* * *

After work, Kate and Flora walked up the hill towards Flora's old house. They had been going for walks most evenings, which Kate said were good for the baby but also a chance for them to catch up on all their news.

'And how do you feel about picking up your things?' Kate asked after Flora had told her about Justin's message. She smiled at Flora. 'How are you feeling about everything?'

'Grand...' said Flora, not able to put any of it into words. 'It is what it is.' She was nervous, but she kept thinking about what Edith had said about Justin being a mistake and how she totally believed the story about him stepping over Marjorie Byrne. But she still loved him, of course she did, and perhaps he was sorry and they could carry on like before and she wouldn't have to sleep in her childhood bedroom. 'How are the Honeysuckle Warblers getting on?' she asked, changing the subject.

'Well, they are the bossiest group of women I've ever met. And the nicest,' said Kate. 'And as a choir, they sound amazing. I need to start thinking of other pieces of music and to come up with some arrangements. I thought "Carrickfergus" would be good...'

Kate seemed happy, thought Flora. 'And your mum,' said Flora. 'Getting a little bit better?'

'A little,' said Kate. 'We've been for coffee by the seafront. It was fine. She talked, mainly, about Paulie. And another time she asked me to come for dinner with her. Fish and chips, again eaten on the sea wall. I haven't told her I'm pregnant because she'll make it all about her. But she's told me she loved me and she was sorry for us not being closer...'

'That's nice.' Flora looked at Kate. 'Isn't it?'

'But what is she sorry for? Sorry for having an amazing career? Sorry for herself?'

'Did you ask her?'

'She says she wants us to have a future as mother and daughter...'

'And what did you say?'

'I said that relationships aren't that easy.' Kate paused. 'Do you think I'm being too hard on her? Do you think I'm too mean?'

'No...' Flora hesitated. 'I think... I don't know... it's easy for me. I don't have a complicated relationship with my mother. Anyway... here we are...' Flora turned into a driveway. 'Oh... Sandra's car is here...'

Sandra's pride and joy was her white Range Rover Evoque, which she drove around Sandycove, with the windows rolled down, her favourite band, Boyzone, blasting out of the speakers, living her best life, a life that could have been Flora's. Minus the massive car.

They let themselves in with Flora's old key. Her house looked exactly the way she'd left it, except for a pink jacket hanging on the hooks which she recognised as being Sandra's. And the

Michael Kors handbag, and the Lululemon running top, thrown over the chair.

Flora's clothes had already been packed in cardboard boxes, her books were in another. In the kitchen, she took out some things from the cupboard, the iron. 'This is mine,' she said. 'Justin has never ironed anything in his life.' All she had been good for was doing domestic chores, she thought, but an iron is an iron and Patsy always needed an extra one for her sewing room. She also took a small picture from the wall. 'I bought this for Justin three years ago,' she said. 'I don't think he even said thank you.'

Kate had been looking around the house. 'It's like stepping back to the 1980s.' She picked up a glass which was on the work surface. 'Who drinks out of crystal these days? How pretentious!' It was one of Justin's special whiskey tumblers, the one which cost an eye-watering sum of money. 'He thinks he's some old-fashioned gentleman...' But as she placed the glass back down, it slipped out of her hand and smashed into a trillion pieces. 'Oh my God.'

Despite Kate's stricken face, Flora would have liked to pick up the second one and smash it as well, but she restrained herself as she started sweeping up the glass. 'He'll be more annoyed that he doesn't have a full set any more,' she said. 'He's one of those people where everything has to match.'

On the kitchen table was a brochure from All Mod Conz, one of Ireland's trendiest interior designers, its showroom a vast space full of marble worktops, engineered kitchens, invisible appliances and hidden handles. Kate opened the page to see an order sheet, the name 'Sandra Donnelly-Joyce' was at the top of the form.

Flora looked at it over her shoulder. 'Well, that's the end of the pine.' She shrugged her shoulders at Kate. 'I almost feel sorry for the kitchen. It's been dispatched as easily as I was.' But then she seemed to rally herself. 'No loyalty these people, to me or to 1980s pine kitchens.'

'Heathens,' said Kate.

'Philistines.' Flora grinned at her. 'If they put the kitchen on a skip, we'll make a bonfire...'

'A bonfire of the vanities.'

'A marital conflagration! Come on,' said Flora, feeling a little better. 'Let's go and leave these barbarians behind...'

'Where they belong,' said Kate, slipping her arm through Flora's as they left the house.

19

LOLA

Lola's rented flat above the boutique on the main street of Sandycove wasn't exactly the Beverly Hills Hilton or the Nashville Hermitage where she had always stayed when she visited Paulie. Right at the end, she had moved into his house, taking over the guest suite, trying to keep everyone calm, while Antonio sobbed and Mick drank heavily and all the other hangers-on kept trying to organise prayer vigils or jostling to know what was in the will. Lola had managed to keep herself together throughout the days and spent the nights counting out all those pills, making him fresh lemonade because that was all he could taste, and talking of Ireland, and life before fame, all over the sound of the ventilator in the quiet of the Nashville night. Antonio was next to useless, spending the whole time sobbing, walking into rooms crying, walking out of them crying. He would go down to the pool, away from the house so they wouldn't hear him bawling but water carried sound and his wailing would drift into Paulie's room. And Paulie would give her a look. 'Jaysus,' he had said, sounding like he'd never left Dublin, 'you'd think someone was dying in here.'

She didn't cry. Not a drop. Nothing. Just kept talking, talking,

talking, as though it was just another stop in their lives. Not the end. But at night, when she was in her room, one ear on the ventilator, she took her guitar and wrote into the early hours, her brain hurting so hard. One of those songs was currently being hawked around Hollywood to film producers. For the first time in her life, she didn't care. Whatever happened, nothing was of any consequence and there was something so comforting, so restful, about being so far away.

She'd been in Ireland for a week now and had fallen into a routine. In the mornings, it was a Chelsea bun and a cup of tea from the nice Man The Van, then call on Kate to see if she wanted to join her for a walk. Kate had come a few times but always seemed busy with her job at the nursing home or going out with Flora. Lola tried to tempt her with food, like you would with a dog or a child. 'A milkshake?' said Lola. 'An ice cream? A bag of chips on the seafront?'

When she did come with her, the walk was short and Kate only either listened or spoke briefly about her time in France or what she was doing in Honeysuckle Lodge. Whenever Lola tried to press for details, Kate would be vague – 'Just helping out, really,' she would say. And then, before Lola irritated her any more, Lola would let the subject drop and bore poor Kate senseless with another one of her stories. *If Paulie was here*, thought Lola, *he would tell me I was going on a bit*. Paulie was the only one who had ever told her the truth. Often, she wandered up to the graveyard to sit on the bench beside Paulie's grave, and have a chat with him.

In the evenings, Lola walked along the seafront, stopping at the old bathing place, The Forty Foot, where swimmers gathered from dawn to dusk, stepping down or diving into the ice-cold Irish Sea, and exiting the water with a renewed vigour that Lola recognised from years of stage performing. Adrenaline, she thought, I see you. It made you feel truly alive, it gave you a feeling as though you were floating above the ground, as though you weighed less than nothing, and there wasn't anything which could bring you down. The feeling never lasted, of course, but it was good enough to make you want more. Stage performing was better than drugs. She used to say it was better than sex, but that was before she met Richie. Just the memory of him made her smile, but even though he had tried to call her a few times, she hadn't taken any of them, nor listened to the voice messages.

She began to sit on the wall beside the Forty Foot and watch a group of women chatting together after their swim, their voices carrying up into their air, their laughter, the intensity of their conversation. *That looks like a nice life*, she thought, *all the adrenaline but without any of the drawbacks entailing performance on a grand scale.* Just normal amounts of adrenaline, manageable levels. The swimmers looked happy, they were all of different ages, and they would pass round a flask of tea, while they sat half-dressed, draped in towels. *If I hadn't been in The Islanders*, she thought, *I would have stayed here and I might have been one of them. It wouldn't have been such a bad life, perhaps.*

She would then meander over to the fish and chip van and eat her salty offerings, staring out at the big blue beyond, thinking. She'd dreamed of this for years, to just sit and be, to be a nobody again, to be alone with her thoughts.

This evening, there was a drizzle in the cool air, the sky laden with low cloud, the sea battleship-grey. She had never been the kind of person who stayed in places or situations where she felt uncomfortable, but for some reason, something had changed. It was like being immersed in cold water and knowing the longer you held on, the easier it would be. Californians, Lola thought, would pay good money for a retreat like this.

Behind her, people were on their evening constitutionals, dogs were pulling at leads, lovers held hands, women power-walked along. A tear dropped onto her chips. What was she crying about? Paulie? There was no need to cry about Paulie, he'd had a good life. He'd achieved everything he ever wanted – fame, fortune, recognition. When he was dying, close to the end, Mick had made him Irish stew and they had all stood around watching him take the first spoonful, his eyes closed, a smile on his face. For a moment, it wasn't dying Paulie there in the bed, it was the Paulie who had spent most of his life laughing and smiling.

Her phone rang. Richie. She blocked the call, again.

'Evening, Lola!' A woman's voice behind her. 'Heard you were back in town.' There were three women and she recognised them as being the swimmers she had been spying on.

'We're big fans,' said one of them. 'Saw you in the Aviva Stadium, a few years back. What a night.'

'Thank you, ladies,' said Lola, graciously.

'You were incredible,' the first one added. 'Best show I've ever seen. *And* I saw Elton John in Wembley.'

'That's so nice,' said Lola. Whenever they were bothered by fans, Paulie would remind her, they are the reason we do this, we don't create into a vacuum. Absorb the love. Easy for him to say.

'Will you answer a question for me, please?' Lola asked.

The three women nodded eagerly and stepped closer.

'Is it better to be a great artist,' said Lola, 'loved by your fans, paid a lot of money and to win awards? Or...?'

The three women waited, ready to respond to this difficult conundrum.

'Or to be a great mother?'

Except the choice wasn't difficult at all.

'Mother,' they all said immediately.

Lola nodded, loving their honesty and knowing they were right. It was that plain thinking and honest talking that was so refreshing. She had arrived, a head full of grief, a heart heavy with loss, searching for love and connection, and instead she was finding a lightness, as though every step she took on the seafront was like therapy. Every breath she took, all that crystallised Irish Sea oxygen was helping her. Her inner voice told her not to rush things with Kate, to let things settle. She was here, and for now, it was enough. Trust in all we don't understand. Let Mother Nature wend her wonderful ways.

20

KATE

Playing the piano had once been one of Kate's great lost joys, but now, as her fingers found notes and chords again, it had come back to her, in the sweetest of ways. At first, her playing was rusty, her fingers stumbling over notes, music tumbling in her head, until it righted itself, finding its rhythm, songs she couldn't remember ever knowing flowed all over again. It was almost like magic. As she sang and played along with the ladies, she found herself smiling along. Working with the Honeysuckle Warblers was proving to be very enjoyable. Finding songs the ladies liked, arranging them to suit their voices, working out harmonies, playing the piano and hearing the ladies begin to sing, was far more rewarding than Kate ever thought it could be.

Kate was also beginning to become very fond of the women. She began to arrive early for work, while the ladies were still eating their lunch, sitting herself down at the piano and working out arrangements, so all would be ready for when the ladies entered the day room. The ladies were also making her laugh a lot. They behaved as though they were each other's family, helping to find someone's knitting basket, or making sure Celia, who was confined to a wheelchair, always had pride of place. Or they would check Marjorie, who was always losing her pen, had a spare to do the crossword. Kitty was one of Kate's favourites, a small, shy woman who always sat beside the window and who explained to Kate that all the bird feeders hanging from the trees outside were hers. 'I like to look at them,' she said to Kate in her soft, quiet voice. 'They are always so busy, so sure about their jobs, so determined to get everything done.' She smiled. 'It's good to be busy.'

The Honeysuckle Warblers' repertoire was growing as well. From 'When The Saints Go Marching In' they had moved on to 'Ticket To Ride' and 'Raglan Road'. Some of the ladies were able to harmonise and Marjorie, who had the greatest range and loved to show it off, sang higher than everyone else.

It was Peggy who spotted her pregnancy before Kate had told anyone. 'I'd say you're seven and a half months?' she said as she and Kate sat drinking their post-choir cup of tea. 'Am I right?'

Kate nodded. 'Is it obvious?'

'It's not hard,' said Peggy. 'Former midwife. Could spot a mid-trimester woman with my eyes closed. That and the way Abigail wouldn't let you push the piano. The way you hold yourself, your back, even your facial expressions. You wince every now and then, and you're too young to be wincing from aches and pains. Except...' She squinted at Kate's stomach. 'You're very small. And you're living in a van? Is it wise? You need a bit of comfort towards the end.'

'But it's a very nice van,' said Kate. 'I'm parked on Patsy Fox's drive and using her shower, but it's just until I find somewhere permanent. Something will turn up.' She hadn't liked to ask Abigail about the house she had mentioned, as she didn't want to be too pushy... At least she had the van, it stopped her feeling too much of a charity case.

'When I had my first,' went on Peggy, 'I was unmarried. Forced to give it up, of course. A little boy. Wanted to call him Sebastian, but the nuns thought it was too fancy. Give him notions. So they put down John on his birth certificate. Thought I'd never get over it. They told me Sebastian was better off with a rich family, who could give him everything he would ever need. I believed them.' She looked at Kate, her bright brown eyes expressionless. 'I went off to London to be a midwife. Seventeen years old, scared of everything, the buses, the noise – took me four years before I caught the Tube for the first time. And I got married. Nice man. John, wouldn't you believe? Then I had my three. But, still, every year on Sebastian's birthday, I used to have a little cry on my own. My children – my three *younger* children – didn't know why the first of March always made me cry. And then, about twenty years ago, I got a call. One of those adoption people. Would I consent to being contacted by a Johnny Sweeney? I knew immediately it was Sebastian.' She smiled at Kate. 'It has a happyish ending. Sebastian and I met, eventually. And he was this lovely, intelligent person and I gazed and gazed at him, taking him all in – his eyebrows, his nose, his hands... his lovely voice. And he was doing the same with me. I knew I could never let him go ever again. And we haven't. He comes to see me here every Sunday afternoon. Brings me a book and an apple tart. Turns out we both love an apple tart.'

Kate smiled. 'You said "happyish"? What's *ish* about it?'

'Because,' said Peggy, 'there is no such thing as a truly happy ever after. You can only ever hope for "happyish" ever after. For all of us. If you have happyish, you are doing pretty well... nothing is like a fairy story. If it was, I would never have had to give him up in the first place. And he would have been called Sebastian.' She took Kate's hand. 'You're lucky. You get to bring your baby back home.'

Kate nodded. Even it was to a camper van, it was better than not bringing her baby home at all.

21

———

LOLA

Lola hadn't been into the sea for years. A few swimming pools heated to the temperature of a bath, a plethora of health spas, a scattering of thalassotherapy centres, Paulie's plunge pool, but the Irish Sea, no, not for some time. Every evening, Lola had been sitting and watching the group of sea swimmers at the Forty Foot, and for some reason she had gone and bought a swimsuit and a dryrobe and was determined to join them. She wasn't doing anything else, was she? There was something that these women had – a freedom, a lightness, a joy. By swimming, could she too have what they had?

She arrived that evening, a towel under her arm, her long hair tied back, her swimsuit already on, under her dress. Feeling nervous, she made her way over to the group, who were changing on the rocks, folding their clothes into neat piles, adjusting swimsuits and goggles and hats, and about to step towards the sea. She stood, slightly tentatively. *Stage fright*, she thought. *Haven't had this for a while.*

But one of the swimmers looked up and smiled. 'Ah, Lola! Good evening,' she said. 'Are you going to join us?'

Lola nodded. 'I'd like to,' she said. When was the last time she'd done something out of her comfort zone? When was the last time she'd done anything where she wasn't treated with reverence as though she was something special? She couldn't remember. 'Would you mind?'

The women were already budging up, moving along the stone bench, to make a space for her. 'Not at all,' said a woman in a zebra-patterned bathing suit. 'I'm Brenda.' She held out her hand. 'This is Catríona.'

A young woman with a beautiful smile reached forward and shook Lola's hand. 'You're very welcome,' she said. 'It's not as cold as you think it will be.'

Another woman gave her a wave from the other side of the group. 'Dolores,' she said. 'And she's lying. It is as cold. Worse in fact.'

Lola laughed. 'Well, there's only one way to find out.'

'Margaret,' said a prim, tall woman, giving a quick smile. 'You're very welcome. We're the Forty Footers. We swim here most evenings. We're missing Malachy, who is on his honeymoon. Cycling around Kerry, currently.'

'I'm Nora,' said a small woman with a long grey plait. 'We were in the same school. I'm a little bit older than you, but I remember you singing that song once... what was it called? I Don't Like Something...'

'Mondays,' said Lola.

'That was it... Mondays.' The woman looked at Lola. 'The nuns had a fierce fright that day. Thought the world was going to end.'

'I was sent to Sister Margaret,' said Lola. 'Who went through me for a shortcut. Said I was bringing the school into disrepute. You see, I'd *told* them I was going to perform "Ave Maria".'

Everyone laughed.

'Well,' said Nora, 'proves how much they all knew. You showed them.'

Lola shrugged. 'It's only singing,' she said. 'It's not nursing or saving lives or anything practical.' She smiled at them.

'Come on,' said Dolores. 'Before you change your mind. Let's go in.'

Lola stood for a moment in her swimsuit in the chill of the evening breeze, her feet on the rough rock, the sound of seagulls above. The women were already making their way to the sea, stepping down into the water, holding the handrail, and then pushing off into variations of breaststrokes. *Come on, Lola*, she told herself. *Aren't you here to challenge yourself? Aren't you here for a second chance, a rebirth? A baptism?*

And then it was her turn, the water on her feet, then ankles, then calves, and then, before she could change her mind, arms stretched out ahead of her, she swooshed in, feeling the cold immerse her, as though she was being cleansed, everything on the outside washed away, everything that didn't matter – the performances, the make-up, the costumes – and all that was left was her true self, who she actually was.

She hung in the water, holding her breath. She felt safe there, held in the sea, suspended in the sea, as though it would take care of her, if she stopped everything and just let things be as they were. *Go with the flow*, she thought. *Be in the here and now.* She had her eyes closed as she faced away from land, the lapping water at her face, the waves gently rocking her. *All I have to be is here, right now, and everything will be fine.*

* * *

Later, she and the women sat talking and she wasn't Lola O'Hare, superstar, she was merely another girl from Sandycove, just like them. Wrapped up in their dryrobes or fleeces, they talked about meals they had eaten, holidays they were planning, books they were devouring. It was the kind of conversation that Lola had been locked out of for too long. She had few friends and no one really brought her into their world, and as she listened and contributed, she realised it had been lonely.

When they were changed and walking back towards the village, she promised them she would be back the following evening.

'Bye, Lola,' said Catríona. 'You'll sleep well tonight.'

'Remember to rinse out your swimsuit,' said Margaret. 'And hang it out to air-dry.'

'I will,' promised Lola.

'And remember to try the scampi from the fish van,' said Dolores. 'To die for. Better than the cod.'

Lola waved them goodbye and made her way home. She felt as though she was singing from the inside, all that music she had within her felt as though it was ringing throughout her. *If this is happiness*, she thought, *then I'm going to swim every night.*

22

FLORA

Instead of heading straight to Waters & Co, Flora stopped to buy a coffee from Peter, who ran Man The Van, a battered red Peugeot vehicle, from which Peter would poke his head out of the side and take your order.

'Morning, Flora,' he said. 'Beautiful day.'

'Gorgeous, Peter,' agreed Flora. 'How's everything with you?'

'Grand, you know yourself,' he said. 'Keeping busy. How's Kate getting on? I was admiring her van the other day. Citroen camper van. 1985. French engineering, best in the world. Apart from German, obviously. But the French knew what they were doing.' Flora passed him her reusable cup to fill. 'By the way,' he went on. 'Don't mind that husband of yours...'

Flora had no idea Peter knew Justin.

'He's a member of my gym,' went on Peter. 'I know I shouldn't say anything, but he and his pal... Robert?'

Flora nodded.

'Ex-pal, am I right? Well, they had a pop at each other. We were all there, in the weights room, and Justin... I know him because I saw you two together a few times... anyway, he comes in, and Robert – I buy my paper cups from him. Anyway, Robert charges at him like a bull in a ring and Justin fends him off with a spray bottle used to clean the machines… got it in Robert's eye, half-blinding him. Screaming mad he was, and anyway, the rest of us were standing around putting two and two together…'

Flora nodded, embarrassed that news of the demise of her marriage had reached the whole of Sandycove. 'I've moved back in with my Mum,' she said.

'Well,' said Peter, 'and I hope you don't mind me saying anything, but my old father used to say men who have blond hair are not to be trusted. They think they are Jesus Christ himself, our Lord incarnated, going around tossing their locks around…'

Flora had to admit that Justin did like to toss his locks and ruffle his hair. He hated anyone else messing with it and had gone to the same – very expensive – celebrity hairdresser since she'd known him. He even used a designer shampoo and conditioner which he bought online and which Flora wasn't allowed to touch. He also went for regular manicures and sometimes Flora caught him holding his hands out in front of himself, as though admiring them.

'Put it away,' Peter said, when she took out her purse. 'Free to my favourite customer.'

She smiled, feeling a bit pathetic, but Peter was so kind. 'Thanks, Peter.'

'You'll be grand, so you will.' He gave her a wink. 'Keep on plodding. It's all we can do.'

Flora took her drink and gazed out to sea. A small fishing trawler with two tiny figures on board made its way around the headland. It made a distant chug-chug sound as the engine pushed through the gentle roll of the waves and she was captured for a moment, thinking of a simpler life, being out at sea, pulling up the lobster pots, the sun shining. The way the light danced, the sparkle of the water, the flash of colour of one of the fisherman's jumpers, the blue of the boat, she had an idea. She took a photograph, thinking, *There's something there, something beautiful.*

Once back in the shop, Flora recalled the trawler. She grabbed some scrap paper and sketched its outline, and then another, a pencil drawing overlapping. *White on blue*, she thought, looking at the angles and the curves of her little boat. *This could be a wallpaper*, she thought. *This might actually work.* The colours would have to be right, nothing wishy or washy. Strong but subtle. Didn't Killian say he was bored of the dark, boudoir colours of hotels these days? And what had he said about Patsy's style? Elegantly feminine.

Inside, it was as though something was waking up, some part of her, which had lain dormant, was finally stirring. Time to start all over again. She had said goodbye to a part of her life. It had never been hers, any of it: the pine kitchen, the gilt wardrobe... even Justin.

* * *

That evening, Flora switched on her computer in her bedroom and began to design. And again, the ideas flowed – the shapes of the old trawlers, the movement of the waves, the light playing over their surfaces, the kaleidoscope of colours, all came together, the patterns and colours finding themselves, as she blocked out all thoughts of Justin and Sandra, of the poor old pine kitchen, the lonely house.

In the morning, she printed off the images and brought them downstairs, feeling nervous. In the old days, she would show her work to anyone, but now she felt awkward about even showing them to her mother. Patsy was in the kitchen, eating her toast and marmalade, her notebook open in front of her, in the middle of writing some kind of list.

'I've finished something,' Flora said. 'Which may or may not work... up to you...'

Patsy put down her toast and wiped her hands on a napkin. 'Show me,' she said. She picked up the first sheet, and then the second. 'Oh lovely... beautiful...' She held them up against the wall, squinting. She turned to Flora. 'They are perfect.'

'They're not *perfect*,' said Flora.

'But they are... the colours, the wash of blues and greens... and then... the trawler. It's as though we are standing on shore watching them go out.'

Flora felt cautiously pleased. 'You genuinely like it?'

Patsy was nodding. 'I think this green-blue for the wallpaper and this lilac for the curtains. And the orange-red for the cushions, with a yellow piping.' She looked up at Flora. 'I love it. Thank you. Now, will you organise getting the wallpaper printed, and the fabric in two colourways and then I can show it to Killian?' Patsy said. 'In the meantime, I am busy liaising with the woodturner – he thinks he could have the benches made in three weeks. And I need to go and meet an artist and see if I can buy some watercolours of the harbour.' She looked again at the designs. 'I love them, I really do. They are exactly what I wanted but couldn't ever have imagined.'

For the first time in years, Flora felt as though she was back on the path she was supposed to take. The hurt was still there. And the embarrassment. But more than anything, she knew she was going to survive.

She cycled to her old printers, Fitzgerald's, at lunchtime. It was part of a small industrial estate incongruously called Flower Meadow, just a short ride away from Sandycove, and situated within the circle of buildings were a glazier, a picture framer, a carpenter and an ironworks. The printers used to be run by a lovely, elderly man called Arthur Fitzgerald but, even though it still had the old sign up: 'Fitzgerald's – for all your printing requirements', there was something shinier and more modern about the place. The door was now painted canary-yellow and the windows seemed brighter, decades of dirt and dust had been washed away.

Flora had her USB in her bag containing her first tentative trawler designs and also another design she thought of as her 'sea creatures and monsters' and was hoping to have them printed off so she could see if they worked. She didn't remember being this nervous all those years ago, she used to have things printed off all the time, and sometimes they looked awful, but other times, the printer released a kind of iridescent magic in the colours and the designs which turned them from a flat image on a computer screen into something which you felt lived and breathed. Good design furthered the dimension on your living space, it brought other worlds into your own.

Flora pushed open the door and stepped inside.

A woman, in a navy denim apron over a long floral dress, her hair half-falling down, a tattoo of a lizard on her forearm, looked up from the desk behind the counter. 'Morning,' she said, smiling. 'Lovely day. Got caught in the shower this morning, but it's brightened up considerably, has it not?'

'It has,' agreed Flora, searching for the USB in her satchel, her heart beating loudly in her ears. She had to show her work to a stranger. 'I wonder...' Her voice sounded strange and she gathered herself a little. 'I would like to have this printed...'

The woman took the USB. 'On what?'

'Just contact paper initially and then... well, fabric and wallpaper... is that something you can do?'

The woman nodded. 'I can send it to Mitchell's in town. Turnaround time about five days. The guys are great and don't mind doing small batches after hours for me. We can go through the paper type and fabric in a moment.' She moved across the room to a desk area with a computer and she put in the USB. 'File name?'

'Trawlers,' said Flora.

The woman squinted as she searched through the files and then clicked on the right one. 'Here we go...' She leaned closer to the screen.

'I've done it in three colourways,' said Flora, leaning into it with her. 'If you could print the three out to see and then I need to order two of them...'

'No problem...' And in a moment, there was a sound of whirring as the printer next to them started into action. 'They look lovely,' said the woman, looking at the computer screen. 'Did you design them?'

Flora nodded. 'It's for something my mother is working on...'

The woman narrowed her eyes. 'It wouldn't be for the new hotel, would it?'

'Yes...'

The woman was smiling. 'It's my brother's. Killian. He's up to his oxters in it all. I don't know how he manages to contain all his stress. But he actually seems to enjoy the chaos of building. He's got quite a few properties now,' she went on, 'but after his divorce, he had to give up half his assets and he's been building it all up again... Anyway, all water under the bridge. Killian's grand. Does yoga and everything these days.' She held out her hand. 'Ailish, Killian's big sister. Good to meet you.'

'Flora.' They smiled at each other.

The woman walked over to the printer and picked up the three sheets of heavy paper. 'Right,' she said, peering at them. 'Colour is good, good representation.' She looked up, smiling, placing them on the large table in front of Flora. 'There you go...'

Flora picked up the first one, the white scribbled trawlers against the blue-purple background, the tones of the colour coming alive. They were subtle but lovely. 'May I?' She propped it up on a shelf and then walked backwards, through the shop, looking at the way the colour reflected the sun streaming in from the roof lights, the blurring of the design to give a warm, happy hue. 'What do you think?' she said to Ailish.

Ailish was nodding slowly. 'I love it. And the others?'

They both stood squinting and staring at the three prints, unable to make up their minds which was the best. They were, Flora dared to think, not too bad. A few tweaks with the proportions, and maybe add a shot of pink, but still quite good.

'Have a think,' said Ailish, 'then come back and we can get them printed.'

The bell above the door rang, and Killian was stepping inside, as Flora quickly took down the prints. She definitely wasn't ready to show them to Killian yet.

'So! How was it?' Ailish said, excitedly, before turning back to Flora. 'He was on another date yesterday and I am all ears, can't wait to hear how he got on. We're all agog. Spit it out. My brother has been single for five years,' she went on. 'He's been lonely and depressed.'

'Ailish!' Killian rolled his eyes at Flora. 'Honestly. You'd think she'd try to make me sound a little bit more dynamic. Not a sad loser with absolutely no life whatsoever. Which, although true, does not do my reputation much good. I want to be known as a heartbreaker, not a lonely heart.'

Ailish laughed. 'You wish... Anyway, don't keep us in suspense. How was the date?'

'Not exactly *great*,' said Killian. 'But not exactly *terrible*. In between.'

'At least that's better than last time,' said Ailish, and then she turned to Flora. 'He went on a date with someone who wanted to see his bank details.'

'No one wants to see *those*,' joked Killian, 'not even my bank manager. But maybe it's a good idea to ask the unromantic, pragmatic questions; you don't want to waste time with the wrong person. With an uneven credit rating.'

'I wasted eight years,' said Flora, without even thinking. 'I should have asked the right questions, such as, *Are you likely to have an affair with your best friend's wife?*'

Ailish and Killian laughed, which made Flora feel suddenly giddy. Up until now, everyone had been carefully and quietly gentle with her, and here were two people who were seeing the humorous side of marriage breakdown. She hadn't realised it could have one.

'Would have saved you a whole lot of bother,' said Ailish. 'My ex was controlling. Not going to make that mistake ever again. Separate bank accounts, own home. The man I've got now is a sweetheart. Couldn't be nicer. Life *should* be improved by a partner. And you have to kiss a lot of frogs before your find your prince or princess. Just don't marry the frog, until you have lived with it for at least ten years.' She turned back to her brother. 'When's your next date, Killian?'

'Day after tomorrow,' he replied. 'Now, she looks promising. Hobbies include wine and reading books and miniature chow chows. Whatever one of those is.'

'Wine and reading books is a very wide personality spectrum,' said Ailish, narrowing her eyes again. 'Most people like them. But she's a dog lover, so bonus points.'

'Ah, it's a dog!' He winked at Flora. 'Well, that's a plus.'

'Flora's been working on her wallpaper and fabric for the hotel,' said Ailish. 'It's top secret... but, and I think I am allowed to say, it's beautiful.' She smiled at Flora. 'I think you're going to like it a lot.'

Killian turned back to Flora. 'I can't wait. What about a sneak preview?'

Flora shook her head. 'Not yet, not until it's all done. On orders of my mother. She's the designer. I'm just the junior partner.' Flora withdrew her USB from the computer. 'I'll talk to you in the morning, Ailish,' she said, turning at the door. 'Good luck with your date, Killian.'

There was a feeling in her chest – a lovely, excited butterfly feeling. The dread and nausea would be back, she knew, but for a moment it was pleasing to know she could feel good things again.

23

LOLA

Sitting on the bench beside Paulie's grave, drinking her coffee and eating a cinnamon bun, Lola thought about what a nice spot it was. If it wasn't a graveyard, then it would actually be a place where people could relax and stretch out. Being a graveyard had its benefits, however: it meant solitude, despite the dead bodies. Lola thought about her swim the previous evening with the Forty Footers and how she had stayed in the water for longer than she had ever done, as though she was becoming acclimatised, and how clear her head had felt after her swim and how much she loved talking to the other women. There had been a discussion about favourite books – they were all big readers – and Lola, who had felt very much lacking in the book department, had written down all their recommendations as soon as she'd returned back to the flat, planning to go to the village bookstore. That would pass some time nicely.

At the next grave, a small woman was planting some flowers in a beautiful silk scarf. Hermès? Surely not. Not in Sandycove, but the woman was dressed surprisingly well in a linen trouser suit and heavy, black-rimmed glasses, hair in a sharp bob.

Lola carried on eating her bun, thinking of Kate and how she could possibly crack her open like a crème brûlée, or was she being too pushy?

The lady with the scarf was now standing up and had glanced over at her. 'Lola O'Hare?'

'Yes?'

'Edith Waters.' She walked towards her, holding out her hand. 'I was sorry to hear about your loss. Your friend, your musical partner...'

Lola nodded. 'Thank you. And I saw you tending a grave... may I ask who you have lost?'

'My parents. It's been some time now.' Edith sat beside her on the bench. Ordinarily, Lola would have hated such an imposition, but in Sandycove, as she was remembering, you *talked* to people. 'They were good parents,' she went on. 'Conventional. Obviously.'

'All our parents were,' said Lola.

Edith nodded. 'It's strange to think of that generation now, isn't it, being so scared of anyone being different...'

Lola let out a hollow laugh. 'Tell me about it. My mother just wanted me to be normal... I asked her what she meant by normal and she said not going around singing everywhere. If she only knew how normal I actually was.'

'My parents,' said Edith, 'didn't think *I* was normal. Gay, you see. A lesbian. They were appalled. Once they made their feelings clear, we never spoke of it again.'

Lola was listening intently. 'What happened?'

'I wasn't brave enough to choose my partner. Instead I chose my parents. The thought of going against their rule was too much. I would prefer to be unhappy than to disappoint them.'

'I was the opposite,' said Lola. 'I disappointed my mother and chose to be a singer. But sometimes I think that drive caused me to overlook other things as well.'

Edith nodded. 'We never get things right completely. There is no such thing as perfect.'

'Are you happy now?' asked Lola.

'Getting there. What about you?'

'Still hopeful.'

'Still hopeful,' repeated Edith. 'That's what should be on my gravestone.'

'Or a song,' said Lola. 'It should be a song.'

Edith was smiling at her. 'I hope you write it. Let it be a commission.' She stood up. 'Are you staying or ready to leave?'

'Ready,' said Lola, joining her. And the two of them walked back to the village together, talking all the way.

24

PATSY

Finally, after weeks of designing, organising and worrying, it was time to start the actual making. Patsy was sewing curtains for the large windows in the reception area. She had seen and loved Flora's fabric designs and knew her own choices would meld so well. Most of the fabric to be made into curtains and cushions had been delivered earlier. There was still the fabric that Flora had designed. Those curtains could be done last, but it was a huge job. All that measuring and cutting and sewing. She'd be flat out until opening day. She turned on the radio, ready to begin.

Her front room was her special place and where she kept everything which was precious to her – her book-lined shelves, her design magazines stacked neatly, her photographs of Flora over the years, her green-painted Chinese cabinet which held her glassware. Her small stove was lit in the winter and kept the room cosy. The sofa was used to store boxes of fabrics, the old dining table held her two workhorses, her Singer sewing machines, plus an overlocker. Sewing had become more than a way to make extra money, it had become therapy; the close concentration, the careful stitching, each tiny loop of thread being made, over and over. The click-clacking of the sewing machine had brought a rhythm to her work, making order out of chaos, turning nothing into something, creating, making, embodying.

The doorbell rang. It was Doodle Matthews from across the road.

'Patsy,' she said, 'I hear you're hiding a superstar. I *need* to meet Lola O'Hare. Hubby says he's seen her a couple of times, in dark glasses, silver space shoes. But I said to him, I will just have to go to Patsy and ask to see her. She knows how much I love Lola... she won't mind.' Doodle smiled.

At that moment, Patsy noticed Lola walking towards them. She considered signalling wildly at her so she wouldn't have to deal with a fan, but Lola was now opening the front gate and had given her a wave. 'Morning, Patsy,' she said.

Doodle turned around and screamed. She seemed to be hyperventilating and was now fanning her face with her hands. 'I don't believe it...' she kept saying. 'I don't believe it. It's you... it's you...'

'Of course it's me,' said Lola. 'What did you think it was, a hologram?'

'I know... I know... it's just that... well... on my street... friends with my neighbour...'

Lola made eye contact with Patsy, who responded with a helpless shrug. 'This is Doodle,' said Patsy. 'She was just telling me how much she admired your work...'

Doodle staggered towards Lola, arms outstretched as though heralding the zombie apocalypse. Lola tried to smile at Doodle, who was now clutching her hands. 'I know I am making a fool of myself,' she was saying, 'it's just that you mean a great deal to me. Your music does, anyway. I mean, you do too, you *are* your music and it has got me through the hardest times in my life. You know, just when you think life is going well, you have another body blow? Of course you know, you've written about it – and sung about it! Oh my God, I'm babbling... I'm going on...' She turned back to Patsy. 'Will you take a photograph? Of the two of us? Please? Where's my phone?' She screamed again. 'OHMYGOD! I've left my phone at home!'

Patsy was already lifting up her own phone. 'Is this okay, Lola?' she asked.

'Of course, of course...' Lola managed to smile at Doodle and then faced Patsy's camera, Doodle's arm around her, clinging on. 'So lovely to meet you.'

'Oh you too! You too!' Doodle peeled herself off Lola and gazed at her with dreamy eyes. 'I'd better get back,' she said. 'I'm in the middle of organising the golf club raffle... prizes need to be sourced...' She looked at Lola. 'I don't suppose you might be able to... I don't know... donate something to be raffled?'

Lola nodded. 'I'll find something.'

Doodle smiled, delighted. 'So lovely to meet you in person,' she said. 'Now, will you come to morning coffee, afternoon tea or evening Prosecco? Any time? Let me know when would suit you? I live in that house, just over there, the one with the wisteria and the Hyundai Tucson hybrid. Well, I'll leave you now. Goodbye.' She skipped down the drive, squeezed past the camper van and was gone.

Patsy turned to Lola. 'Does that happen much?'

'Not usually in Ireland,' said Lola. 'But can't complain. Without fans, you don't really exist. You don't make your music for no one to listen to, you want an audience. Paulie always loved our fans.' She looked at Patsy, and cleared her throat. 'I'm here to see Kate, actually,' she said. 'Is she...'

'She's at Honeysuckle Lodge,' said Patsy.

'Of course... but what is she doing there?'

'A choir, actually,' replied Patsy.

'A choir?'

'Would you like to come in? Cup of tea? I was just about to make one.'

'Only for a moment,' said Lola, her voice shaky. 'If it's not too much trouble. I hope I'm not disturbing you.'

She seemed humbled and vulnerable, thought Patsy, her heart going out to her.

In the front room, surrounded by the piles of fabric, Patsy removed a pile from one of the armchairs, so Lola could sit down.

'What's all this for?' Lola asked, seeming to have gathered herself a little.

'I'm the... well, you could say... I'm designing... working on...' began Patsy, clearing her throat and shifting slightly awkwardly on the sofa. Lola was staring at her as though she was mad. 'I'm the...'

'What are you?'

'Well... I'm making the new hotel... doing the insides... designing, you could say... paint, furniture...'

'You're doing the *interior design*?'

Patsy nodded.

'Why didn't you just say so?'

'It sounds too much,' said Patsy. 'I mean, I've only just done a course... and I did the café...'

'In the village? It's very nice,' said Lola. 'And you've been hired for the hotel? What's the problem?'

'What if it's *bad*?'

'How bad can it be?' said Lola, with a shrug. 'I've seen a lot of hotels and cafés in my time and ninety-nine per cent of them are awful. I imagine yours will be better than the majority. Paulie's place in Nashville was absolutely horrible. He paid a fortune to this interior designer from Palm Springs who thought wallpaper with tigers on was a good idea. And a black carpet in the

bedrooms.' She paused. 'You're not thinking of *black* carpet, are
you?'

Patsy laughed. 'No...'

'Well, then,' said Lola. 'It's already better than that charlatan's
design.' She smiled at Patsy. 'Anyway, do you need help? Because I
am not exactly busy these days. I swim a bit, eat a lot, walk for
miles...'

'You can sew?'

'I used to make all my costumes growing up,' Lola said. 'I
know my way around a sewing machine.' She swallowed and kept
talking. 'I could do whatever you needed.' She seemed to need
Patsy more than Patsy needed her. 'If you'll have me?'

'How about starting now? As soon as we finish our tea?'

And Lola smiled back at her. 'I would love that. Thank you.'

25

KATE

In the evening, Kate and Flora had fallen into the habit of meandering towards the beach. The roads were wide and leafy, the front gardens all distinct, some with neat lawns and cherry trees, others with professional landscaping and even one overrun by gnomes.

'That's my favourite,' said Flora, pointing at one gnome who was performing a handstand.

'I couldn't possibly choose between them,' replied Kate. 'I can't believe they're still adding to their collection. Last time I saw them, there was only half the number...'

They carried on walking, the evening bright, the day stretching itself as far as it could.

'Nothing changes,' said Flora. 'And yet...'

'Everything changes,' finished Kate. 'Walking around, it's exactly the same. I could be eight years old again, or eighteen...'

'Are you glad to be back?'

They had left Sea Road, and were crossing in front of the shops, heading towards the sea. Beyond was the small, curved stone pier which held the golden beach.

'I think so,' said Kate. 'I mean, we're hanging out together, and I love working at Honeysuckle Lodge... and...' She turned to Flora. 'I didn't realise how much I wanted to come home and how much I missed it. I don't think I was listening to myself...'

Flora laughed. 'Tell me about it. I wish I listened to myself more.'

'How are the designs coming along?' asked Kate. 'Your mum says they are beautiful...'

Flora blushed a little at the compliment. 'Well, they're not quite there yet... but I'm enjoying it, you know? When you allow yourself to be creative and when things just flow... it's the best feeling...'

'Wait...' Kate squinted, and there, in a billowing white coat, her hair flying in the air, was Lola. 'It's her!'

Lola was walking along the seafront, her back to them, her figure getting smaller and smaller, carrying a bag, from which a rolled-up towel was poking out. 'Is she going swimming?'

'She told Mum that she goes every evening,' said Flora. 'She's met a group of women at the Forty Foot.'

'She's been talking to Patsy?'

'They're working together. She's been helping Mum with the sewing all week.'

There was something so poignant about seeing Lola all on her own. Kate wished Lola would just go back to the States before feelings were awakened which she didn't want to have to deal with.

Parked beside the beach was an ice cream van, a small queue of people waiting their turn. 'Ice cream?'

Flora nodded and they took their place. Once they had their 99s in their hands, they walked towards the end of the beach where a small pier jutted out into the high tide.

Flora took off her sandals, and, her ice cream held up high, edged her body out towards the sea, her toes submerging into the water. 'Ahhhhh....' She closed her eyes. 'Come on, Kate. It's good for the baby!'

Kate sat down beside her, feet melting into the cool of the water, and the two ate their ice creams. It was moments like this that made her think she could never leave Ireland again. But she still couldn't stop thinking about Lola, all on her own, and Kate wished she could just love her in the uncomplicated way Flora loved Patsy. Now she was nearly a mother herself, she could see that perhaps there was another perspective. And perhaps it was Kate who had been selfish and had refused to allow room for any reconciliation to take place. Kate's stubbornness was just as strong as Lola's and it was so hard to come down from your mountain of self-justification and righteousness.

26

FLORA

The following afternoon, Flora was hiding behind the hawthorn tree in the front garden of her old house. She felt sick, her heart was beating so loud she couldn't hear the voice in her head, telling her she still had a chance to leave. Instead, she was listening to the other voice which was whispering intently: *You shouldn't be thrown away like this, you deserve answers, an explanation, an apology!* Wasn't her marriage worth fighting for?

Her heart thumped, blood rushed through her brain like a stream after a week of rain, she was possessed with a madness like a Brontë heroine. She had thought she was doing really well... but she had been compelled to come back. She knew she should make those feet turn around and keep on walking back down the hill and carry on with her day like any other normal, sane person. Hadn't Edith said that she had a month left to grieve all this? Well, she was still just about within the time frame.

Perhaps Justin would be working in his study and they could talk. Sandra's Range Rover was in the drive, but she could be at tennis with her friends, while Justin worked. Sometimes he would update her on the work he was undertaking. But mainly, it all went way above Flora's head. How had she managed to marry someone who was so different from her?

On her wedding day, she had noticed a look pass between Patsy and Kate and she had turned to them, suddenly desperate. 'What?' she had said. 'What are you thinking?'

Kate, who had recently returned from India with henna tattoos, said, 'Nothing.'

'Except,' Patsy had said, after a pause, 'you're very young.'

'Yes, you're very young,' Kate had agreed.

'As long as you're happy,' Patsy had said.

Sense was beginning to prevail, and she had a moment of clarity. *Leave now*, she told herself. *Leave before you are discovered.*

She turned to go... except... oh God, there was another voice. This time in the house. Sandra's.

Through the window to the right of the front door, into the living room, Flora spied Sandra sitting on the sofa. And then Sandra looked up, her eyes fixed on Flora. Her face was a mixture of surprise and amusement.

Flora lifted a hand to wave. 'Just seeing if everything was okay,' she said, loudly. 'Making sure you were settling in all right.'

Sandra came to the window. 'What?' she said, wrestling with the catch.

'You need to force it down,' said Flora, 'wiggle it and then gently push it open.' Her smile was manic, she knew, teeth on display like a horse.

Sandra looked concerned. 'Are you all right, Flora?' she said, looking at her with pity. 'I was going to call. Annette and Lisa told me you fell over in the supermarket.'

'I didn't fall over,' said Flora. 'I overbalanced.'

'Right...' Sandra didn't look convinced. 'Justin dropped your things to your mother's... she gave him an earful...' That amused smile again. 'He said it was like being savaged by a mosquito.'

Flora managed to keep herself calm. 'I'm just here for my design books, actually. I need them because I'm so busy with my work...' She had forgotten all about them until now, but they were on the lower shelf of the bookcase in the living room and at least she could pretend they were why she had returned.

'Busy?' Sandra looked almost put out. 'You mean in the *shop*?'

'I'm actually designing wallpaper for the new hotel in the village and some fabric,' said Flora airily, 'so my books are a useful source of inspiration. Haven't quite finalised the design yet... still some tweaking to do... So could you pass them to me? Out of the window is fine. The whole lower shelf of the bookcase in the dining room.'

Sandra returned with a heavy pile of books. 'Do you need a bag?' She passed them out, loading up Flora like an aged mule.

'No, no!' Flora's legs buckled beneath her. 'I'll be fine. And how are you, Sandra? How's the tennis?'

'Oh, I'm looking for a new club,' she said. 'I've been excommunicated. You know what women are like. Bitches. The lot of them.'

Flora shook her head. 'Without my female friends, I'd be lost.'

She noticed Justin now, standing behind Sandra, trying to listen in.

'Well...' Sandra shrugged. 'I've just been unlucky with my friends. I'll find a new club. And new friends. They'll just miss out on the villa in Portugal this year. More fool them.'

'I'd better go and get on with my work,' said Flora, brightly. 'Thanks so much, so sorry to disturb you...'

'Right...' Sandra looked as though she was sucking on a lemon. 'Well... good luck with it.'

'You too! Good luck with everything!' Flora turned and jogged out of the gate, and down the road, wondering how she would ever make it home with this huge pile of hardback books. She briefly considered dumping them in one of her old neighbour's green bins, but just as she was contemplating fly-tipping, a car pulled up, and a voice called out through the window.

'Need a lift into the village?'

Oh God, Killian Walsh. She wanted to refuse, but she was already tired from lugging the books.

'I'm going to Sandycove. Save you the walk? And why are you carrying so many books...' He looked amused.

'Oh, they're for... research,' she said. 'And yes, a lift would be very kind.'

She sat in beside him, the books piled on her lap. While she was a sweaty mess, Killian was freshly shaved and wearing a smart pair of jeans, shirt and blue cotton jacket.

'Going to a meeting?'

'Kind of.' He gave her a half-smile as he pulled out onto the road. 'Another date, actually. Coffee in the café. Women don't want to go for dinner these days, even though I'd be happy to pay for a nice meal. They don't want to be stuck with a weirdo for a whole evening.'

'I don't blame them,' said Flora. 'No one does.'

He laughed. 'Apparently, it only takes thirty-two seconds to work out if the person who you are looking across the café table at is a psychopath, forty-seven seconds to work out if they are merely unsuitable and three minutes twenty-three seconds to decide if you want to see them again. Dating is now done with the efficiency of a ninja warrior. Small talk is out. They want to know what you do, how much you earn, what car you drive...'

'What's this then?' said Flora, peering over at the steering wheel.

'A nine-year-old Volkswagen,' he said. 'Not new enough, it seems.'

'What else do they want to know? Who you vote for?'

He shook his head. 'Not that,' he said. 'More like do I watch

Love Island...'

'And *do* you?'

'I don't really know what it is. I googled it and was even more confused. Another asked me what my star sign was. Again, no idea.'

'You *don't* know what your star sign is?' laughed Flora.

'Why would I?' He was laughing as well. 'It's never seemed relevant. One of them worked it out for me. I'm on a cusp apparently. Sounds about right. I'm on a cusp of everything.'

'But they must like the fact you own a hotel?'

'Yes, I think that's what lands me the date in the first place, but then I am just a series of disappointments. The car, my clothes, the lack of interest in reality TV...' He was smiling as though his lack of success wasn't the end of the world.

'Well,' said Flora, 'what do you think of them?'

'I'm still hopeful,' he said. 'Who knows, Ms Right might be waiting for me at Alison's. In three minutes twenty-three seconds, I may be about to meet the love of my life.' He pulled a face, making Flora laugh again. 'And then I have my yoga class... which is an antidote to everything.'

'Yoga?'

'You should try it,' he said. 'I told you, it's been part of my post-divorce healing journey.' He gave her a look. 'Except you don't do journeys, do you?'

'Not if I can help it.'

'It really helped,' he said. 'I was feeling so bad about myself, but it worked. The breathing, the bending into ridiculous shapes, the tight Lycra... something shifted...'

'Lycra is never a good idea,' said Flora. 'Not if you want things to shift...'

He laughed again. 'Well, we're in Our Lady's Hall. Come and join us. It's nice to have an excuse not to do anything for an hour.'

He pulled into Sandycove's main street. 'I make a lot of decisions in my yoga class. But if yoga isn't your thing, counselling also helps. My counsellor made me *thank* my wife for the experience, the love... and even how it ended. I wrote it all down and tried to remember the good times and not dwell on lingering anger and bitterness. Well, not dwell *too* much. But it worked. Just glad I didn't have to send the bloody letter. And now, I sincerely wish her well. My counsellor used to say we grow as people at our darkest times.' He smiled. 'I finally got there. Mostly. And now, I'm ready to find someone. Eternally optimistic, that's me.'

'Good for you. I'm not, though,' she said. To be honest, she was beginning to realise, she hadn't really liked Justin for a long time. He wasn't a particularly nice person. 'Never.'

'Never what?'

'Going to find someone. And I have to tell you, Killian, the relief is enormous. I can now spend the rest of my life just pleasing myself, I never have to eat food I haven't chosen, I never have to share a bed, or listen to anyone's boring stories.'

Killian was smiling. 'There are definitely many benefits to being single,' he said. 'Except, I got a bit lonely. Began craving affection, someone to talk to, someone to look after. Someone to hold hands with...'

'Justin's hands were always sweaty,' recalled Flora. 'I never told him, just had to put up with them. It was like holding hands with a damp facecloth.'

Killian laughed again. 'Where shall I drop you? You can't carry those books. Your arms will fall off.'

They were opposite Alison's café. 'Here is fine.' She smiled at him, wondering if he saw her as a mad, old hag who needed rescuing. Actually, she realised that being a mad, old hag wasn't the worst thing to be in life. Maybe it was something she should embrace.

Killian reversed the car into a space and turned off the engine as Flora peered through the window into the café.

'I wonder if the next Mrs Walsh is there yet?'

'I'm not sure. I've seen her photograph and she looks nice… brown hair. Loves the colour pink apparently, loves Zumba and guinea pigs. She's got two. Mr George and Big Ears.'

'And how do you feel about guinea pigs?'

'I have absolutely no feelings whatsoever. I mean, I like *pigs*…'

'These are rodent versions,' said Flora.

'Rodents!' Killian tried to look horrified, turning off the engine. 'No one mentioned rodents!'

Flora laughed again. 'Well, I think she sounds perfect. Anyone who gives a home to rodents has to be a nice person.' She opened the car door and began to clamber out, managing to balance the books under both arms. 'You will be stepfather to Mr Ears and Big George, or was it the other way round?'

Now Killian laughed, as he exited from his side and they faced each other across the roof of the car.

'Thanks for the lift,' Flora said. 'And say hi to your wife-to-be.'

'And my future step-guinea pigs.' He smiled across at her. 'How are the designs coming along?'

'They are… well… not sure, hopefully I'll have something completed soon.'

'Well, good luck with everything.'

'I should be saying that to you.'

'Thank you,' he said. 'I need it.'

She watched him walk across the road, and just before he ducked into the café, he turned and gave her a wave. She hoped he found Ms Right, he definitely deserved to be happy. Seeing how Killian had dealt with his wife's adultery, the loss of his marriage and half his bank balance, there was hope for her. She might even consider yoga if it had the same effect on her.

27

LOLA

After patiently waiting for Kate to soften towards her, Lola realised that the time had come when she would have to be a little bit more forceful. Leaving Patsy's after lunch, she walked down to Honeysuckle Lodge and stood outside. Someone had tried to make an effort with the geraniums and the hanging baskets. There was even a ceramic sign saying, 'Home is where the honey-suckle grows', which looked as though it had been made by one of the residents' grandchildren. Paulie would have turned his nose up at ending his days on earth in a place like this.

'Lorraine?'

'Lola,' she said automatically, before turning round. Oh God, it was Abigail Duffy from school. 'Abigail, hi!' she said.

'Couldn't miss *you*, Lorraine,' said Abigail, coming in for a hug, and squashing Lola tightly.

'Lola,' said a muffled Lola.

'Sorry, *Lola*,' said Abigail. 'It must be so good to have different identities. I've only the one, unfortunately.'

'It has its benefits,' replied Lola. 'You can get rid of the things that aren't working...' *Like mothers*, she thought. 'And concentrate on the things that are.' *Like music.* Becoming Lola had given her so much. But it hadn't given her everything, because if it had, she wouldn't be outside Honeysuckle Lodge, waiting for someone who no longer cared for her. She should have shown Kate that she was the most important thing to her. How selfish she had been.

Don't blame yourself, Lola. Paulie's voice was in her head. *You didn't know any better.*

But, Paulie, I made a choice. I could have had it all. I could have done it so much better. I did it all wrong.

Lola, stop it. You did the best you could at the time. And anyway, it's not too late. Look, you're here now.

But Lola suspected it was just that: too late.

Kate was now older than Lola had been when The Islanders' first album came out, the one that went platinum on three continents, the one that got them their first Grammy. There was a photo on the back sleeve of Lola in a long green velvet dress, the sleeves like those of a medieval princess. Paulie was there in a crinkled silk suit, looking mystical and pensive. The photograph still made Lola laugh when she remembered the shoot. They had spent most of the day laughing and trying to straighten their faces for the photographs. It was taken on a summer's morning, at sunrise, the day before they were about to go on their first big tour. She and Paulie never thought they would be bigger than playing at Dublin's Olympia Theatre, but their manager, Zachary, had changed all that. 'I think we have something here,' he said to them, over chips from Burdocks.

Kate was also a nicer person than Lola. Always had been. She'd put up with a great deal, being dragged around to gigs for all those years. No wonder she got tired of it. And when Kate had said that she would be all right and not to worry about her, Lola had taken her at her word, ignoring any voices in her head. It was amazing what you could choose to ignore if it suited you. She wanted to tell Kate again that she loved her, that she had always loved her, and that she was sorry. But how would Kate react? Would she rush off, refusing to talk to her? Just being in the same airspace as her was a major step, and she didn't want to frighten her away.

Abigail was talking away, about how she'd lost her own mother the year before and how they were delighted to have Kate with them for the next while. 'She's just like you,' said Abigail. 'But you know what they say about mothers and daughters? A mother is one who can take the place of all others but whose place no one else can take.' Abigail's eyes filled with tears. 'I'm sorry, Lorraine, I mean Lola, it's only when I think of Mammy and how glad I was to be close to her at the end.'

Lola felt could feel a rush of something in the centre of her chest. Fear. Loss. Grief. Not the same as Paulie, but as though her body was absorbing the tragedy. Being here now, her beautiful daughter so near and yet further away than ever, Lola said to herself, *You could have handled it all so much better, you really could.*

What shall I do, she asked Paulie, in her head.

Give her time.

28

KATE

The Honeysuckle Warblers were sitting to attention in the day room, the photocopied songbooks Kate had made in their laps. Flora had designed the cover – a little bird fluttering over a tangle of honeysuckle – and Kate had photocopied and stapled the booklets at the library.

'Right, everyone,' she said, sitting down at the piano, 'all ready? I am hoping that we will be able to perform in front of an audience soon, but we've got some work to do... lots of practice and we need to work on our harmonies. If we could start with "Carrickfergus". Altos, you are doing the harmonies in the first verse, sopranos in the second... everyone ready? Bernadette, do you have your glasses? Marjorie, are you all right on the end there? Do you need an extra cushion? No? Okay, then, one... two... three...'

There was a knock on the door. And then a head appeared, framed by long silver hair. 'Mind if I join you?'

A rustle went through the ladies.

'Who's she?' Kate heard Marjorie say.

'No idea,' said Celia. 'Looks like a banshee...'

'It's the thin lips,' remarked Kitty. 'And the white hair...'

'For a moment,' said Dorothy, 'I thought it was one of God's angels, come to beckon me...'

'No wings,' noted another.

'You don't need *them* to go down,' replied Marjorie.

The ladies all laughed together, as Lola stepped into the room.

Kate had watched her mother stride on to stages, every single person in the stadium bellowing out one of The Islanders' hits. Lola would stand, arms raised, hair flowing behind her, her face replicated in multiple on the huge screens behind her. There was one time in a stadium in São Paulo, when Kate was about seventeen, when she had watched Lola run along the peninsula as though she was running along the hands of her fans. Her mother was big, she had thought, bigger than all the other mothers. Kate had felt pride but also as though she was such a small part in her mother's life. *How can I compete with this? Where on earth do I fit in? I'm just an afterthought, a duty, someone to be slotted into her world.*

And now, in the day room of Honeysuckle Lodge, Kate realised Lola looked uncertain. Smaller, almost tentative.

Lola walked towards her. 'Do you mind if I joined in or gave you a hand?'

Kate didn't know what to say. She was aware that every one of the Honeysuckle Warblers was watching the two of them, probably judging her for not being a good and loving daughter. Even Chico the chihuahua had its ears pricked.

Lola cleared her throat. 'I wondered if maybe I could join the choir? I'm in need of a new band...' She gave a laugh and turned to the ladies. 'I'm Kate's mother... her long-lost mother...' She laughed again, looking at Kate uncertainly, as though she wasn't sure how her joke would go down with her.

'Tea,' said Marjorie. 'You can make us our tea. A cup would do very nicely.'

'Wets our whistles,' said Celia.

'And a biscuit,' added Dorothy. 'I find the sugar does my singing voice no end of good.' And then, in a lower voice, 'Chico is partial to a custard cream.'

Kate turned to them, and she realised, as a whole, they had somehow assessed the entire situation and had chosen a side: they were on hers.

'Would you mind?' said Marjorie to Lola, in her most head-mistressy voice. 'Poor Kate does such a wonderful job with us, that she also could do with a cup of tea.' She turned to Kate. 'Milk and sugar? And the rest of us like a large pot of tea. And an extra pot of hot water, just off the boil. Full-fat milk and china cups. Abigail will show you where everything is.'

'And the biscuit cupboard,' said Celia.

To Kate's amazement, Lola nodded obediently and disappeared from the room.

'Will you tell us the story of you and your mother, Kate?' asked Bernadette. 'Maybe bring us up to speed, as my son says. He works in finance and he's all about the jargon.'

'Mine's like that,' said Kitty. 'He told me he was going to *reach out* to someone the other day... and I said, you can't, they are not here...'

'It's very confusing,' agreed Peggy. 'My daughter says she is "touching base" when she calls me. I've given up asking her what on earth that means. She also says that she needs to get her "ducks in a row" and she likes to "get bang for her buck".' She shrugged. 'She's head of some big company. Always on her phone.'

'Quick,' said Celia, 'we need to hear from Kate before her mother returns...'

All the ladies turned to face Kate. 'Well,' she began. 'She lives in California and we're... well, we're... I think the word is estranged.'

'She does look strange,' said Bernadette. 'Didn't I say she was a banshee?'

'No,' said Marjorie, 'estranged. As in not talking to each other. Like a divorce but worse because they are always there, in your mind, you don't ever get away entirely. Divorce you can move on from. Estrangement is something you have to learn to live with.' She looked at Kate. 'Is that what it's like for you?'

Kate nodded. She had expected them to look shocked and appalled, horrified that any daughter wouldn't be speaking to her mother. But they seemed to be nodding understanding, as though in their long years they'd seen it all and nothing shocked them.

'What brought about your estrangement?' asked Dorothy, leaning forward, and almost squashing Chico.

'It was a long time coming,' said Kate, sitting down on the piano stool. 'She was a singer. *Is* a singer. And when I was a teenager, she went on tour with her band... and left me behind.'

'How old were you?' asked Kitty.

'Sixteen,' said Kate.

There were nods of the heads all round. 'That's young,' said Peggy.

'Very,' agreed Bernadette.

'I mean, you can fend for yourself, and in our day, some of us did. But not these days,' said Marjorie.

'It's cruel,' agreed Celia.

'You'd be locked up,' remarked Dorothy.

'It wasn't that bad,' said Kate, feeling terrible, because when you compared it to others, or what women of the Warblers generation dealt with, it wasn't bad at all. Now, she felt foolish, as though she'd made more of something than it warranted. She was allowed to be hurt. But all these years later? She was now officially ridiculous. But the ladies were being so kind and so generous towards her.

'Relationships aren't easy,' said Peggy.

'Particularly family,' noted Kitty, with feeling.

'My son hasn't spoken to me in fifteen years...' said Peggy. 'Came home one day and told me he needed time away from everyone and that was it. Last I heard he was in Melbourne.'

'My daughter didn't speak to me for six years once,' said Kitty. 'It was because I said I wasn't sure about the man she was marrying. I said that his nose was too thin and that men with thin noses weren't to be trusted. What I wanted to say was that I had a bad feeling inside about him, and I thought the nose thing was a good way. But she went mad. Married him. Didn't invite me. And then, the poor loveen, knocked on my door at 2 a.m. with my little granddaughter in her arms, and just a suitcase.' She paused. 'I don't think I've ever hugged anyone so tightly as I hugged the two of them that night. My little granddaughter, Rosie, is not so little any more. She has just graduated from the Royal Irish Academy.'

There were nods of approval from around the room.

'My mother was tricky,' admitted Marjorie. 'That's the word we used to use for impossible...'

'We say narcissistic these days,' said Kate.

'Well, mine was that,' went on Marjorie. 'You could feel her mood from the sound of the key in the door. We'd be terrified of her, waiting for her to explode.'

'What about you and your mother, Kate?' asked Peggy. 'What happened?'

'She...' It sounded ridiculous now. 'She just put her career before me... I didn't feel I mattered so much.'

'You didn't think she loved you?' asked Celia.

'I thought she loved music more than me...' said Kate.

'Ah, that's never good,' said Celia. 'A daughter should know she is the most important thing.'

'She should *feel* it,' said Peggy.

'I thought she was selfish...' added Kate, realising that she was suddenly in a group therapy session.

The ladies were nodding, thinking, taking it all in.

'Selfishness isn't a good trait,' acknowledged Kitty.

'It's the worst,' said Peggy. 'My husband was selfish.'

'You can't live with someone like that...' said Dorothy.

The door began to open and all the ladies immediately stopped talking and looked up expectantly as Lola shuffled in, backwards, pushing open the door with her behind, and then turned, as it closed, holding a large tray of pots, cups and a tin of biscuits. 'I'm going to buy some decent biscuits for you all,' she said, smiling. 'The selection in the kitchen wasn't the best. Cheap ones. The list of additives in them went on and on. And I found supermarket-label tea. Tonight, I am going to buy Barry's Gold Label and decent biscuits.' She smiled at them all, and then turned to Kate. 'I don't have to stay, if you don't want. But I can still buy the tea and biscuits.'

The ladies turned to see Kate's reaction. 'I don't mind,' she said.

While they still had their tea in their hands, they began to sing, Kate standing in front of them, Lola at the piano. They went through 'Carrickfergus', 'Down By The Salley Gardens' and 'The Fields of Athenry'.

There was a feeling of elation in the air. The ladies, Kate noticed, were sitting up straighter, they were all smiling, as though they had just completed a Zumba class. Kate wondered if they should break for more tea or finish for the day. She was about to speak, when Lola stood up.

'Does anyone know "It's a Long Way to Tipperary"?' she said, beginning to play the introduction. 'My grandmother used to sing it to me. Join in!'

Of course everyone knew it and Lola was good, Kate thought. Really good. But wasn't that what she had been doing for the least thirty years, leading a band, bringing people together, creating a sense of togetherness around music?

There was a rustle of excitement as they all began to sing, Marjorie finding a harmony on the top notes and Lola finding one which swooped low and deep around them all. Kate joined in, bringing the altos and the sopranos together. And then at the last few bars... '*Goodbye Piccadilly... farewell Leicester Square... it's a long long way to Tipperary, but my heart's right theeeerrrrreeee...*' Every single voice in the room clung to their note, their voices merging and mingling in the air, the last word and note soaring like a lark in flight. Even Chico was howling.

Finally, they all stopped and everyone started giggling. They looked, thought Kate, like schoolgirls, bright eyes, shiny faces, laughing.

'Brava!' called out Marjorie.

'Brava!'

'Let's give ourselves a round of applause!' said Lola, standing up. 'Everyone was tremendous. What do we all think?'

'We were tremendous,' agreed Dorothy. 'Especially Kate.'

'Kate is magnificent,' said Celia.

'What a wonderful young woman she is,' remarked Peggy.

All the ladies nodded their heads.

'She certainly is,' said Lola, catching Kate's eye. 'Now, I'll gather up all the teacups and take away the tray.' She began piling up the crockery. 'Back in a sec.'

When she'd gone, the ladies paused for a moment, to make sure the door was closed, and then turned to Kate. 'How are you getting on?' asked Dorothy. 'Is she going to come again?'

'She doesn't have to,' said Marjorie, 'we're on your side... whatever you want.'

'But she's very good, isn't she?' said Kitty.

'She's a professional musician,' explained Kate, sitting down, suddenly exhausted, on the piano stool. 'She leads a band... she tours... she's... well, she's pretty successful.' But she felt invigorated by the music and every day she returned from the lodge wishing she could make this her life, that she could always run a choir, always bring music to people's lives.

The ladies nodded. 'I'm sure she is,' said Celia. 'She looks the type.'

'I like her sandals,' remarked Marjorie. 'They look so comfortable. And in silver.'

They all nodded again.

'Birkenstocks,' said Kate, absent-mindedly. She wasn't sure how she felt about Lola being involved in the choir. Lola was a professional, she knew how to bring people together, she was better than Kate on the piano. And there was something about seeing Lola playing and singing, her eyes closed, completely and utterly happy, in that moment. She didn't just *love* music the way Kate did. Music, she realised, was what Lola did to stay *alive*. And it was infectious. The ladies loved her too.

'Is she going to stay?' asked Marjorie.

Kate nodded and the ladies smiled back at her.

'Maybe this will be the end of your estrangement?' said Bernadette.

'Lola needs to behave herself and learn to be less selfish,' said Dorothy.

'Yes, she must learn to be a better mother to our Kate,' agreed Peggy. The ladies all nodded approval.

'Only if it works for Kate,' said Celia. 'You need to decide, Kate. Do you want your mother in your life?'

'I'm going to have to talk to her, properly,' she said to the ladies. 'We're going to have to clear the air.'

The door began to open and they all went silent again.

'Well,' said Lola, walking in, smiling, 'thank you all so much for a lovely afternoon... I have had a very nice time, thanks to all of you.'

'Are you coming back?' asked Bernadette.

'With the tea and biscuits?' said Dorothy.

'Well...' Lola looked at Kate. 'It depends...'

Kate nodded. 'Yes,' she said. 'Yes, she's coming back. Right...' She was speaking more briskly than she felt on the inside. 'We start again tomorrow. And we're going to have a concert. One week's time... here at the home. We'll invite everyone's families...'

'The ones speaking to us anyway,' said Kitty, making everyone laugh.

Kate looked across at Lola who was smiling as hard as anyone, and she turned to Kate and smiled and Kate, despite herself, found herself smiling back.

29

FLORA

In the printers, Ailish smiled when Flora walked in. 'I was just about to ring you,' she said. 'I was on the phone to the lads at the industrial printers and there's been a big cancellation. If I send the order to them now, we'll get the fabric and the wallpaper back in two days.' Ailish placed the clipboard on the counter between them. 'Let's fill this in and send it off. If you give me the files...'

Flora stood beside her, filling in the form and choosing paper size, quality, and for the fabric, Irish linen, weight, weft and weave. This felt a little like the old days, when she would think nothing of designing and creating... but now she felt a little stiff like getting back into exercise after years behind a desk.

Ailish began uploading the files, checking that the correct colours were ticked, cross-checking order numbers and file codes, and then she pressed send. 'I'll quickly call the lads and say it's on the way. They'll be delighted for the work. They are the kind of people who hate hanging around. One of them is my partner, you see. Lewis is one of those who won't sit down. Even on Christmas Day he hovers around looking for tree lights to fix or a turkey to baste.' Ailish smiled at her. 'This time next year, you'll have quadrupled the order...'

Flora swallowed. 'Actually... well... I've done something else... and I wouldn't mind hearing your honest opinion.'

'For the hotel?'

Flora shook her head. 'For me. Well, not for me. But I've had an idea. My own range of tablecloths and napkins. Based on the trawler print, but taking it a bit further.' She stopped. 'It's just an idea...'

'Why not?' said Ailish. 'Sounds like a great plan. Right, let's see the other designs. Shall we print them again? How would you have them made into napkins or tablecloths? Do you have a producer, someone who could make them up for you?'

'My mother, actually,' said Flora. 'Initially. After she's finished the hotel. I don't know. I don't have anything that would qualify as a plan, as such. More... musings.'

'Plots and plans,' said Ailish. 'Where would we be without them?' She clicked on the file, staring again at the screen, and then the printer beside her began whirring. 'I think they are beautiful. Stunning. I've never seen anything quite like it. Dark, mysterious, unique.'

'Really?'

Ailish nodded. 'Let's have a look at them, full-size, in full colour.' She plucked the first sheet from the printer, peering at it. 'It's amazing. The dark pink. The way the net gives shape and structure. Like a garden trellis, except it's not flowers...'

'It's the seabed,' said Flora, pleased that Ailish could so easily see what it was meant to capture.

'Why don't you order some linen? Have some samples made up?'

'Maybe.' Flora was suddenly losing confidence. It had seemed safe to create alone in her old bedroom, but making the dream of her own business real was a step too far.

The bell above the door rang out.

'You again,' said Ailish, looking up. 'Honestly. I know you love me, but this is ridiculous.'

'I was just passing,' said Killian. 'Thought I'd call in and see my favourite sister.'

'There's only the two of us,' said Ailish to Flora. 'He doesn't have another sister.'

'Oh, Flora!' said Killian, as though surprised to see her. 'I didn't see you there.'

'She's ordered the fabric for the hotel,' explained Ailish. 'It's beautiful.'

'Your mother showed me the samples,' said Killian. 'I absolutely love them. They really stand out. I had never thought of wallpaper being something other than a wall covering. Patsy was explaining about the need to look a certain way from a distance and how colour and light can change things. And pattern...' He was smiling at Flora. 'It's fascinating.'

'Anyway,' said Ailish, 'tell me how it went with the cat lady?' She turned to Flora. 'He's moved on from the guinea pig obsessive to a wine-drinking, book-reading cat lover,' she explained. 'Which I am sure is what everyone puts on their dating profiles?'

'They do,' said Killian. 'Apart from the narcissists. But the thing is narcissists are hard to discern. The only way to find out if someone is one, you have to be in a serious relationship with them for six years – at *least* – and only then do they reveal themselves.'

Flora silently agreed.

'They are very good at hiding in plain sight,' agreed Ailish. 'So, how did it go?'

'Well,' said Killian, 'she was very nice. And yes, we talked about wine. My sommelier qualification – a prerequisite for the hospitality industry – came in very handy. And then we talked about books. Luckily, I can read and we discussed our favourite books. And then we talked about cats. She has a hairless Sphynx cat...'

'Oh dear,' said Ailish.

'She's passionate about them,' he said. 'So, that's good. We all need to have a passion in life...'

'Really?' said Ailish. 'You don't.'

'I do!' Killian insisted. 'I have businesses...'

'More like obsessions,' Ailish countered.

'And yoga,' he went on.

She laughed. 'You only go because you think you might meet someone...'

'I don't,' he said. 'They are all twice my age and treat me like a teenager. I'm the one who has to carry all the blocks and the mats. I had to help Carmel stand up last night because she was stuck in pigeon.'

Ailish laughed again. 'You need a passion,' she said. 'Something that makes you happy.' She motioned at Flora with a jerk of her head. 'Flora here is passionate about designing... she's setting up her own company, aren't you, Flora, to make napkins and tablecloths...'

'Well...' Flora didn't want to get into a big conversation about her ever-so-tentative business plans. 'So, are you going to see the hairless cat lover again?'

He looked at her. 'I don't think so, because... well, the thought of having to spend time with a hairless cat sort of puts me off. I googled one last night, and I couldn't sleep...'

Ailish laughed again. 'The quest goes on,' she said. 'My brother, the handsome prince, sets forth once more to find the beautiful princess...'

Killian looked at Flora. 'She's hilarious, is she not? Any other sister would be supportive. And actually I do have another blind date coming up. It's a walk around the National Gallery, and then tea and a scone in the café.'

'I like the sound of that,' said Ailish.

'So do I,' said Flora.

'Can we come?' Ailish gave Flora a nudge.

'I think you might spoil the opportunity for chat,' he said. 'Luckily, I have a Leaving Cert in Art so I feel relatively confident to chat away about paintings.'

'He *was* going to be an artist,' explained Ailish. 'And then he met his ex-wife and suddenly he was going into hospitality.'

'Sounds like me,' said Flora. 'Changed all my plans for my husband... my ex-husband. Soon to be ex-husband, anyway. Once I get a solicitor.'

'It's not easy,' said Killian. 'But I'm five years on, and look at me...'

'He's a man about town now,' said Ailish. 'Making small talk about cats...'

Killian shrugged. 'We can't all be as interesting as you.'

'*You* can't, anyway,' said Ailish, smiling. 'You need to find someone as weird as you, someone who likes yoga, drinks expensive wine and wants to live in Rivendell... from *The Lord of the Rings*.' She laughed again.

'I was fifteen!' said Killian. 'I said that when I was fifteen and she won't let me forget it!'

Siblings were always fascinating to Flora, but she had to leave. 'I'd better go,' she said. 'I'll leave you two to your bickering.'

'Oh, don't,' said Killian, as though disappointed. 'We need a referee.'

'Edith will be wondering where I am,' said Flora, laughing. 'See you both soon...'

Outside, she unlocked her bike and just as she was cycling off, she heard Killian's voice calling her. She turned to see him running after her. 'Your USB,' he said, holding it out to her. 'You can't be a designer without your designs.'

'Thank you...' It was nice to make new friends in Ailish and Killian. Maybe after the hotel was finished the three of them could hang out. As she biked back to the shop, she thought about community and the fact you only noticed it properly when you really needed it and it was there, ready to break your fall.

30

PATSY

Over the following week, Patsy and Lola worked side by side, measuring, cutting and sewing, talking together, or singing along to songs on the radio. Or they were both silent, deep in thought. When Patsy looked across at Lola, silver hair falling over the vast swathes of fabric as she cut long, straight lines, Patsy realised that she found her deeply impressive. Lola held a well of resilience and strength, a quality which Patsy had never noticed before. They'd never spent much time together and even when Kate came to live with Patsy and Flora, the arrangement had almost been rushed. Lola was on tour, Kate was refusing to fly to meet her, and Patsy remembered poor Kate in tears, on the landline in their hall.

'She won't be home for Christmas,' Kate had said, when she'd returned to Patsy and Flora in the kitchen. 'She says she can't. But she wants me to come to her, says I could do my schoolwork on the road with them... but I said no way. And I put the phone down.' Kate's expression had been a mixture of pure fire and total devastation. Patsy couldn't ever imagine putting Flora in that position, forcing her to leave her life, just so she could have hers.

She had put her arms around Kate. 'You can stay here,' she'd said. 'For as long as you want.' You never knew why people did the things they did, and who was she to judge?

Across the room, Lola was on her hands and knees, a mouth full of pins, frowning as she concentrated.

'Curtains are the most difficult things to make,' said Patsy. 'Far harder than making a dress. You can make a mistake in a dress, but a curtain has to hang perfectly or it's totally ruined.'

Lola sat back on her heels. 'When something has only one job, it has to do it well. A curtain's job is just to hang there, and if it can't do that properly, then it doesn't deserve to be called a curtain.' She smiled then, and Patsy realised it was the first time she'd seen Lola smile in a long while. Yes, she did the gracious I'm-a-star smile, she'd seen her do it on stage or at awards, but since she'd been back in Sandycove, she hadn't smiled properly. She was grieving. It was such a hard place to be. Patsy used to think it was like being at the bottom of a well. Somewhere up there was sunlight, but you never thought you'd reach it again. But you did... somehow. One day you realised that the sunlight was a little brighter, and you were getting closer. Flora was the reason why Patsy reached for the sunlight. Maybe that was why Lola was back in Sandycove, she needed Kate to help her out of the dark?

'It's hard, isn't it?' She hadn't meant to speak out loud.

'What is? Curtain making?'

'Yes...' Patsy pretended that was what she meant, but Lola was looking at her curiously.

'You lost your husband, didn't you?' she said, suddenly.

Patsy nodded. 'Jack.'

Lola stood and walked over to the mantelpiece and picked up the photograph of Jack. 'He was a very nice-looking man... and he looks so young...'

'He was...' Patsy sat on the edge of the sofa. It didn't hurt her any more, thinking or talking about Jack wasn't something which stopped her breath any longer. 'It was a long time ago...'

'How long?'

'More than thirty years...'

'And you've never met anyone?'

Patsy shook her head. 'Too busy...'

'I've always found the time for men,' said Lola, still staring at the photograph. 'I've always had someone.' She shrugged. 'Why have I prioritised men? Why?'

'You tell me?'

'I like their company,' said Lola, coming over and pulling out one of the old dining chairs and sitting at the table. She propped the photograph of Jack in front of her. He looked strange, away from his usual place, where he'd been all that time. 'Or rather, I used to. Not to talk to. But you know what I mean. I like *talking* to women, and *sleeping* with men.' She laughed suddenly. 'Makes me sound awful, doesn't it? I did like talking to Paulie, though. And he was a man.'

'But you weren't sleeping with him.'

Lola laughed. 'I most certainly wasn't.' She paused. 'I *was* living with someone in California. Richie. I've set him loose though, like a horse, unshackled him and hopefully he's off riding free.' She shrugged. 'It was time for him to meet someone less complicated and younger. But he was nice to talk to. Actually asked questions. Listened. Which is a bonus.' She gazed off in the distance for a moment. 'My mother didn't like me. My daughter doesn't.'

'Of course Kate likes you,' said Patsy. 'She *loves* you.' She remembered how sad Kate had been when Lola was on those long tours.

'I made our relationship complicated,' said Lola. 'It's my fault.'

'You need to give her time,' said Patsy. 'Or find another way of reaching her. Slip back into her life, rather than forcing your way in...'

'Is that what I'm doing?'

Patsy looked back at her, wondering how she was going to take it. 'A bit.'

Lola was silent, thinking.

'Maybe be a part of her world this time, rather than Kate having to fit in with you.'

Lola smiled at Patsy. 'Thanks.'

'For what?'

'For everything.'

Patsy paused for a moment. 'What's that quote? Success is not final. Failure is not fatal. It is the...'

'...Courage to continue that counts,' finished Lola. 'We had a nun in school who used to say that. Sister Philomena, remember her?'

'Was she the one who ran off with Father Eamon?'

'The very same.' Lola laughed. 'She was right though, wasn't she? We all strive for success but it's fleeting. It doesn't mean anything. It's just nice. Failure is uncomfortable, so we try to avoid it. But both don't mean much, not really.'

'What about your awards?'

Lola shrugged. 'I thought they meant something. I thought they were the point of everything. But they aren't, are they? It's the life you build around the successes and the failures.'

Patsy was nodding. 'How do we get up every day and carry on...?' She thought of those days and weeks after Jack was gone. It seemed quite incredible now she had survived.

'Courage,' said Lola. She and Patsy looked at each other for a moment, as though taking in everything they had done and survived in life. And then Lola laughed. 'It must have taken courage for Sister Philomena to abscond with Father Eamon.'

'Fair play to her,' said Patsy. 'Hope she was happy.'

'I hope so too,' Lola agreed. She gave Patsy a look, an eyebrow raised. 'Talking of which, do you want to sleep with a man again?'

Patsy laughed and shook her head. 'I can't even conceive of the idea. I think it's all over for me.'

'Nonsense! That's all in your mind. You're telling yourself it's over... I'm only a couple of years behind you. You can't close yourself away like a nun. Well, not Sister Philomena but the other ones. Take a risk.' She picked up the photograph of Jack. 'What do you say, Jack? Would you mind if Patsy met someone else?' She twisted her mouth and dropped her voice. 'No,' she said. 'No, I would be very happy if Patsy met someone else. She deserves to be happy, and she's a really beautiful woman.'

And then Patsy laughed. 'Thank you for the permission, Jack.'

'You're welcome,' said Lola, still in her Jack voice, and then she was laughing. 'I hope you don't mind... that was probably insensitive...'

'Not at all,' said Patsy, 'it's about time I got out there a bit more... except... I don't know... perhaps I should?'

Lola was nodding. 'Why not? It's not as though we are old or anything? We're just getting going? Are we not?'

And as the afternoon wore on, they spoke of life and love and everything in between.

31

FLORA

At the haberdashery, Edith and Flora were eating cakes from Sally-Anne's for their usual elevenses.

'I know we shouldn't,' Edith was saying. 'It's just that... well, I think Sally-Anne makes the best cakes in Ireland. The world, probably. Since she opened up, there has been a collective weight gain and definitely an uplift in disposition. Wouldn't you agree?'

Flora laughed. 'I would. Justin would never let any cakes in the house. Or biscuits, because he was always watching his weight. He would get on the scales every morning and if they were half a pound over his usual weight, he wouldn't eat anything all day.'

Edith rolled her eyes. 'I rest my case. People who don't eat cake aren't worth knowing. That should have been a warning shot across your bow.'

'And,' went on Flora, warming to her theme. Focusing on Justin's bad points was immensely helpful in her healing journey, she noticed. 'He was always scrimping. If I bought anything, he would remind me that we had a mortgage to pay. He'd say, how are you going to contribute to the mortgage if you keep spending money?' Flora's laugh was hollow as she picked up a piece of her custard slice.

'Another warning shot,' said Edith, shaking her head. But then she put down her cake as though something had struck her. 'Wait. How exactly did your finances work?'

'Seventy-five per cent of my earnings went into the joint account for insurance, bills, holidays and mortgage.'

'And he did the same?'

'He put in seventy-five per cent as well... yes.'

'And this was fair?'

'It seemed fair. And he is an accountant after all...'

'But didn't the house belong to his parents?' said Edith.

'Yes... but...'

'So, there can't have been a mortgage...'

'But there was... he said there was...'

'And you believed him?' Edith narrowed her eyes.

'Yes, of course... why would he lie? Unless...' Flora thought rapidly. Justin was an only child. His parents had both died. There *couldn't* have been a mortgage. That house was bought and paid for decades earlier. He had lied. He had actually, blatantly, to her face lied. He was worse than she had imagined. But worst of all was that she had believed him, that she had been so guileless, so foolish, so stupid as to let him take control of her money, when he was a liar and a cheat.

'I think, Flora dear, he was stealing off you.' Edith was still looking at her through narrowed eyes. 'Mark my words. Do some detective work. Get your mitts on some papers. Once a *sleeveen* always a *sleeveen*. Make sure you don't let him get away with this.'

* * *

Later that evening, Flora worked out how much she had paid in 'rent/mortgage' over the last eight years – €48,000. Surely not. She did it again: €500 a month, times twelve, times eight. Yup, €48,000. And she was supposed to pay for everything else, all her medical bills, clothes, everything. Presents for him! That stupid Mont Blanc pen she'd bought him for his thirtieth birthday. Those Paul Smith shirts he wore. And he was taking *her* money.

She knocked on Kate's van door. Her whole body trembling.

'What's happened?' Kate looked as though she'd been asleep.

'I'm sorry,' said Flora, 'did I wake you?'

'No, no, come in...'

The van was neat and tidy, but although the bed hadn't been set out, there was a pillow on the bench where Kate had obviously been sleeping and Flora felt awful for disturbing her. She should have talked to Patsy, but she didn't want to worry her and anyway, Patsy was out somewhere.

Perhaps there was a simple explanation? Justin wouldn't have made her pay rent, not when she was on a lower salary than he was. But then again, he'd never told her what his salary was. He'd always said he was 'building the business'.

'What's happened?' said Kate, sitting on one side of the table. 'Tell me.'

'I was paying rent,' Flora said. 'Rent! I was a tenant in my own marriage. He took money off me for the mortgage, but I've realised that we mustn't have had a mortgage. It was his parents' home. It was *free*.'

Kate stared at her, trying to take it in. 'How did your finances work?'

'He worked out how much we should pay into a joint account. And then I had whatever was left over. Which wasn't much. I had to save for *everything*. Holidays... nights out. I was so careful with money. God, I was so naive.' She wondered if she might find any letters to a bank, anything to say that there had been a mortgage. After all of Justin's betrayals, she would feel better if there had been a mortgage, and that she hadn't been paying rent. She needed to get into the house when she knew the coast would be clear.

'You need a solicitor,' said Kate. 'You'll have to find one anyway to get away from him.'

Flora nodded. 'First, I was hurt and upset, then I was desperate and now I'm just numb...'

'The anger will kick in soon,' said Kate, confidently, putting the kettle onto the stove. 'And then you lawyer up...'

Flora laughed. 'Lawyer up? Have you been reading potboilers again?'

'I've borrowed some crime books from the library,' admitted Kate. 'They are quite compelling. There's nothing like police procedurals to take your mind off...' Her words trailed away.

'I'm going to go and have a look,' said Flora, 'see if I can find bank letters. I can't let him get away with this. We just need to find the right time.'

32

PATSY

In the foyer of the Sandycove Arms, carpenters, electricians and plumbers were rushing about, all busy at work. Killian was on his phone and waved Patsy over. 'Be over in a moment,' he mouthed.

Ever since their first meeting, she had been down to the hotel every day, measuring and remeasuring, or carrying out random jobs, such as checking the light filtering in from the front and side windows at different parts of the day, or worrying about flow of people and where to put them if suddenly a huge group arrived at once, or how to make the space warm and inviting on cold days and cool and breezy on hot days.

If you removed the stress, the anxiety and the constant feeling of inadequacy, you might even say she was enjoying herself. *Why wasn't I like this before*, she thought. *Why have I waited so long to do something which excites me?* But more than anything, she was pleased for Flora. Flashes of the old Flora were coming back, the happy person she used to be. She'd hear her singing in the house, or from her bedroom in the early evening, working on a new project – one which was top secret. And then she'd come downstairs and go for a walk with Kate. Patsy had watched them heading down the road together, towards the beach, just like the old days.

Killian ended his call and walked over to her. 'Happy with everything?' he said.

She nodded, taking out a notebook from her bag. 'I've a few more ideas, actually,' she said. 'A place to have a cup of tea, people-watch...' Killian was listening carefully. 'And the carpenters can start tomorrow?' she went on. 'They'll have finished in the bedrooms, won't they? I need them to start on the bookcases before the furniture arrives.'

'All going to plan,' he said. 'And how is the curtain making going? I've never heard of an interior designer making her own before? That's a lot of work...'

'I have help at the moment,' she said. 'We'll work night and day to finish on time.' She smiled at him, trying to present a confident demeanour, but oh sweet Mary and baby Jesus, there was still so much to do.

Killian looked across the room at an older man who was assisting some of the builders to carry in planks of wood. 'Dad! Will you stop bothering the carpenters. They don't need your help!' He turned back to Patsy. 'That's my father. Thinks he's actually being useful.' He then turned back to his father. 'You're a hindrance, not a help. Go home!' He began to make a shooing action. 'Get away with you. Scritch. Scram.'

The older man laughed, walking over towards them. He was dressed in long shorts, a bright blue cotton shirt, and looked just like an older version of Killian.

'I hope you are not finding my son hard to work with,' he was saying. 'I hear he's impossible.'

'Oh, he's all right...' said Patsy.

'Dad, this is Patsy Fox, my formidable interior designer. Patsy, this is my incorrigible father, now retired, Dermot Walsh...'

Patsy shook Dermot's hand. 'Good to meet you,' she said.

'As my son said, I am retired,' said Dermot, 'and I could apply to be your able and eager assistant. I would like to apply to be your driver, your gopher, your runner, your delivery boy...'

'Delivery *boy*.' Killian shook his head, smiling. 'He still thinks he's sixteen...'

'So do I,' she said. 'I can't believe I am sixty-two. I look in the mirror and wonder who is that elderly woman looking at me.'

'Elderly?' said Dermot. 'Spring chicken.' He was still smiling. 'So, if you need me, I could help? I have a car and a bicycle and too much time on my hands... I like to be busy and useful. I am obedient and pliable.'

'Pliable?' Killian laughed again.

'I can hang curtains,' Dermot went on. 'Drill some holes. Fling scatter cushions about. Hoist heavy boxes. I am nothing if not willing and relatively able.'

Patsy found herself smiling at Dermot. 'Yes, I don't see why not?'

'So, am I hired?'

She nodded, hoping he wouldn't spot she was a little flustered. It was those blue eyes of his, they were really quite startling in their intensity. She liked this cargo-short, check-shirt and runners look retired men were adopting, as though they were on permanent holiday, which, now she thought about it, was exactly what they were.

After saying goodbye to Killian, Dermot carried her folder outside. 'My first assignment,' he said. 'Look, I hope I wasn't being pushy there. I mean, I know I was. So just say no, but I like being busy, that's all...'

'I don't mind,' she said. 'I mean, it might be useful... *you* might be useful... because...' She stopped talking, wondering what she was trying to say. What she wanted to say was actually, yes, it would be nice to have someone to help.

'Well, then, good.' He smiled at her again. 'Do you live far?'

She shook her head. 'Just on the other side of the village. A five-minute walk.'

He nodded. 'I'm in Shankhill,' he said. 'I cycle everywhere now on my electric bike. I feel like I could keep going all day. My dream is to take it to France and cycle around Provence... you know, up and down the hills, through the lavender fields, stopping off for a glass of rosé, maybe a picnic lunch in the fields of the Abbey de Senanque...'

'Sounds like heaven.' She found herself liking these thoughts of cycling through lavender fields, glasses of rosé and picnic lunches in Provence. 'You know the area?' she asked.

'Not as much as I would like to,' he replied. 'I was watching a programme last night on medieval churches in France, and I thought how much I would like to do a little tour.' He handed her the folder and stood at the front gate of the hotel, as though seeing her off from his home. 'Shall we exchange numbers?'

'Oh yes, one moment...' And she scrambled for her phone.

'And maybe,' he went on, 'you might like to go for a walk some evening? I could cycle to Sandycove and we could take a little stroll along the seafront?'

She found herself nodding. 'That sounds very nice. Very nice indeed.' A new friend was always welcome, especially one who appreciated rosé and medieval churches. It was the exactly the kind of combination she liked.

33

FLORA

The yoga class was full. Women had their mats placed wherever they could in Our Lady's Hall. There was a waft of incense in the air. Flora didn't quite know what had brought her to the church hall to do yoga, except that she knew she used to be that person and she wanted to reclaim all of her, to see what else remained of that confident, excited twenty-something. She had to still be in there and maybe the more of her old self she excavated, the happier and stronger she would feel. She had to do something to help her feel calm about what she thought Justin had been doing. She'd gone from sadness and despair to utter rage, but that fizzing, bubbling fury was unbearable. Breathing deeply and stretching was a known cure for anger and so she found herself in leggings standing a little uncertainly at the corner of the room.

The teacher – long, frizzy hair, paisley harem trousers, vest top and arms like an Olympic athlete – came over. 'Ashanti Elaine,' she said, bowing. 'First time?'

Flora nodded.

'Have you done yoga before?'

'Not since college...' Flora didn't want to say her husband had convinced her it was a waste of time.

'Take it at your own pace,' said Ashanti Elaine. 'See how you get on. Why don't you settle yourself at the front of the class, close to me.' She turned around to have a look. 'Perhaps go next to Killian?'

Flora looked over and there, sitting cross-legged on a mat, dressed in tracksuit bottoms and hoodie, with bare feet and closed eyes, was Killian. At the sound of his name, he opened his eyes and turned around and smiled, waving her over.

This is awkward, she thought. *He's going to think I am here because I like him.* Didn't Ailish say this was where he went to meet women? But Killian didn't seem at all fazed by her presence, in fact he seemed entirely at ease, as though they were old friends, meeting for yoga.

'Right everyone...' Ashanti Elaine stood in front of the class. 'We're going to begin with a little circular breathing...'

Throughout the class, every time Killian caught Flora's eye, he made her laugh. But he was surprisingly good at it, easily moving between postures, and then, most impressively, balancing on two hands in 'crow'. And his arms, when he had removed his hoodie, were muscular and tanned, straining as he pushed himself up into a handstand.

'You should put that on your dating profile,' she whispered. 'You'd receive a lot more swipes.'

He laughed again. 'Able to invert body. Very useful if you need me to find something down the back of the sofa.'

The two of them giggled like schoolchildren. By the end of the yoga class, when they were lying down, draped in the blankets Ashanti Elaine had handed around, Flora got the giggles so badly, she had to try to think of serious things to recover. She thought of Justin, hoping the image of him would sober her up, but for some reason, all she could see was that ridiculous mop of hair of his and being jabbed at by Robert and it took a supreme effort to manage to stop laughing. But when she thought she was over the worst of it, there was Killian, lying spreadeagled, cross-eyed, his tongue hanging out. Flora began laughing again.

Eventually, before they were thrown out, Ashanti Elaine namasted to everyone, and they got to their feet, and rolled up their mats.

'Feeling okay?' Killian asked.

'I think so...' She did feel good. Bending and stretching and breathing could only be good for you.

'See you again!' called Ashanti Elaine. 'Bye, Killian. Looking forward to the hotel. I'll see you at the bar at the opening. Mine's a soda and lime. With tequila!' She cackled suddenly, shattering the earth-mother vibes entirely, being more Elaine than Ashanti for a moment.

Killian waved goodbye, and then, as they walked out, all the other women waved to him. 'See you next week, Killian,' said one, looking particularly fetching in, Flora noticed, camouflage leggings.

Another gave him a dazzling smile. 'Bye, Killian. Hotel looks fab-u-lous. Can't wait to see the inside.'

He really wasn't the unlucky-in-love person he tried to convey. Killian could have gone on a date with any of those gorgeous, flex-ible women.

Flora glanced at him from the corner of her eye. There was something so nonchalant about him, so unassuming, as though he wouldn't have noticed in a million years those women were interested.

He walked her to her bike. 'Will you return to the land of Ashanti Elaine?'

'Maybe...' Flora laughed.

Her phone rang. Justin. What did *he* want? 'Sorry, Killian,' she said, 'I have to take this...' He smiled and gave her a wave and walked away. 'Hello? Justin?'

'Flora? How's it going?' He sounded his usual ebullient self. But of course he did. Nothing took the wind out of his sails, he never faltered. His self-confidence had been one of the things that had attracted him to her... but surely he could have sounded a little contrite. 'Gorgeous day, isn't it?' he went on. 'Hotter than Portugal... talking of which, I think I left my baseball hat behind in Quinta... I was looking for it earlier... you wouldn't know where it was...'

Was he really calling her to ask about his baseball cap? For the first time since she'd met him, she didn't want him to call her. She wanted the space and time to be left alone.

'I have no idea,' she said.

'It's a special one, remember? None of the others fit over my head because of my...'

'Hair, I know. You have a lot of it.'

He laughed, pleased with himself. 'It's not my fault I am luxuriantly thatched. Unlike Robert... have you seen the top of his head? Shiny! Could see the clouds reflected in it the other day...'

'Justin, is there anything I can help you with?'

'Yes, well, first of all, I want to say thanks for everything,' he went on. 'You've been absolutely brilliant about everything. So understanding. Most women would have gone full *Fatal Attraction*, but not you, you were always able to rise above things. Sandra was worried you might attack her, you know with a bread knife or long nails or whatever... but I said there was no way on God's earth would you ever do something like that...'

Flora wished she was that kind of person who *would* attack Sandra. And Justin. She felt her ice-cold blood begin to warm. *Keep calm*, she told herself. *Don't give anything away.*

'Of course I wouldn't...' Was it really her speaking? 'I just want everyone to be happy and get along.'

'Really?' He sounded almost disappointed. 'So! Okay, so the reason I'm calling is that I can't find my passport. Anywhere. I don't know *where* you used to keep them. We're going away,' he went on. 'To Paris. You know how much I love the place. Go for a meal. Few drinks.' In all the years Flora had known him, he had never mentioned going to Paris. 'So, I need my passport,' he went on. 'And I said to Sandra, Flora will know. She'll know where it is.'

'How could I forget?' she said, drily. 'It's in your study, actually. In the cupboard above your desk. Mine's in there too. In the zipped envelope. I had better pick it up.'

'Ah, great. Thank you!' He paused. 'And thanks again. You've been amazing. Surprisingly amazing.'

What was actually amazing was that Flora didn't throw her phone against the wall and scream. Revenge, she remembered, was a dish best served cold. If only she had the recipe.

34

LOLA

Lola had developed a little bit of a rhythm to her day. In the morning, around 9 a.m., she would knock on the door of 45 Sea Road and she and Patsy would begin the curtain making. And then in the afternoon, just as the ladies of Honeysuckle Lodge had finished their lunch and would be ready for their choir rehearsal, she would head over to assist Kate and to help do whatever other jobs needed doing around the Lodge. One day, she'd helped Abigail bleed every single radiator in the building, trap and release a pigeon which had flown into the scullery, and had even started helping in the kitchen preparing the dinner. If only Richie could see her now, she'd thought, as she pinged on her washing-up gloves and set about unblocking the huge stainless-steel sink, he wouldn't believe it. He wouldn't care, actually. He'd stopped the texts and the calls, her phone remained Richie-free. Which she told herself was what she had wanted. Good for him.

Sitting at the piano, while Kate stood in front of the ladies leading the ladies, was where Lola was finding the greatest joy. Who would have thought accompanying a choir in an old folks' home, hearing the sweet voices of the ladies, seeing her own daughter singing away, leading the altos one moment and the sopranos the next line, could bring such deep satisfaction. She and Kate hadn't spoken much, but there was something of... she tried to think of the right word... an *acceptance*. It was better than nothing.

This morning, as she and Patsy sewed together, the sound of Irish radio reminded Lola of being back in her mother's kitchen. On a Sunday, they weren't allowed to have the same kind of roast dinners everyone else on the street used to have. They had a small piece of boiled ham, boiled potatoes and carrots. No gravy, no butter, nothing which would elevate it above what was essentially a very plain meal. Lola would he tasked with making it while her mother stayed behind at Mass to help with the subsequent services of the day. It was the one day where her mother seemed to achieve something close to happiness. Lola would listen to the radio, and all the voices in her head would swirl around. She hadn't eaten boiled ham and boiled potatoes since.

'Are you glad to be home?' asked Patsy, hand-hemming a huge and heavy curtain.

Lola nodded. 'I am,' she said. 'Much to my surprise, I really am. I mean, there's a lot of unfinished business... with Kate.' She paused. 'And... I don't know... coming home. Everything is different and yet everything is the same. The same smells, sights... I walk the seafront every evening and it's like I'm sixteen again. Paulie and I used to walk along and talk about the band we were going to form and the music we were going to create and the millions of pounds we would have.' She smiled at Patsy. 'Funnily enough, we never discussed all the mistakes we were going to make.'

'What mistakes?' asked Patsy.

'Too numerous to mention,' said Lola, threading the needle on her machine. 'Kate. She's the big one. I couldn't wait to be away from my mother. I thought she was the same. But the thing with daughters is that however much they look like you, they are entirely different and separate people and what worked for you doesn't work for them.' She felt suddenly a swell of emotion rise within her. 'I put music first. I put myself first. And I could have waited. I *should* have waited.'

'Hindsight being everything...' said Patsy.

'Yes, but at the time I thought this opportunity, those big tours, would only come once. Who knows what would have happened had I stayed? I would have a better relationship with my daughter.' She looked up at Patsy. Her lips pressed together.

'I think about that too,' said Patsy. 'All the things which have happened, all the decisions – the big and the small – we make. My husband... Jack... well, he wasn't meant to be driving that morning and I hadn't slept well the night before and I was tired and with Flora being so small, I didn't go and wave him off at the door.'

She and Patsy gazed at each other, contemplating all those micro-decisions – and the macro-decisions which changed the entire course of their lives.

'Afterwards,' continued Patsy, her voice shaking a little, 'I was consumed with the thought I hadn't said goodbye properly. It took years to forgive myself.'

'Hindsight...' said Lola, with a wry smile.

'Indeed.' Patsy smiled back. 'I miss him, though. Still. After all these years.'

'Of course you do. You loved him. You're lucky to have had it.'

Patsy nodded. 'Have you ever been in love?'

Lola sighed. 'Yes... once. The one I left behind, actually... Richie.' Lola smiled thinking about him. 'He was one of the best guitar players I've ever worked with. But he's the kind of musician who knows people and relationships are more important than music. And let me tell you, he's a rare breed. But I've been grieving

Paulie and I haven't been the best company. I want to be close to Kate more than I want to be close to any man.' She shrugged. 'I don't have anything left for him.'

'What did he say? Did he understand?'

Lola shook her head. 'I didn't really tell him much. Just said I was going away.' She thought of Richie, his broad chest, those eyes of his which softened when he listened to music. The first night they had spent together, they'd lain in bed and she'd talked about her mother and about the pressures of being on tour, and he had listened, his arms around her, and she had felt for the first time in her life as though she was safe. 'You know, Patsy,' she said, 'sometimes you need to stop fighting, don't you? Sometimes you just need to give in and surrender. And let the past be the past and be open to whatever the future has in store.'

35

KATE

The concert for the Warblers was all arranged. Abigail had notified family members to come along and was writing lists of refreshments they could serve, while Kate finalised the songs and was making a songbook with the words and music of each piece. Her back was hurting her now. She'd noticed her clothes were getting tighter. She had borrowed a book from the library, *Your Baby and You*, and every day tried to imagine what size her baby was. She was now more than thirty weeks pregnant, but her bump was still small and she had a surprising amount of energy.

'Have you ever thought about teaching professionally?' asked Abigail, when she walked into the day room, to find Kate at the piano, making changes to the arrangements.

'Never,' said Kate. 'I couldn't imagine me in front of a class.'

'But that's exactly what you are doing.' Abigail began picking up some of the squashed cushions from the sofa, and banged them together violently. She turned and faced Kate. 'You could have a choir.'

'But I have a choir.'

'Another choir then,' said Abigail. 'A *school* choir. Become a music teacher.'

It was one of those moments in your life when everything just stops, as though time is waiting for your thoughts to catch up with whatever the universe is trying to tell you. 'A music teacher?' Kate repeated.

'Yes,' said Abigail, banging another two cushions together, causing a cloud of dust and feathers to explode in the air. She turned to face Kate. 'Why not?'

'Because...' But Kate was thinking. Could she train? Was she too old? What did you need to be a teacher exactly?

Abigail was reading her mind. 'You'd need to do a degree,' she said. 'There's a course in Dun Laoghaire, starting September.' She smiled at Kate. 'Just an idea... Now, those windows need a good clean...'

Kate thought about the course, the baby and if she could afford everything. She had to start being serious about her life, she couldn't drift any longer. She had to anchor herself, somewhere. 'Abigail,' she said, 'you mentioned the caretaker's cottage... it's just that I need somewhere to live...'

Abigail nodded. 'I'm already on it,' she said. 'It needs damp-proofing, relining and rewiring. I have a team of lads there at the moment.' She smiled at Kate. 'It should be ready in a month.'

'That would be wonderful.'

When Abigail left the room, Kate sat back at the piano. A month. The baby wouldn't be here yet, so that would give her time to get things ready. She wondered how Jacques was and if he was thinking of her. She had been trying to push memories of him to the back of her mind but there were moments when all she wanted was to see him again. She should have told him. At least they would have parted as friends. Typical of her, another estrangement. Was this what she was going to keep doing all her life? Run away when things became complicated?

The door opened again. Lola.

'Hello,' she said. 'Excited?'

'About what?'

'The concert! What did you think I meant? I was thinking we need lighting. Maybe a few spots. We could open the concert in darkness, and maybe just one voice – Marjorie's? – perhaps singing *a cappella*. I thought the poignancy of "It's A Long Way To Tipperary", sung slowly and quietly, dreaming of home. And then, there should be a moment of complete silence, the lights slowly come up, as the other voices join in, building to a crescendo...' She smiled at Kate. 'What do you think?'

'No. Definitely not. What is this? Jesus!' She stood up, wincing in pain for a moment, her back spasming. 'Spotlights? Darkness? Someone would fall over and break something...'

'I was just trying to make it more interesting...'

Typical of Lola to take over and to make it something it wasn't. 'We don't need interesting,' said Kate. 'Or, rather, we have enough interest without you trying to showbiz the arse out of it.'

'Showbiz the arse?'

'Yes,' said Kate, 'because that's the only important thing to you, lights, cameras, crowds... what's wrong with a really nice choir, singing really nice songs, in front of a really nice audience?'

'Nothing,' said Lola, 'except...' She stopped.

'Except what?'

'It's a bit boring?'

Kate rolled her eyes, irritation rising within her. 'I suppose nice, normal things are boring to you. Like being at home...'

'Kate, if this is about me leaving you...?'

Kate felt immediately foolish. Wasn't it time to put all this behind her, behind them? Didn't she want a better relationship with her mother? They were never going to be Flora and Patsy, but they could be better than they were currently. It was just Lola was annoying with all her talk of lighting effects, as though the Honeysuckle Warblers were going to be performing at Wembley Stadium. Except... maybe she was a little bit right. And Lola was hugely experienced in how to put on a show. Maybe there was something in what she had said.

'I like the poignancy bit,' Kate conceded.

Lola came closer. 'It's a performance, you see. It's not just singing. It's about connection.'

Kate was nodding. 'I see...'

Lola was becoming more animated. 'You're right about the spotlight though,' she said. 'Too much. It would be showbizzing the arse out of it, which is unnecessary...' She gave Kate a look. 'But perhaps we could have low lighting? The room is dark enough, but we want the ladies to gleam and glow... We want them to sparkle.'

Lola was right, of course: they wanted the ladies to shine. 'How should we do that?'

'Leave it to me,' said Lola. 'I'll have a think.'

As Kate nodded, she felt the baby move, just a quick bolt, as though she was changing her sleeping position. Instinctively, Kate put her hand on her stomach but then removed it quickly as Lola was looking over. 'Well,' said Kate, 'maybe we can come up with few ideas. Not too showbizzy...'

'The very idea!' Lola gave her a wink.

'But perhaps a *little* bit showbizzy...'

'I think that can be arranged,' said Lola. 'Dial it down, less is more, et cetera, et cetera.'

'Exactly.' And they smiled at each other.

36

PATSY

All afternoon, Patsy continued sewing, singing to herself, listening to the radio, thinking about the project, and what she had to do. The sewing room, her old front room, was her happy place, and where she thought more clearly and had her best ideas. If she hadn't found sewing, she sometimes thought, life would have been far more stressful. Without this retreat and time to think, she wouldn't have known how to cope. Her phone rang.

'Hello, Patsy. It's Dermot.'

'Ah, Dermot, how are you?'

'I'm very well,' he said. 'Now, I was thinking of taking a little stroll along the seafront at Sandycove this evening, around 6.30 p.m., and then go for a glass of rosé in the wine bar. I wondered, if you weren't too busy, if you would like to join me? I thought we could pretend to be in France, even if we aren't actually there.'

She laughed. 'You mean Fantasy France?'

'Exactly.' He chuckled. 'Well? Are you free?'

'Yes,' she said, 'why not?'

'Right-o. Harbour at 6.30?'

After she had hung up, Patsy wondered what on *earth* was she going to wear. In the end, she found her navy chinos and her Liberty-print blouse. She even put on some lipstick – something she hadn't bothered with for years.

At six thirty, she walked to the harbour and there he was, sitting on the bench, wearing a cream linen jacket, a bright blue shirt, and a pair of long shorts, doing that day's crossword in *The Irish Times*. He rolled it up, quickly, when he saw her, and stood to greet her.

'Ready for our trip to Fake France?'

'Faux France?' Patsy suggested, as he offered her his arm. And away they went.

They didn't stop talking, covering every topic imaginable – from grown-up offspring to life as a retiree, to politics (they were on the same page) to the best holiday they'd ever had. When they'd walked the full length of the seafront, four times, Dermot stopped.

'Now, do you think we deserve that rosé?'

'Definitely.'

They sat outside the wine bar, at a table for two, under a string of fairy lights.

He held up his glass. 'To new friends,' he said.

'Yes, to new friends.'

And their smiles matched each other's – big, wide grins. *I remember feeling like this, before*, Patsy thought, happily. *I remember this feeling.* She kept smiling, unable to stop.

* * *

Dermot walked Patsy home, the two of them laughing and talking and occasionally her hand would brush his or his would brush hers and it would feel so wonderful.

'Is that your van?' he asked.

'Unfortunately not,' said Patsy. 'It belongs to my friend's daughter. She's staying here for a bit.'

'That would be good for sojourns in the south of France, would it not? When the sun was too hot for the old electric bicycle. And you could have the rosé chilling in the fridge. Solo holidays are all very well, and I've had some of the best times on my own... But there are times and places where it would be nice to have someone with you...'

She smiled at him. 'I agree...'

'Now, we haven't discussed me being your assistant. Is there anything you need shifting, lifting or doing?'

'I'll let you know.'

'Thank you,' he said. 'I've had... I was going to say a wonderful evening, but it's been... I want to say the best evening I've had in a long, long time... Let's do this again. Soon. Tomorrow. Or the day after. You say the day and I'll be there.'

After saying goodbye, Patsy stood for a moment inside her hall, letting the events settle upon her, hoping to be able to remember every moment of this lovely evening. She'd have a shower, and then bed. There was another long day of sewing ahead but for now she could bask in the warmth of the memory of this lovely evening.

Under the hot water, Patsy sang to herself, thinking of Provence, rosé, lavender fields, good company, good food. It sounded like heaven. It was funny, she thought, just when you wanted a little adventure and fun in your life, it arrived.

She reached down for her sponge and began soaping her body. And then, as her hand brushed over her breast, she felt something. It didn't feel like a lump, as such, but a foreign object. Hard. Small. Wrong.

She stopped breathing. The water streamed down her body.

Any strength she'd ever had was being washed away. She turned off the water, and wrapped herself in a towel, not knowing what on earth to do next. As in, literally she did not know what to do. Should she keep standing or sit down? Have a cup of tea or go to bed? Start crying or start googling? *When do I start panicking and who do I call? This could change everything. This could be how it all ends.*

37

FLORA

Justin and Sandra were in Paris, the house quiet, the hum of the boiler, the alarm set. Flora quickly disabled it and walked to Justin's study, feeling like a thief. Right. Deep breath. Inside, it was its usual jumble of papers, old coffee mugs and a smell of damp.

Flora opened the cupboard above the desk, where, inside, she knew was a zipped envelope containing her passport, but her eye fell upon something which was poking out from underneath the blotting pad. When she slipped it out, it looked like a printout of a spreadsheet and a list of employees, with their personal public service numbers and bank details. And then a name caught her eye.

Flora Fox. Her exact PPS number. But *not* her bank account number.

Maybe there was another Flora Fox? But with the *same* PPS number?

She looked to see who the spreadsheet belonged to. Robert Dunne's business – Sandra's *husband*. He owned a large paper factory and Justin did the accounts. But why was *her* name on the list of employees? It didn't make sense. She glanced again at the other names; there were around one hundred. Robert's was the very first one, and then there were a couple of names she recognised, but most of them she didn't. And there was hers. Followed by two more – a Mohammed Khalil and a Zahara Farid. She knew what she was doing was wrong. Reading the accounts of a company surely was illegal. And yet... something told her to open up the locked filing cabinet where Justin kept all the files from the companies he worked for.

The first file was for a local firm of estate agents, the CEO was one of Justin's golfing buddies, and again, there was the list of employees. Around sixty this time, and again close to the bottom was her name. And again the name of Mohammed Khalil and Zahara Farid.

She pulled out another file for another firm, this time it was the chain of family-run DIY shops, the owner of which was another of Justin's friends. And the fourth file belonged to the business owned by David Geraghty, who had been at the barbecue. Again, the long list of employees, and the same names at the bottom, all earning a salary. She could see what she, Mohammed and Zahara had been paid every week. Justin was falsifying accounts. He was claiming there were more employees than there were. She definitely did not work for these companies and she had a hunch neither did this Mohammed or Zahara. She had another look, to make sure. The money was being paid into the same account number, same sort code... everything.

Breathing hard, Flora put the files back into the cabinet and locked it and left the room.

Back at home, there was a lamp on in the camper van. She knocked on the door. 'I found something...' she told Kate. 'I went to Justin's house to look for some bank statements – which I didn't get! – but I found something which is worse...' She swallowed, and blinked at Kate. 'I found a spreadsheet for accounts Justin was doing. Robert's company, Sandra's husband? My name is on it,' went on Flora. 'There could be other Flora Foxes, obviously, but this had my actual PPS number...'

'No...' Kate came over and sat across from Flora.

'Yes. And it had bank account details. But they weren't mine. And then I checked other company spreadsheets in his filing cabinet... And there were other names on the spreadsheets, a Mohammed and a Zahara... both with PPS's, on all the spreadsheets I managed to look at.'

They looked at each other wordlessly. And then Kate spoke. 'So what do you think he's doing?'

'I think he's pretending these people – and me – are working for these companies and they are being paid. My theory is their salaries are going into *his* account.'

'Oh my God.'

'I know.'

'Did you take a copy of the spreadsheet?'

'No, how would I do that?'

'Take a photo with your phone.'

'I should have done that! Why didn't I do that?'

'Let's go back.'

In no time at all, after a brisk, breathless walk up the hill, they stood on the doorstep of Flora's old house.

'Do we break a window?' Kate asked. 'Shimmy up a drainpipe?'

'We use my key,' said Flora, opening the door, and letting Kate go first.

'What is shimmying anyway? I thought it was dancing,' mused Kate.

'Shh,' said Flora, half-laughing. 'You're not taking this seriously! Come on, to the study,' she said, leading the way. 'Look here,' she said, pulling out the first spreadsheet and finding her name and that of Mohammed and Zahara. 'Weird, isn't it?'

Kate stared at it, taking it in. 'Take the photo, quick,' she said, as Flora took out her phone. She then opened the filing cabinet and photographed all the files she'd seen earlier. 'Go to the bottom and see if it's the same with all of them?' said Kate. 'If so, then you can presume he's doing it with everyone he does accounts for.'

Flora pulled open the bottom drawer and found a random file, quickly she flicked through and saw her name. 'It's here,' she said.

The immensity of the crime hit her. He was stealing from perhaps fifty companies? Perhaps claiming tens of thousands from each one? How much was he getting every month?

'Take another photo,' said Kate, who was looking through one of the drawers of the desk. Inside was another zipped folder containing social welfare letters to different people. 'Who has this kind of information about other people?'

Flora read a letter over her shoulder. 'Dear Mr Khalil, we enclose your services card and your PPS number...' She looked at Kate. 'What exactly is going on?'

'I've no idea...' began Kate, but then they heard the sound of a car pulling into the driveway. Flora had never felt panic like it, a cold sweat enveloped her and every hair on her body stood on end. The two of them froze.

'It's Justin,' whispered Flora. 'And Sandra!'

'Quick!' said Kate. 'Get your passport!' Flora pulled down the zipped envelope, took her passport quickly – Justin's was still there, so he wasn't in Paris, she must have got the dates wrong – and also grabbed a random bank statement from the desk. They heard car doors being slammed shut and then voices.

'The window!' Flora began fumbling with the handle. Once she had pulled the window open, she clambered up. She landed on the ground and then saw Kate's look of horror. The baby. Oh my God. Flora turned around so Kate could crawl onto her back and then slipped to the ground. Holding hands, they raced to the side of the house, and peeked out. 'Coast is clear,' she said to Kate. 'Come on, we're going to run for it. Or...' She looked at Kate. 'Jog.'

They ran as fast as they could, which wasn't particularly fast, but they kept going until they were far enough away to slow down. Kate lay down on a grass verge, panting heavily, and making a strange sound. Was she sobbing? Flora desperately hoped she was all right, and then realised she was laughing.

'Oh my God!' she cried. 'I can't believe we did it!'

And Flora began laughing too, her fear had now given way to complete and total elation. It was only when they were nearly home that the magnitude of what they might have uncovered hit them. Justin wasn't just a mop-haired adulterer, he was a criminal.

38

LOLA

They were sitting in the sewing room at either end of the old dining table.

'Just to let you know,' said Patsy in a strained voice, looking up over her machine, 'I won't be here tomorrow morning... I've a medical appointment.'

'Oh yes?' Lola eyed her, hoping she would say more.

'It won't take long,' said Patsy. 'Should be back before you head off to Honeysuckle Lodge.'

'Anything serious?' asked Lola, casually.

'I've found a lump,' said Patsy, trying to smile. 'So it's a mammogram... see what it might be.'

Lola nodded, waiting for Patsy to continue.

'I'm a little...' began Patsy, '...scared, to be honest.'

'Of course you are... who wouldn't be?'

'I feel,' admitted Patsy, 'that I am being punished for being cocky, as though I have to be taken down a peg or two. Taught a lesson.'

'You? Cocky?' If Patsy only knew the kind of people Lola had been spending time with the last thirty years, she'd know what cocky really meant. Most of them wouldn't get out of bed unless someone told them the sun shone out of their backsides or that their song was the best thing since The Beatles.

'I know it doesn't work that way,' went on Patsy. 'It's just how it feels. I need to get back in my box, stop reaching too high.'

'Well, that's bollocks,' said Lola. 'And anyway, I'm coming with you tomorrow. I've got very particular skills that are very useful to take one's mind off medical appointments. I can bore you with stories about tours... or, I don't know, the time I was on stage with some old has-been.' She paused. 'I'm a bit of a has-been myself. I shouldn't be throwing stones in my has-been glasshouse.'

'You? A has-been? You've got to be joking,' said Patsy, laughing.

* * *

The following morning, the two of them sat in the waiting room. Lola was reading out the posters on the walls in funny voices to a nervous-looking Patsy. 'Quit smoking,' she said in a low growl. 'Before you quit life.' She looked at Patsy. 'That's a bit harsh, don't you think? Can't they soften it up a bit?' She put on a high voice. 'Have you ever considered perhaps maybe giving the old ciggies a little break? Perhaps you might be healthier?'

Patsy laughed. 'Did you ever smoke?'

Lola shook her head. 'Never did anything, to be honest. Paulie pushed things too hard. I was the sensible one. Older and wiser.'

'Aren't you cold?'

Lola shook her head. 'Warm as toast. That's the good thing about getting older. Your internal thermometer goes up a couple of degrees.'

'I'm frozen.'

Lola took of one Patsy's hands. 'Let's get some blood going.'

She began to rub Patsy's hands with hers. 'Now, how are you feeling? Still scared?'

Patsy nodded again. 'But thank you for trying to distract me.'

'You are welcome,' said Lola, still rubbing Patsy's hands. 'You know everything is going to be all right, don't you? Even if it isn't, it will be eventually. We women prevail. That's what we do. Whatever it is, we keep going, mountains, valleys, on we plod.'

'It's the courage to continue...' said Patsy.

Lola nodded. 'The courage to continue that counts. So we will continue and, whatever happens, I am going to be here for you. You're an exceptionally brave woman, Patsy Fox.'

'I don't feel very brave,' admitted Patsy.

Lola took her hand. 'Well, you are. Jack dying. Minding Flora. Starting your business. Taking on your course. The hotel. All of it.'

'Patsy Fox?' A nurse stood calling her name. 'Ready? Do you want to bring your friend in?'

Patsy turned to Lola and opened her mouth to speak, but Lola was already on her feet.

'Yes,' she said to the nurse, 'her friend is coming with her.'

The tension was allayed by the nurse being a fan of The Islanders and wanting to tell Lola which album was her favourite and why. Lola remained as polite as she could, holding Patsy's hand all the way through.

Finally, it was over, and they walked out into the corridor, down the staircase and out into the fresh air. They would have the results in two days, said the nurse. 'Dr Lambert, our oncology consultant, likes to give the news in person. I'll book you in.'

39

KATE

That afternoon, Kate watched her mother as she sat among the ladies of Honeysuckle Lodge, charming them all. They were all eating a bowl of Lola's 'famous' trifle.

'I made this for a dinner party I held a few years ago. Jane Fonda loved it,' she said. Celebrity anecdotes always went down well with the ladies and Lola had a plethora – 'Barack was as charming as you'd expect and Michelle and I talked for most of the night.'

Kate watched, with some admiration, how Lola was so ready to give part of herself to the ladies. The day before, she had arranged a fashion swap shop, where the ladies gathered in the day room with items of clothing which they no longer loved and Lola showed how they could be styled differently – 'I would try it with a belt, show off your amazing waist.' She, it had to be said, was a blast of sunshine. Charisma, personality, likeability. Kate remembered this was how she always had been on tour; she gave so much of herself, knew everyone's names and those of their children and pets, made a fuss of birthdays and created a sense of family on those long weeks and months away. If Lola wasn't her mother, she would really like her, she realised. She might even want her to be her mother. It was complicated.

After the events of last night, Kate was feeling tired. She'd gone straight to bed when they had arrived home but had come early to the Lodge to start planning the concert. She needed to contact all the families to invite them, there was music to print out and a repertoire to finalise. But suddenly, she felt she couldn't drag herself around any longer. She needed to lie down and sleep. She left Lola clearing away the teacups and modelling the socks Bernadette had knitted – 'I am transformed,' she said, doing an Irish jig, making the ladies laugh and clap their hands in time to the song Lola was singing.

She sat on the wall at the front of Honeysuckle Lodge; she breathed in the fresh air. The baby was moving a lot lately, it felt as though Kate's insides were being twirled and twisted. And she had a headache... and... most of all, she missed Jacques and wished she could call him and tell him everything. He'd still be in Greece, she knew. But wasn't there a way of getting a call to him?

Behind her, she heard Lola's voice. 'Fancy a walk?'

Kate turned. 'Is that a suggestion or an order?'

'A suggestion,' said Lola. 'I just thought we could talk...'

'I thought you wanted to walk...'

'Both.'

'I'm tired,' Kate said. 'I'm just going to go home.'

Lola nodded, as though she was expecting her to say no.

But Kate stopped. 'What did you want to talk about?'

Lola shrugged, but she looked hopeful. 'Nothing important,' she said. 'If you don't *want* to. We can talk about unimportant things...'

'Okay then...' Kate began walking and Lola fell in beside her.

'I'm still waiting to hear from Zachary,' Lola was saying. 'He's sent my song out to film producers and he says it's wait-and-see time...'

Zachary, The Islanders' manager, had first come over to Dublin to take a look at this Irish band who he'd listened to a demo of. Kate remembered him wearing Hawaiian shirts and smoking big cigars. He had *loved* Paulie and Lola, and after a dinner of chip-shop fish and chips – and a battered sausage – Zachary had been completely charmed. Kate had listened as Paulie, Lola and Zachary sang songs and told stories. She'd fallen asleep to the sound of their voices, feeling as though they were all in some magical adventure together.

'I always liked his Hawaiian shirts,' Kate commented.

'Well, he's in the right place,' said Lola, who looked suddenly so happy, as though Kate's interest was all she had dared to hope for. 'He's in Maui full-time these days and lives in accordance with the sun. Wakes at dawn and goes to bed at dusk. I can never work out when to phone him. Richie was always so good at working out time zones...'

'Tell me about Richie?' Kate asked.

Lola's eyes lit up for a moment. 'Richie? Well, he was... I suppose... my partner. I'm too old to say boyfriend.' She smiled almost shyly at Kate.

'But you love him, don't you?'

Lola nodded. 'Of course I do... who wouldn't? He's a peach of a man. He's the cream on the apple tart, he's the head on a pint of Guinness...'

'So, be with him?'

'Ah, I can't... And anyway, I've let him go...'

'Why don't you let yourself be happy?'

'I am,' said Lola. 'Enough.'

'I let mine go too,' said Kate, half-smiling but thinking with a stab of pain of Jacques.

'You have?' Lola was smiling back at her. 'Maybe we're...' She trailed off.

'What were you going to say?'

'Maybe we are more similar that we thought...?' There was that shy look again. Forget Jacques, it was Lola who was breaking Kate's heart.

'Maybe.' Kate felt a sharp twist of pain in her stomach. She put her hand on her stomach and closed her eyes.

'Are you all right?' said Lola.

'I am absolutely fine,' said Kate. 'Just hungry...'

'Well, let's go and eat,' said Lola. 'I need to eat or I get light-headed. Richie always says it's because I drink too much coffee and I should switch to caffeine-free... but I say, what's the point of that? It's like drinking alcohol-free wine or sugar-free sweets. He says it would help with my insomnia. But I gave up on sleep when Paulie was sick... Although I'm sleeping so much better since I came home. Do *you* sleep?'

Kate wanted to tell her that she hadn't really slept well in years. Years ago, she would wake up in the middle of the night, and work out where Lola was and what she might be doing. So, it's 9 p.m. in Tokyo so she's about to go on stage. Or it's 12 p.m. in LA so they are soundchecking. She'd look out of the window at the night sky and know if she floated up and carried on going either east or west, she'd fly straight to Lola. But she didn't know how to say any of that, and anyway, seeing Lola's face, so eager to please, so sad about Paulie, she decided it was better just to keep it light.

'I sleep like a baby,' Kate said.

'You're lucky.'

They were now on Sandycove's main street.

'That's my flat, up there,' said Lola. 'It's actually quite nice. There's a sea view if you stand on a chair and stick your head out of the skylight. And it's close to the seafront so I can buy fish and chips...' She turned to Kate. 'Would you like some? They have scampi and tartare sauce. Your favourite.'

'It *was* my favourite,' said Kate. 'When I was a child. Haven't eaten it in years.'

'Okay... well, then, what about this place?' They stood outside Alison's. 'I need a coffee. Fully caffeinated. And a sandwich. That all right for you?'

Kate needed to sit down and so found herself nodding and following Lola inside.

'I buy my morning coffees from someone called Man The Van at the harbour. Peter is his name. He reminds me a little of Paulie... there was this time when we were in Bogotá... and there was a lightning strike and everyone was panicking...'

'I don't want to hear another story about The Islanders,' Kate said. Her headache throbbed. There was that sharp stomach pain. She hoped the baby was all right. She knew Lola was trying and so was she. But bridging an estrangement wasn't that easy. You couldn't just click your fingers and be back as you had been, before. 'I don't want to hear another war story of life on the road, or the music, or of Paulie! He wasn't Jesus Christ, you know! He wasn't even that good a guitar player!'

As the words tumbled out, she felt awful. *Forgive me, Paulie, I am not in full control of myself*, she intoned. *Why does everyone else I know have their shit together and here I am still being triggered by my own mother?* She walked out of the cafe, Lola on her heels, like two demented power-walkers out for their evening constitutional.

'What's wrong, Kate? I just want to spend time with you...'

Kate kept going, her eyes lowered, her legs pumping.

'Kate, just talk to me, will you?'

Kate could feel herself start to cry. *I'm such a fool*, she thought. *These are feelings I should have grown out of years ago.*

'Evening, Lola,' said a short woman with a dark bob. 'I'll drop in the book I was telling you about. I'll leave it in your letter box.'

'Thank you, Edith,' said Lola, before turning back to Kate, gripping her sleeve. 'Kate, tell me...'

'I don't know,' said Kate. 'I'm behaving crazily. I didn't realise I was so unhinged.' She gave a nervous laugh. 'It's just that...' She stopped.

'Just that what?'

'Nothing.' Kate hated feeling so helpless, so unmoored, that feeling where a current could take you and you had no control. Travelling had been a way of taking control of the chaos, of staying one step ahead of uncertainty. Coming home to Sandy-cove had been a bad idea. 'You fecked off on tour,' she went on. 'Because that was what was important to you, not me! Can you imagine what it feels like not to be loved by your mother, not to think you are the most precious thing in the world to her, to be rejected? You have no idea what it's like!'

Lola blinked back at Kate.

'Just leave me alone, okay?' Kate blundered on.

Three women walked by. 'Will we see you later at the Forty Foot, Lola?' said one. 'Margaret's bringing cake for Dolores' birthday!'

Lola smiled and waved to them quickly, but turned back to Kate again. 'I do know,' she said quietly.

'Know what?' Kate was forced to say.

'Know what it's like to be rejected by your mother. I was actually rejected by two.' She looked at Kate. 'I had two mothers. Neither of them wanted me.'

'Two mothers? That's a biological impossibility.'

'But not a legal one,' said Lola. 'I was given up when my mother gave birth to me, she was sixteen and gave birth, apparently, in the back bedroom, and was told to keep the noise down so no one on the street heard. The local midwife was there, apparently, and her mother. And then they had to find a home for me.'

'Your mother *isn't* your mother?'

Lola nodded. 'She adopted me. She lived two streets away and she told me from when I was young that she hadn't wanted me. But had done that family a favour. I was given away, like you give away unwanted things.'

'But she must have wanted a baby?'

'She couldn't have one of her own, and if you didn't have one, then people talked. And she probably thought that she had to have one to be normal. But she was an utterly horrible person. "I don't want you here!" she would shout. "Nobody wants you."' Lola looked up at the sky for a moment, blinking.

Was she *crying*? Lola didn't cry. But she looked back at Kate, dry-eyed, which was a relief. The *one* person Kate *never* wanted to see cry was Lola.

'I was sworn to secrecy. I *knew* who my biological mother was, she knew, probably the whole street knew, but I was not allowed to talk to her.'

'So you saw her?'

Lola nodded. 'Every day, practically. She didn't want to know me. Shame – that brilliant Catholic tool of oppression, I suppose. She'd gone on to get married and have another child a year later. Her *golden* boy.'

It was the way she lingered ever so slightly on the word 'golden'.

'Paulie,' said Kate, staring at Lola.

Lola nodded. 'My little brother. We met in Sunday school and put two and two together. His mother confirmed the story but said I was bad news and he should have nothing to do with me, and told him if anyone found out about it, then she wouldn't be able to show her face around the place.' Lola shrugged. 'So, I was her secret, and he and I were each other's.'

Kate shook her head, trying to take all this in. 'He's your brother?' It all made sense, their connection, their protectiveness of each other. 'But why didn't you tell people once you were grown-up?'

'Because Paulie loved the old wagon and didn't want anyone to know for *her* sake. You remember how loyal he was. And I felt I had to take care of him, you know? And he took care of me. He was my family.'

Kate was trying to work out where she fitted into this psychodrama. 'But I was your family. I was more important than Paulie...'

'I know that,' said Lola, quietly. 'But I thought you would come with us and I thought I was making a life for us, an interesting life. I thought I was giving you more than I had, but you chose to stay in Sandycove. I was wrong, I know now. And I'm sorry. I *thought* you'd be fine. You gave every impression of being independent and self-sufficient. You told me to go!'

'Mum, every sixteen-year-old gives a very good impression of being independent and self-sufficient,' said Kate. 'But they are not. And *of course* I told you to go, but I didn't think you would.'

There was a day, once, years ago, when Kate had asked to go to the beach. 'No,' Lola kept saying, 'I hate the beach. Too hot. No shade. And horrible sand.' Kate gave up asking, but one day, Paulie arrived at the door. 'Your mother has ordered a taxi,' he told Kate. 'Apparently, the little princess wants to go the beach.'

From the kitchen, Lola had appeared with two large bags. 'Towels, swimsuits, umbrella,' she'd said. 'Right, we're ready.'

They sang all the way to Wexford, the three of them in the van, until they arrived at the most beautiful beach Kate had ever seen. Large and golden, already filled with sun-worshippers and children making sandcastles, and the sea stretching on forever. Lola set up camp and sat under a large black rain umbrella, handing out sandwiches and warm lemonade and melted choco-late biscuits. Paulie snoozed for most of the day, while Kate built sandcastles and jumped the waves in the sea. Who knew life could be magical and dreams came true? That day, she loved Lola even more than she thought was possible, and on the drive home, as she half-slept between them in the front of Paulie's old van, she felt as though she was floating, the sand in her shoes, the salt on her lips, her whole body aching with exhaustion and happiness.

Lola was silent for a moment, as though listening for the first time, the weight of Kate's words finally falling. 'I shouldn't have gone,' she said. 'And I'm sorry. But it happened. I can't do anything about it, but I want to be in your life more than anything I have ever wanted. I am so incredibly sad about the thought of not having you... I thought we would find our way back, I thought we'd always be involved in each other's lives, but I realised I was in danger of losing you completely... And I know no one invited me, I know I just came, but I have been spending the last few months not doing very much but missing you. Kate, *you're* my greatest achievement, you're the greatest and most wonderful award. I was stupid and I'm so, so sorry. And I will do *anything* if you give me another chance.'

We all make mistakes and do things that years in the future we will regret. It is called being human, Kate realised. She had been okay... and to be honest, she wouldn't change a thing. If Lola had been a different mother, she wouldn't have had the life she'd had so far. She'd loved travelling, seeing the world, the experiences she'd had. And what's more, she loved Lola. Always had. Always would. She'd carried on the hurt for so long, it had become a habit and now it was time to leave it behind. 'I wish I'd gone to Paulie's funeral,' she said.

'He wouldn't have minded you not being there,' said Lola. 'He knew you loved him.'

'Well, I'm glad you had Paulie. He was an amazing friend to you. Brother, I mean.' She smiled at Lola.

Lola half-smiled back, but she still looked in agony. 'Kate, I really am sorry. I didn't deserve to be a mother. I let you down.'

Kate shrugged. 'What's done is done.' She thought of Paulie. He would hate them to be arguing. 'So Paulie's mother...'

'Noreen. She hated me. *Hates* me, I should say.'

'She's *alive*?'

'Of course she is, the old bat. People like her don't die, they wither away. At Paulie's funeral, she wouldn't let me dress him in one of his stage outfits. There was this amazing one, this long blue shimmery shirt. Anyway, Noreen made us put on this horrible brown suit. He looked like he was going to his own communion.' She shook her head. 'Poor Paulie.'

40

LOLA

'How did you end up with two mothers who didn't like you?' Kate asked, as they wandered back to the village.

Lola shrugged her shoulders. 'Bad luck, I suppose.' She gave Kate a smile. 'It *used* to matter to me. But my revenge was having a daughter that I *really* liked. Negated everything.'

Kate smiled at her. 'Yeah... well...'

'Not just do I *like* her,' went on Lola. 'I love her.'

Kate rolled her eyes, but she was still smiling.

'Now, Kate,' said Lola, 'when are you going to tell me about the baby?'

Kate stopped. 'How do you know?'

'Of course I know!' said Lola. 'The whole village knows. The way you stand, your face when the baby moves, the fact that you haven't touched a drop of alcohol and you obviously like wine working in a vineyard...'

Kate nodded. 'I do...'

'But why didn't you tell me?'

Kate sighed. 'I suppose it was me trying to control something... in a situation where I didn't feel like I had much. And I was scared... and I thought you might make the drama worse...'

'What? Showbiz the arse out of your pregnancy?' Lola said, making Kate laugh.

'Perhaps,' she said. 'Sorry...'

'Look,' went on Lola. 'I've been there. Unmarried. Single. Scared. Certainly didn't want my mother interfering. But look how well it turned out!' She winked at Kate, making Kate smile. 'So, tell me everything. If you want to. Why aren't you with the father?'

Kate sighed. 'Jacques...'

'French...'

'No, Mum, Icelandic. Of course bloody French! But not into conventional families. I thought I wasn't either, until this happened.' She put her hands on her stomach. 'And he's currently on a sabbatical in Greece, working with refugees... so I came here...'

Lola was nodding, taking it all in.

'The thing is,' said Kate, 'I miss him. I hope one day he will forgive me.'

'How could he not?'

Kate looked as though she was going to cry. 'I miss everything about him. He's such a good person. Too good. He wants to leave the world a better place, you know the kind of person?'

Lola nodded. 'Few and far between, unfortunately.'

'Even the way he made me coffee... and his smile.'

'He sounds lovely,' said Lola, slipping her arm through Kate's, who, much to her surprise and delight, allowed her.

'The irony is,' said Kate, 'that he'd make a great dad.'

'I never thought that about *your* father,' said Lola. 'Mick O'Loughlin. Guitarist, balladeer, along with being an untetherable waste of space.'

'The infamous Mick,' said Kate. 'He's following me on social media these days. Looks like he's got about fifteen children now. I was invited to a party for his sixtieth a couple of years ago. Maybe I'll turn up one of these days, now all the family skeletons are on full display, with his grandchild.'

'Well, your baby is going to be loved,' said Lola. 'By you, by me, by Patsy, Flora, everyone. Come on, let's go and get a drink. Mocktail for you.' She moved towards The Island, where people were already gathering outside, chairs spilling onto pavements, groups of post-work revellers talking and laughing in the evening sunshine.

'Mum, wait a minute,' said Kate, pulling on Lola's arm. 'I want to say this... I am proud of you... really proud. You're amazing and what you've achieved has been incredible. You survived your horrible mother, you endured your other horrible mother. You went on to become one of the best musicians in the world and you did it through talent and determination.'

Lola thought she was going to cry. 'Really?'

'I wouldn't swap you,' said Kate. 'I'd rather have you than anyone.' And she looked, to Lola, as though she actually meant it.

'I'd rather have *you* than anyone.' And Lola opened her arms and pulled Kate towards her. 'I love you,' she said. 'Let's never be strangers again, okay?' Kate felt so right in Lola's arms, and she remembered all those years ago, bringing her home from hospital, this tiny baby, and it felt exactly the same. 'I never stopped loving you,' she said, 'I'm sorry you thought I did.'

41

FLORA

It was nearly 10 p.m. and Flora's phone rang with a number she didn't recognise.

'Flora, it's Robert here. How are you doing?'

'Fine,' she said, surprised to hear from him. She and Robert had never had much to say to each other. 'How are you?'

'Grand, listen, I meant to call to see how you were...'

'I'm fine...'

'Good... right. Well, I'm also calling about a very delicate matter, which I ask you to keep as private as possible. But... well...' He coughed awkwardly. Last time Flora had seen Robert, he had his head in his hands and was looking venomously at Justin. Now, he seemed back to his old self. 'Were you aware you are one of my paid employees?'

Flora froze. Oh God, she should have told someone straight away, not sat on the evidence.

'Actually, I was,' she said. 'But the thing is, Robert, I only discovered this the other day when I had to go back to the house to get my passport. There was a spreadsheet sticking out from beneath Justin's blotter thing and... Well, I saw my name... How did you find out?'

'I have employed a new accountant,' he said. 'And he is forensically looking through my accounts, asking the kind of questions that should have been asked before, such as why is the wife of my accountant on the list of my employees...'

'And other names,' said Flora.

'He found those as well.' Robert was ice-cold. Flora had never witnessed this side to Robert before.

'Yes, he's used their name in every account,' went on Flora.

'What do you mean every account?'

'It's not just you,' said Flora. 'It's everyone else.'

There was silence on the other end of the phone.

'You know,' he finally said, 'I've known this man since we were six years old? He was best man at my wedding and I was best man at his? *Yours.*'

'I know,' said Flora miserably.

'I'm going to have to take this to the Guards, you know that? For everyone's sake.' Robert sounded flat, as though he'd lost more than a marriage, more than a friend. He'd lost faith. 'I'll let you know if I hear anything else,' he said, and ended the call.

42

LOLA

The rooms of the oncology consultant Dr Lambert were on the top floor of the hospital, a sweepingly beautiful panoramic view of Dublin bay, with a rather intimidating secretary standing guard. Finally, after forty-five minutes she beckoned Patsy and Lola in.

'Well...' Dr Lambert glanced at his notes. 'Patsy.' He peered up at her. 'Is that short for anything?'

This, thought Lola, was probably his attempt at repartee. He had been told along the way to improve his bedtime manner and this was him, trying it out.

'Patrick,' said Lola, making Patsy laugh. 'It's short for Patrick.'

Dr Lambert did not smile, just bared his teeth as though he was wincing in pain. It didn't bode well, thought Lola. The man looked as though he was about to deliver the worst possible news. She and Patsy had left Sea Road earlier that morning, not telling anyone where they were going. As far as Flora knew, they were just sewing as normal, not sitting in the less than salubrious environs of St Vincent's hospital.

'Now, Patsy...' he went on. 'Your results are in...'

Lola reached over for Patsy's hand. 'And...' *Go on*, urged Lola. Jesus. The man was a masochist.

'And...' His face winced again. 'And everything is clear. The lump is a collection of tissue. Easily removed. We can whip it out in a jiffy.'

Patsy turned to Lola, nodding. 'Well, that's a relief, isn't it?'

Lola nodded. 'You could say that.' They smiled at each other.

'My secretary will book you in for the procedure. What do we say? A month's time?' He looked down at his diary. 'No, golf,' he mumbled. 'Um... conference. Um... maybe...? No, golf again.' He looked back at them. 'We will find a mutually agreeable date and we will give you a call in the next few days.'

Patsy stood up. 'Thank you, Dr Lambert,' she said.

'You are very welcome, Patrick.'

Patsy and Lola managed to get out of his room, past the secretary, before bursting out laughing in the empty corridor.

'Thank God for that,' said Patsy. 'I've decided how much I like being alive.'

'Oh, so do I,' said Lola. 'You can do so much when you're alive!' And she began to sing. 'We're alive, we're alive, we're alive! And it feels bloody wonderful!' She danced around for a moment, and then Patsy joined in. They held hands, above their heads, and danced down the corridor. 'Drink?' said Lola. 'Something stronger than tea?'

They went to The Island pub in Sandycove and Lola ordered them two whiskey and ginger ales. 'We deserve them,' she said to Patsy, as they sat tucked away in the corner of the pub's courtyard at the back of the pub, surrounded by a small jungle of ferns and vines.

Lola held up her glass when it arrived. 'To whom are we cheersing?'

'Our daughters,' said Patsy, immediately.

'Our daughters,' echoed Lola. 'To the greatest daughters two mothers could ever have.'

'And to us,' said Patsy. 'And to courage.'

Lola smiled. 'To courage. May we never run out of it.'

Patsy laughed. 'Then we'd be in trouble.' She paused. 'After this, I will never waste a single second of life being scared or worrying that I am not good enough.'

'Quite right,' said Lola.

'First I have to finish the sewing... but I don't think we're going to be able to do it all. I think I may have taken on too much. I was looking at the piles of unsewn fabric and I know Flora could lend a hand and perhaps Kate, but it's not enough. We'll have to delay everything. Killian would understand. He's a lovely man.'

'It's all right,' said Lola, patting her hand. 'I thought we might need a hand and I phoned my new best friend Doodle Matthews...' She winked at Patsy. 'And she has asked a few others to help out. If that's okay with you?'

Patsy smiled. 'Lola O'Hare, you're a wonder, so you are. You're absolutely amazing. I don't know what I'd do without you.'

Lola blushed and shook her head. 'Au contraire, Patsy,' she said. 'You're the wonder. It's me who owes you.'

* * *

Within a few minutes, they heard voices coming up the drive, before ringing the doorbell.

'Excuse me a moment,' said Lola. 'I think the troops have arrived.'

In the hall, Patsy could hear Elizabeth from next door, along with Mary Costello, Doodle Matthews and Valerie Kelly.

'It's so lovely to see you again,' Doodle was saying, as though talking to the queen. 'I couldn't believe it when Lola O'Hare needed an army of sewers. Anything for Lola, I said. Pass me my scissors.'

They all walked into the front room.

'We hear there is sewing to be done,' said Elizabeth.

'I'm not much of one,' said Doodle, 'but I can sweep, make tea and basic in-and-out stitches.'

'I'm a pretty proficient sewer,' said Mary, which they all knew was an understatement because she used to teach curtain making in the local further education college.

'I'm not too bad,' Valerie added. 'Can sew a straight line. Can thread a machine. Know my way round a pair of scissors. Put me to work.'

'I'm what might be thought of as adequate,' said Elizabeth. 'I'm slow but neat.'

They began to organise themselves. Mary threaded all the machines, while Patsy worked out what needed to be done, and gave everyone jobs. 'This pile needs hemming. Here for ironing,' she said. 'And we still need to cut out these cushions.'

They set to work and, for the next few days, they did nothing but sew, hem, iron, stitch and trim, and a great deal of chatting, laughing and telling stories. For the first time in years, Lola wasn't a star, she was just like everyone else, and it was wonderful.

43

FLORA

Ailish called to say the fabric and the wallpaper had been delivered and did Flora want to see them or should she ask her dad to drop them off.

'I'll call down,' said Flora, and cycled over to the printers at lunchtime.

Ailish looked up when Flora entered. 'I haven't seen them yet,' she said, smiling. 'But the lads in the printers were very impressed. One of them said he wants it for his living room. He's brought home a sample to show his wife. Said the saturation of colours was... what was the word he used? Immense! That was it.'

'Immense?' Flora grinned at her. The past week had been difficult and this was something good. She took one of the rolls handed to her by Ailish. 'Shall we look?' She peeled back the sticker at the end of the roll and then she flattened it out, Ailish carefully unrolling it until the entire counter was bedazzled with colour, the trawlers and sea creatures in magenta, cerise, aquamarine, turquoise and neon.

'Wow,' breathed Ailish.

Flora felt a lump in her throat, thinking of Patsy and how

she'd brought her in to this project. *She did it for me*, she thought. *She wanted me to rediscover myself and I have... I didn't go away. I was here all this time.*

'Happy?' said Ailish.

Flora nodded. 'Yes... thank you. It's... beautiful.'

The fabric was just as dazzling, but there was a shimmer and a movement that suited the theme perfectly. Flora could see the wallpaper behind the reception area of the hotel, and the fabric made into cushions on the upholstered sofas.

Ailish was brushing her hand across it. 'You had better show it to your boss...'

'Edith?'

'Yes, Edith. Maybe ask if she wants to sell it? Get your business up and running. Should I deliver this to the hotel for you?' asked Ailish, smoothing the wallpaper.

'Fabric to my mum's house,' said Flora, 'and wallpaper to the hotel, please.'

The bell on the door rang again and there was Killian.

'Ah!' said Ailish. 'Talk of the devil...'

Killian looked quite pleased at this introduction. 'What were you saying? How nice I am? Drop-dead gorgeous?'

'Don't be ridiculous,' said Ailish. 'We were just working out the deliveries of Flora's lovely wallpaper and fabric...' She turned to Flora. 'Can we show Killian? Or is it still a surprise?'

'No, go ahead,' said Flora, feeling nervous again as Killian stood beside them, studying it.

'Beautiful,' he said, when he looked up. 'I've never seen anything like it. It's...' He gave a shake of his head. 'It's stunning.'

She smiled back at him. 'That's a relief.'

'I can't wait to see it all done... your mother has done a gorgeous job. The two of you. Good team.'

Flora nodded. 'Well, we've known each other a long time...'

'And when are you coming back to yoga?' he went on. 'I've had no one to talk to this week.'

'You're not meant to *talk* in yoga,' Ailish said. 'I think you are *supposed* to be silent.'

'Supposed to be,' said Killian. 'But Flora here is quite the troublemaker...'

Flora laughed, just as her phone rang. It was Justin. 'Excuse me a moment,' she said, and stepped aside, feeling nervous. What was he going to say to her?

'Flora? What the hell is going on? I've spent all morning in Dún Laoghaire Garda Station. The house is being searched... I'm waiting for my bloody solicitor to turn up. Robert has turned out to be the biggest snake in Ireland... all because his wife fell in love with me...'

Flora didn't feel it was quite the time to remind Justin there were no snakes in Ireland. But he sounded rattled, appropriately enough, and Flora had never heard him like that before, the sheen of charm chipped away to reveal a harsher voice.

'Where's Sandra?'

'At her mother's. Won't take my calls. Robert told her... those lies, that fiction he is fecking well making up. Revenge is a terrible thing. Can't trust anyone, can you...?'

'No...' Flora said, vaguely. 'No, you can't...'

'Sandra is a total bitch. I should have listened to you...'

'I didn't say anything...'

'Yes, but you should have... I *would* have listened to *you*. And now... well, I'm going to have to fight for my good name...' His voice wobbled, the first time Flora had ever heard him show anything akin to vulnerability. 'But I knew you would answer... you're a good person...'

'Justin...' she began.

'Flora,' he interrupted, 'I've got nothing with me and I'd kill for a decent coffee and something to eat. And I need a shower and I thought that perhaps you could drop in some clean clothes, maybe a McDonald's – Big Mac Meal, extra-large chips and a chocolate milkshake. And a McFlurry. And extra ketchup. They never give you enough. And... now, this is important... go to my study and remove *all* my files... take them to your mother's house and then, when I am out on bail, I will come and get them. Okay? And... one other thing...'

Flora didn't wait to find out what that was, because she ended the phone call and stood, blinking a little, trying to take it all in.

Killian and Ailish looked at her. 'Everything all right?' said Killian.

'It's my husband,' she said. 'Well, soon-to-be ex-husband. He's been arrested. Fraud. He's been stealing money from his friends, lying to me, charging me rent and now... it's all caught up with him.'

'Come on,' said Killian. 'I'll take you for a drink, you look like you need one.'

She and Killian went to The Island and sat in the garden courtyard at the back. Flora's hands were shaking. She felt a mess of panic, fear, relief, disappointment and, more than anything, she felt sad. How could the man she loved – past tense – have fallen so low?

Killian returned with a gin and tonic for her and a pint of Guinness for him.

The TV news was on in the corner and she realised they were showing her old house. A reporter stood holding a microphone. 'Assets were seized this morning of accountant Justin Moriarty, who is being accused of falsifying the accounts of the companies. Bogus employees were used, the money going straight to Mr Moriarty's own bank accounts held in Zurich. Mr Moriarty rejects all allegations and is currently being held in Dún Laoghaire

Garda station. There is a further allegation Mr Moriarty bought
the identities of people recently arrived to Ireland to use their PPS
numbers. The inquiries continue...'

'Is that him?' asked Killian.

She tried to nod. 'Why would he do it? He didn't need the
money.'

Killian shrugged. 'Why does anyone commit crimes? Because
they can? Because they think they are better than anyone else? I
suppose it comes down to a complete lack of empathy for others,
some kind of wiring gone wrong...'

Flora nodded. 'I'm in shock...'

Killian looked at her, his eyes full of concern. 'I don't blame
you...'

'I mean, all of it. The last few weeks. I tried to manage the fact
he had an affair, and then me having to move out and now this. It's
as though I never knew him. You meet, you fall in love. Or you
think you do. And you expect there to be a growing closeness, a
greater understanding about this other person you share your life
with. But thinking back, it never happened between me and
Justin. I thought I knew enough about him to want to marry him.
But it stopped there.'

'It's scary,' said Killian, 'the leaps of faith we take as humans.
The bravery we all have when we fall in love. We open ourselves
up to being hurt and all that pain, so we can perhaps experience
all the wonderful things.' He smiled at her. 'It's a risk. But one we
are willing to do over and over again. If I was to channel Ashanti
Elaine, I would say being human is a beautiful thing.' He smiled.
'But I'm not Ashanti Killian and all I would say is we are all fools
for love.'

'Would you do it again?' asked Flora. 'Fall in love? Open yourself up? Be vulnerable?'

He nodded. 'Most definitely. Hence the rather desperate

dating I've been doing. But I'm stopping all that now. Taking a break from it. Think I will concentrate on...' He shrugged. 'Oh I don't know... other things...'

The gin and tonic was having an immeasurably calming effect on Flora. Her heart was no longer pounding, her hands had stopped shaking, the tightness in her chest had released a little.

'I'm probably going to be interviewed by the Guards,' she said.

Killian nodded. 'Would you be okay with that?'

She thought of Patsy and everything she had gone through with Jack dying, the daily courage she exhibited. 'I'll be fine,' she said.

'Would you like another drink?'

She shook her head. 'I have to go back and see how the sewing army are getting on.' She stood up, feeling strangely reluctant, as though she didn't want to leave him.

44

LOLA

Finally, the last cushion was made, the curtains steamed, ironed and folded, ready to be hung in the hotel. Lola went to Alison's café and returned with platters of sandwiches and brownies.

'Thank you,' said Patsy, with a brie and grape sandwich in one hand and a cup of tea in another. 'I don't know what to say, but it wouldn't have been done without you.' Kate and Flora were there, along with Valerie, Elizabeth, Mary and Doodle.

'I should have brought some alcohol,' said Lola. 'We can't cheers with tea.'

'Wait,' said Kate, standing up. 'I have wine! In the van. Gilles gave me a case of his very best. It's incredible. The family save it for Christmas Eve normally.' A ripple of excitement fluttered around the room, as she and Flora went outside.

'I like a nice glass of red wine,' said Valerie. 'Especially the good stuff.'

'I think we deserve a glass,' remarked Mary. 'A small one... though.'

'Small glasses are objective,' said Doodle. 'One woman's small is another woman's teetering tankard.'

Flora carried in the box of wine, meanwhile Patsy had retrieved the wine glasses from the cabinet and Kate began to pour. 'I obviously can't have any,' she said, putting her arm around Lola. 'I think everyone knows by now...'

'We all knew,' said Doodle.

'Still lovely news,' added Valerie, 'despite it being old.'

'We were just wondering when you were going to announce it publicly,' said Mary.

'It's the worst-kept secret in Sandycove,' remarked Elizabeth.

'There are no secrets in Sandycove,' said Lola, looking at Kate. 'Not any more.'

Once the glasses were filled, Lola held up her glass. 'Patsy, we need a speech...'

And so, Patsy stood up and began to speak. 'I want to say thank you my dear friends for working and sewing so hard these past couple of days.' She smiled at all of them in the room. 'And also to my darling Flora, who is the best thing in my life, and to our wonderful Kate, who we have been so delighted to see again after all this time, and of course the brilliant Lola, who has shown us you can live a life of glamour and success, but you can't beat a sandwich and a glass of wine.'

'Hear, hear,' said Valerie. 'Right, can we taste it yet?'

And they did. First they sipped, letting the flavours of the wine float over their taste buds. It was, said Valerie, 'almost like drinking a completely different drink'. Mary said it 'tasted how one always wants wine to taste'. Elizabeth pronounced it 'very nice', while Doodle had already finished her first glass. 'Nectar,' she said. 'And, Kate, tell me this Gilles is single because I'm going to divorce Hubby and marry him.'

Kate laughed. 'If only Gilles and Elise could be here,' she said, 'it would make them so happy.'

The sewing army sat back in their chairs.

'You know *my* favourite song of yours?' Doodle said to Lola.

'"Just A Girl"? That's usually what people say,' said Lola. 'Well, women do. Or "At Last I See Me".'

'It's "Finally Free",' said Doodle. 'Oh my God. I love that song.' She turned to Mary. 'Do you know it?'

Mary shook her head. 'No, sorry...' She looked at Lola, shrugging. 'I don't...'

'I've never heard a single song of yours,' said Valerie. 'I am sure they are very good however...'

'Good!' Doodle was aghast. 'She's just the greatest Irish export since Kerrygold!' She turned back to Lola. 'I do apologise. I will be holding The Islanders' appreciation classes as soon as possible. This wrong will be righted.'

Lola laughed. 'I couldn't care less. It's just singing...'

'But you bring people together,' persisted Doodle. 'You are a conduit through which people process the emotions they wouldn't be able to do so ordinarily. Your music helped me, particularly. "Feeling Free" became my battle cry at a time in my life when I was feeling... well, vulnerable.'

Lola was struck by the sincerity of Doodle. Before she had dismissed fans as people who didn't care about who you were, but she realised that your music was theirs... it didn't belong to Lola, or Paulie, or any other songwriter. Once it was released, it belonged to whomever grasped for it, finding and making their own meanings and finding secrets in there that they felt were just for them.

And then Doodle began to sing. '*Say goodbye to all I've left, leave it all behind, I've shed my skin, I've turned my back, to find the real me...*'

And then Lola joined in and the two of them sang together. '*I'm not scared to show my face, I've nothing to fear, I'm the only thing I really need, because I'm finally free.*'

Doodle stopped singing, so it was just Lola. Low and throaty, her voice vibrated with emotion, with more feeling than she had ever felt before. She thought of Paulie, wherever he was. She thought of her mother, who no longer really mattered. But it was Kate who captured her heart and she thought of how much she loved her, and how much she loved her unborn grandchild. *A second chance*, she thought, *is all I want.*

'*I'm the only thing I really need, because I'm finally free.*'

When she finished singing, there was a round of applause and a whistle from Doodle, who was able to do one of those fingers-in-mouth whistles which everyone was quite impressed by. 'Misspent youth,' explained Doodle.

'That was lovely, Lola,' said Mary.

'Very nice,' said Elizabeth. 'For popular music. I prefer Cliff Richard. Anyone know any of his?'

Lola began to sing, her voice low, words tumbling out of her. She really needed someone to accompany her. Richie and his mandolin. Richie and those arms of his.

Doodle joined in with the chorus, and all the women swayed from side to side. Mary had a dreamy expression on her face, Valerie's eyes were crunched shut, her lips moving along with the words, a beat too late.

'*All your dreams have led you here...*' sang Lola. '*All those tales you wove... But loss is just another name for love and did you really think you'd had enough? Oh no, because on you go... don't even stop to breathe, you're defiant, brave and free. For this time, it's your time, it's not just you no more... I'll bring you everywhere in my heart, Because where there's you, there's me...*'

She looked over at Kate, who was singing along. Lola had no idea she knew the words, never mind would sing it with her. Her heart was full. *I love you, Kate*, she thought. *I'm never going to let you down again.*

Lola realised this was her new beginning. Part two of parenting, her second chance had started.

45

JACQUES

Jacques Roux was back in France after what felt like a lifetime away. He'd missed everything about home – the long, straight, tree-lined roads, the sight and smell of an early-morning bakery, families going about their lives. Guilt wound its way around him. He was lucky because he could return home here. His time in Greece had been chaos. Those poor people seeking refuge in Europe had been thrown into that inhumane whirlpool, their whole worlds turned upside down, leaving them scrabbling for the only thing they had left: life. He had thought a great deal about life and the world while away. He wanted to grow food, he had decided, he wanted to work with his hands, feed people. He wanted to give back. And there was only one person he wanted to do it with. Kate. He'd come home a few weeks early because he missed her so much and needed to be with her. Just as he had from the first time he'd met her.

He'd noticed her around, the blonde hair, the decidedly non-Frenchness of her, and he'd been intrigued. And then, he'd found himself standing next to her at a stall at the Saturday market. She was buying apricots, and when he'd heard her accent, he'd asked her if she was Irish. 'I'm half-Irish,' he'd told her. 'My mother is from Cork but grew up in France…'

Kate hadn't looked particularly interested in taking the conversation much further, as though she wasn't keen on men who found tentative lines of connection. But he kept seeing her around, a small figure heading into the cinema, or drinking a coffee all alone in the café. He had asked around, and being a journalist he knew how to ask the least amount of questions for the most amount of answers. Her name was Kate O'Hare and she was working for the Auberts.

He had decided a story on the vineyard might be of interest to his editors. After he'd interviewed Gilles and Elise about their biodynamic wines, Gilles had asked if Kate could pick up a case of wine to give to Jacques. 'I'll come and get it,' said Jacques. 'I can bring my car. It will be easier, no? We can go together.'

The office was at the far end of the vineyard, in the old barn, and in the eight minutes it took to drive there, Jacques managed to ask Kate all the questions he'd wondered about. And then, just as he made his goodbyes, Jacques asked her to go for a drink and she agreed. She wasn't remotely interested in having a relationship but she was funny and intelligent and he was given the distinct impression she'd come a long way. Her mother was some sort of singer and Kate had told him she was offered a big tour and had chosen it over her.

'I was old enough,' Kate had told him. 'But it still pissed me off.'

Pissed her off. He loved that phrase. He loved listening to her, the way she'd look away when saying something she needed to think carefully about, or how she'd wrinkle her nose when saying something important. Or the way she laughed, and he loved making her laugh.

'You're the Frenchman,' she'd once said, 'with an Irish sense of humour.'

'My mother,' he'd shrugged, as a way of explanation. But it was possibly the best compliment he'd ever received.

She had told him early on, she didn't want to settle down. And neither did he. His parents had divorced when he was four and all he could remember was being shunted from his father's home in Draguignan to Paris, where his mother ran a small clothes shop, selling Irish cashmere, linens, tablecloths, the kind of thing Parisians adored. He didn't want to make any mistakes and he and Kate were perfectly happy. He'd call over to see her at the house on the estate and they would cook dinner, enjoy a glass of wine and talk.

One night, in bed, full of love for this woman, he'd said, 'Let's do nothing to change this, no babies, no marriage, no living together. I think that's the secret.'

And she'd agreed. 'Suits me.'

'Suits you?' Sometimes there were still phrases he'd missed the meaning of.

'I mean, that's fine by me,' she'd explained, and he pulled her closer to him thinking he'd never been happier. They'd cracked the code.

He thought about all this as he got off the train at Tournon, and then walked to his flat in the centre of town. He'd tried to call ahead to Kate, wanting to tell her he was in Athens and he'd missed her and was on his way home. And then, a couple of hours later, when he was on the train, making its way through Europe, he texted again. Still no signal. But then Kate wasn't one of those people who was constantly on their phones and he'd see her in a matter of hours.

He called when he was in his flat and finally he thought something might be wrong. The call didn't connect. 'This number is no longer in service,' said a voice.

Something was wrong.

He found his car keys and drove to the Auberts'. He'd see Kate soon, Jacques told himself. She'd lost her phone, she'd had to get a new one. Maybe, he thought, she'd had an accident? Maybe, something terrible had happened to her and they couldn't contact him because he'd gone off to be a fucking saviour of the world, to do something which served to make him feel as though he was doing something. Recently, he'd wondered what kind of discernible difference he had made. Yes, he'd helped build shelters, and he'd cooked and cleaned. And he'd written articles which he'd sent back to the newspaper, and yes, it might have meant an uplift in donations, but he had returned to France with the very real sense that life could change in an instant and that you shouldn't take a second of it for granted. He'd been desperate to talk to Kate about all this... but now... where was she?

He kept driving, down tree-canopied avenues, past acres and acres of vineyards and there, as he crested a hill, the Auberts' estate spread around him. Usually, at this point, he always had a little lurch of excitement, *I will see her soon*. Now, he felt fear.

Her camper van was gone and he peered through the window of the barn looking for signs of life, before knocking on the door of the chateau. One of the children answered.

'Is your mother here?'

And the child nodded, shouting, '*Maman!*' And ran away again.

Jacques felt sweat on his body. Why had he gone away in the first place? He had left her behind and then *this* happened? How stupid of him.

'Jacques!' Elise Aubert looked shocked to see him. 'You're back? I thought...'

'Where's Kate?' he managed, dreading the news. 'What happened?'

'Did she not tell you?' Elise looked confused. 'I thought... I *assumed* she'd told you...'

'Where is she?'

'She's gone to Ireland,' said Elise.

For a moment, Jacques stood entirely still, taking it in. 'She went to *Ireland*?'

Elise nodded. 'She said she wanted to go home. I thought everything must have ended between you. Have you called her?'

'Her phone's off...'

Elise shook her head. 'I've been waiting for her to call with her new address and number.'

'How long has she gone for?'

'Forever,' she said. 'I think. The children were devastated, we miss her so much. But she said she had things to sort out.'

'You don't know where she's gone?'

'Ireland,' she said again, shrugging. 'I am sorry. I don't know any more.'

He nodded, walking backwards, towards his car. He would find her. He would knock on every door in Ireland if he had to. 'Thank you, Elise!' He turned and ran to his car.

Jacques tried to remember any place names Kate had mentioned in the past. Sandycove. She'd grown up there, she had spoken about friends of hers. He remembered looking at pictures of the place and had sworn he would visit James Joyce's tower one day with her. She had laughed.

He packed a bag, started up the old 2CV, and headed north, towards Cherbourg and the ferry to Ireland. There was a ferry leaving that night at 9 p.m. If the car didn't decide to have one of its funny turns, he would make it. 'Come on, Joséphine,' he said to the car. 'Don't let me down.'

46

RICHIE

Richie wasn't much for travelling and hated being on the road so he had long ago realised the life of a musician wasn't the best career for someone who got jittery on planes, felt ill in cars and became claustrophobic on tour buses. Playing with The Islanders had been both a dream and a nightmare. Being in the backing band of a successful group had given him experiences he could never have imagined. They were fun, they knew how to have a party, Paulie was hilarious and told these crazy stories. And as for Lola... he'd fallen for her even before they had met. She was the kind of person who didn't care if people liked her or not – the problem was, people did. Paulie worshipped her, her other friends – blow-ins from Ireland, mainly – Siobhán, Sarah, Anna, were a pretty cool bunch of women. And they loved Lola. And so did he.

There was a party once, which she threw for Paddy's Day, invited anyone Irish she knew, anyone half-Irish, anyone who'd ever heard of the Irish, and of course all the musicians were there from the tour, the crew. Richie and Lola would chat about this and that, but it was at this party that everything changed.

He could see her talking to Liam Neeson, and Richie couldn't tell if Liam was into her or if she was into Liam or if that was the way Irish people talked to each other, but he'd felt suddenly jealous. It wasn't because he thought he had a chance with her, but it was because he knew he liked her a lot. And he also thought that perhaps he understood her more than she wanted to be understood.

But that evening, he'd had enough. He went and found his leather jacket, went over to Paulie to say goodbye, squeezed past Colin Farrell who was talking to Saoirse Ronan, and went outside to find his motorbike. He'd played with The Islanders for eight years and he was ready to call it a day on a life of touring. He wanted the simple life, a home, no more travelling, maybe teach guitar to local kids, set up his own band which played in local bars, that kind of thing. Nothing fancy. Just him, the bike, his guitar. A couple of beers. And the same bed night after night. And the same woman.

'Where'd you think you're going?'

And there she was. Lola was standing at the top of the steps, looking like she always did. Magnificent. Like a queen. But it was that voice which stayed in his head. Sometimes, late at night, he'd put on one of the albums and listen to how she sang, how she bent the notes, how she was able to pour her whole self with so much emotion and feeling into those words. She sang with her soul and it gave him chills every single time. She sang songs of love, loss and longing. And he had all three right there.

'I'm going to head home,' he'd said. 'Get an early night. I'm kinda tired.' He felt shy, as he always did around her.

'Now, why would you do a thing like that?' she'd asked. 'The party's just getting started.'

Something had shifted at that moment. Richie still didn't know what had made him fix her with a gaze which rooted her to the spot. Or what had possessed him to place his hands on either side of her face and kiss her the way he had wanted to kiss her for years. He could feel her skin against his hands, her lips giving way, her body against his, and when he stopped, his face millimetres from hers, his breath heavy, his voice raspy. 'I was just heading home...'

'If you go,' she'd said, 'I'm coming with you.'

And that was it, the two of them, on the back of his motorbike on their way to his place, and they went to bed and didn't get out again for three days.

And now, she was back in Ireland and it had been a living hell without her. Richie missed her, he hadn't been able to sleep, to eat, he'd lost ten pounds in weight, the whole house was too quiet and he just wanted her back. She'd said not to call her, and every time he'd picked up the phone, he'd put it down again. But this time, he thought, he'd go and see her, see this place she'd told him about and ask her when the hell she was coming home. His big fear was that she wasn't, and he wanted to grow old with her. He wanted to watch the ocean, play some music and spend the rest of his life with the woman he loved.

He patted his jeans pocket. The box was still there. Phew.

He squinted up at the departures board. He had an hour until his Dublin flight, time to go and get a coffee.

47

JACQUES

Joséphine, the orange 2CV, edged its way off the ferry, behind the camper vans and family-sized cars, and joined the queue leaving the terminal. Jacques had spent every holiday in Ireland, as a child, his mother leaving Paris behind for the whole of August and driving her and Jacques all the way to Goleen in West Cork. He would return to France knowing a few more Irish swear words, with a bag of Tayto and a pack of Club Milk, the kind of delicacies you couldn't buy in Paris, and a sense that he had stepped into another world. Everyone was so different, in every way. No one even looked like the people at home, they wore different clothes, talked about politics as though their lives depended on it and never resisted the opportunity to find some way of teasing you. He was called French Jacques and would be greeted every summer like a returning local. 'We can have our holidays now French Jacques has arrived,' someone would say. 'You brought the good weather with you, French Jacques, I see,' said someone else. They'd ask him to say hello in French and ask about who was in charge over there and talk about the time they went on holiday in France and had to pay to use the roads. Jacques loved it. But once he left school and friends were backpacking to warmer climes, he fell out of the habit of going.

But now, seeing the green of the fields, the jumble of the road-side hedges, the sight of someone selling strawberries on the side of the road, he felt his heart lift. Ireland, he thought, was always a good idea.

He looked at his petrol tank, better fill up before he got on the main road. He had already put Sandycove into the satnav on his phone and as far as he could see it was going to take two and a half hours.

Once he'd filled Joséphine up, he went into the small shop attached. There was a woman behind the counter, who smiled at him as he swiped his card. 'Beautiful day today,' she said. 'Aren't we lucky with the weather?'

'We are,' he said. He never knew if these were questions or comments and therefore if he was expected to answer.

'French, is it? Just off the boat?'

'I am,' he said.

The woman looked out of the window to the forecourt. 'Travelling by yourself, are ye?'

'Yes...' He really had forgotten how much people wanted to know about you here. 'I'm here to see someone. A friend. My...' He searched for the word. What was she? More than a girlfriend. His partner. His *life* partner. His *love*.

The woman listened, nodding, waiting for him to say more.

'She's Irish and came back some weeks ago.... I'm not sure exactly when...'

'Did she now?' The woman seemed to be thinking of something.

'Yes, she's...'

'Her name's not Kate, by any chance in heaven? Was she in a camper van? One that'd seen better days?'

'Yes...' Maybe Ireland really was as small as everyone said it was and everyone did know everyone else.

'Lovely girl, she was. Felt very tired because of the baby...'

'Baby? She doesn't have a baby...' He looked at the woman, taking it in. 'You mean...?' Oh my God. 'She is carrying a baby? You mean, she's...?'

The woman nodded, confused. But a bomb exploded in Jacques' chest. He ran straight out of the shop, across the old fore-court, past the strange-looking man in the hoodie, and into Joséphine.

Oh my God, he kept thinking. *Oh my God.*

Joséphine's tyres had never actually squealed before, nor had her accelerator ever been pressed with such force, but true to French engineering and her desire to help Jacques, who'd always been a good owner and changed her oil and never expected too much from her – until yesterday, that was – she complied. The two of them found the motorway and began driving as fast as possible.

Sandycove, j'arrive!

48

KATE

Thanks to Abigail and her crew, Honeysuckle Lodge gleamed and shone. Even the dandelions had been plucked from the path that led to the heavy double front doors. Inside, the parquet floor in the hall had been given an extra polish, every corner and crevice had been dusted – even the old stag horns above the porch seemed less laden with dust. Abigail herself was wearing a smart navy dress and large crystal earrings but was still wearing her old trainers. 'I have the heels in my office,' she told Kate. 'I'll put them on when I actually have to.'

The two long sofas in the day room had been pushed against the far wall and the piano moved beside them. A table had been placed to one side in front of the bookcase, stacked with teacups and plates, a giant urn, and platters of ham sandwiches and custard creams. Sally-Anne's bakery had donated a huge, square cake, iced to perfection with the words CONGRATULATIONS HONEYSUCKLE WARBLERS on the top. Chairs were laid in five rows at the other side – they looked like a jumble of deckchairs, folding kitchen chairs and an old school bench.

Lola had been in and out of the kitchen all day, helping the cook make sandwiches, carrying trays of miniature pavlovas and millionaire's shortbread from the kitchen to the day room. When Kate was running through the songs with the ladies, Lola arrived with a huge tea urn carried on one shoulder.

'I'll be there in a moment,' she called, placing the tea urn on the trestle table's white linen. Lola ran over and took her place at the piano. 'Right,' she said, 'what are we running through first?'

After their run-through, Lola and Kate and some of the other staff set up a grooming area, where each lady had their make-up and hair done.

Chico the chihuahua was wearing a bobble hat and scarf for the occasion and all the Honeysuckle Warblers had on their best blouses and cardigans and sparkliest jewels.

Abigail went around dabbing lipstick on them all. 'Just a little bit, dear,' she was saying. 'Spruce ourselves up a bit.'

Kate faced everyone. 'How are we all feeling?'

'Nervous,' said Bernadette. 'Never thought I'd feel that again, aged eighty-seven.'

'Ah, don't be silly,' said Marjorie. 'When you're our age, we don't do nerves. We've done it all, seen it all. I marched for the women in Ireland. I marched for the workers... this is just a bit of singing.'

'I think,' said Kate, 'that it's a bit more than that.'

'Absolutely,' called out Lola. 'It's a performance. It's a culmination.'

'A culmination,' said Kitty. 'I like that. I've always wanted to culminate.'

'We're octogenarians,' remarked Bernadette. 'We don't have much choice other than to culminate.'

'It's better than Christmas,' Abigail said to Kate. 'Christmas can be a little on the poignant side, everyone remembering their younger days. Today, our ladies themselves are feeling young!'

She smiled at Kate. 'Thank you for everything. You've been a tonic. You and your mother have brought a lot of fun to all of us. Hearing your rehearsals and the ladies laughing has been wonderful.'

Kate suddenly felt a little faint. She had been feeling strange all day, a weird woozy sensation as though she was still on that ferry from Cherbourg.

'Are you all right? Are you having a funny turn? Have you eaten?' Abigail grabbed a plate of ham sandwiches. 'Take one of these. You've got to keep your blood sugar up.'

'I'm fine, I'm fine.'

The doorbell rang and Lola shouted, 'That's for me! I might need a hand with this!'

Brenda, who was doing hair and make-up, found herself being pulled along to the front door. Within minutes, they were back, carrying a huge cardboard box, and dragging another behind them.

'Ladies,' said Lola, 'gather round. I have something for you all.' She began pulling out shoeboxes. 'Right, size four, who is size four? Size five? There's even a size three for Kitty.' She handed them out to the ladies and they all sat with them on their laps. 'Right, all got one?' asked Lola. 'Now open them? One, two... three!'

They took them out, and inside were pairs of silver Birkenstocks.

'Oooh! I love them!' said Kitty.

Bernadette gasped. 'Ah now... look at this finery...'

'Rock-star shoes,' said Marjorie.

'They remind me of a pair I had when I was a tiny child,' went on Dorothy. 'My mother had us all dressed up every Sunday. Immaculate, we were. All the neighbours used to say my sister and I were like little princesses. I had silver T-bar shoes. My mother saved up for them, a penny a week, until she could buy us both a pair. We wore them until our toes were pinched raw. But we never let our mother see that we were in pain. She gave them to next door and Mam had to avert her eyes every time she saw them kicking a ball in them.'

'They are comfortable,' said Lola, 'for ladies such as ourselves. We all deserve happy feet.'

'And silver,' said Kitty. 'It's the silver which makes them.'

Kate and Lola helped each of them off with their old shoes and helped slip their feet into the new sandals.

'Now, you don't have to wear them all the time,' said Lola. 'Special occasions...'

'I'm going to wear mine *all* the time,' said Peggy.

'Mine are for special days,' said Celia.

'Better wear them every day so,' said Bernadette. 'Our special days are numbered.'

'And one more thing... we can't have our stars not looking like the stars!' Lola began taking out silver sequin jackets from the other cardboard box. 'Ladies, put them on, drape them around your shoulders, whatever works for you... but, above all, sparkle!'

Lola then placed two lamps, one on either side of the sofas and a couple more on low tables, in front of the ladies. With the silver jackets, lights bounced around the room, illuminating the ladies' faces, making them glitter.

'There,' she said, standing back. 'You all look like stars now.' She looked over at Kate, who smiled back at her. 'I told you, I'd make them glow. Happy, ladies? Need anything?'

'No, thank you, Lola,' said Marjorie. 'I think we look the part now, don't we, girls?'

'Oh, yes,' said Peggy. 'We really do.'

* * *

Kate was still feeling a little strange as the time for the concert drew closer. The ladies were all in the dining room having their lunch, and she and Lola were on their own in the day room, putting the finishing touches to the room.

'This is a bit of a comedown,' she said to Lola, as she watched her mother heaving one of the long sofas closer to the other. 'Aren't you used to concerts on a slightly bigger scale?'

Lola looked up at her. 'It depends on what you mean by scale? Doesn't it depend on your heart? If your heart is in something, then it's on the biggest scale imaginable.' She sat down for a moment on the arm of one of the sofas. 'All those people who organise school shows or community theatre or whatever it is... is that not more important than the huge events? My heart' – she clutched at her chest – 'is here. In this room.'

'Oh God, you're always so dramatic,' she teased.

'Well,' said Lola, 'that's what I feel. I'd far rather be here than anywhere else.' She smiled at Kate. 'With you, I mean. And *our* ladies.'

Kate found herself smiling back.

'And anyway,' Lola went on, 'I told you I was in need of a new band. And I love being part of the Honeysuckle Warblers.'

Kate felt a little dizzy and sat down on the wooden bench by the front door.

'You look pale,' went on Lola, concerned. 'Are you feeling okay?'

'I'm grand,' said Kate. 'Just need some water... or sleep....'

The audience had been gathering steadily – relatives, family, friends, the sewing army were all present, including a nice-looking youngish man who hugged Peggy. Flora took a place at the back of the room as Lola rushed from the piano stool, when she saw Patsy and patted the back of a very comfortable armchair.

'Guest of honour coming through,' she said, beckoning her over. 'Come on, Patsy, this is for you.'

She went back to the piano and all the ladies were in their positions, sitting in a line on the two sofas, all with their silver shoes on. Someone had even made tiny shoes for Chico out of tinfoil.

The room hushed.

Kate stood nervously, in front of them. She felt as though she was going to faint. These last few weeks had been a whirlwind. A wave of nausea surged through her. 'Thank you all for coming,' she said. 'It's a pleasure to see you all here. It's been wonderful to work with the ladies of Honeysuckle Lodge and it's so lovely to see their family and friends. I hope you enjoy today's concert. I want to thank Abigail and her amazing team here and also we have been honoured to be working with the great Lola O'Hare...'

The audience clapped and cheered.

'Love you, Lola!' a male voice called out.

There was a wolf whistle. Doodle. Of course.

Lola and Kate were smiling at each other.

'My honour,' said Lola, 'is to work with my fabulous daughter. The woman I could never be and who I love more than anything.' She held Kate's eye.

Kate looked away. She couldn't start crying now, not in front of everyone. And she needed all her strength to get through the concert. She couldn't let the ladies down.

'I just have a few words to say,' she began. 'I want to thank the ladies of Honeysuckle Lodge, our wonderful choir. They've all been such a pleasure to work with. And I was thinking about the importance of music... how it brings people together, whether we are performing it or listening to it, it's a pleasure to be shared.' She smiled at Lola. 'Without music, life is...' She gave a laugh. 'Well, it's pretty rubbish. Music makes us all better people. So, without further ado, I bring you the ladies of Honeysuckle Lodge, the Honeysuckle Warblers.'

And so, it began. The voices were sweet and pure, the songs beautiful and redolent of other lives, times past, songs sung in the kitchens of childhood, from Carrickfergus to Tipperary to the Salley Gardens. Even Chico was quiet, the beauty of the singing, the faces of these lovely old women thinking of their own mothers and grandmothers, of their children when they were tiny toddlers holding their hands, of a whole life, spread like a cloak behind them, facing bravely into their next journey.

Kate turned to the audience for their finale. 'We're going to end today with a beautiful song, sung by the great Count John McCormack, this is "I'll Walk Beside You"...'

Lola began the introduction, and the ladies started singing.

'I'll walk beside you through the passing years... Through days of cloud and sunshine, joys and tears... And when the great call comes, the sunset gleams... I'll walk beside you to the land of dreams...'

Every adult was wiping their eyes. Doodle had her face in her hands, Flora had her arm around Patsy, even Abigail was red-eyed. The people who weren't crying were the teeny grandchildren and great-grandchildren, who looked around at their adults and wondered what on earth had caused them to start crying.

Kate was about to stand up and thank everyone again when she felt a stabbing pain. She put her hands to her stomach, falling back.

Lola was instantly kneeling beside her. 'She's in labour!' she shouted. 'Call an ambulance!'

49

ABIGAIL

Abigail tried to think how she could help. She had worked with the older generation for so long, the fact that she was now dealing with the very opposite end of the age spectrum momentarily floored her. Someone was busy ushering out the families and relatives, who were all making swift exits, leaving by the front door and heading away in their cars. Another woman in a navy dress and very nice earrings was keeping the ladies calm. But as Abigail closed the door on the last remaining family member, there was a knock. As she opened it, a tall and extremely handsome man was standing there, like the most perfect apparition. And then he spoke and she realised he was French. *Zut alors*!

The apparition spoke again, asking for Kate.

'Kate?' said Abigail. 'She's in the day room, having her baby.'

The apparition turned white, and he dashed inside, leaving Abigail blinking, and wondering if all of this was actually happening or if that sixth custard cream had been a mistake.

50

JACQUES

Jacques stood for a moment, trying to make sense of the scene in front of him. The last time he'd seen Kate was eight weeks ago, in France, and now here she was lying on the ground, her eyes scrunched up in pain, her hands on her stomach. Beside her, kneeling on the ground and clutching her hand, was a remarkable-looking woman with long white hair falling down her back. There was another woman trying to force cushions under Kate's head, and a line of elderly ladies, sitting in a row of two sofas, calling out instructions.

'Stand back and give her air,' one said.

'Peggy,' said another, her voice sounding squeaky, 'you go and give a hand...'

'I can't untie the laces!' the woman shouted, panicking.

'Pull them off then!' roared the white-haired woman.

Another woman came up to him. 'You must be Jacques?'

He nodded, panic now setting within him like concrete. What had he walked into? Some kind of crazy women's cult? He'd arrived in Sandycove an hour earlier and had begun asking in shops did anyone know a Kate O'Hare. It was a fabric shop, the kind his mother used to drag him into when he was small, and the woman behind the counter knew exactly who he was talking about and drew a map to the house on Sea Road. When he'd arrived, parked in the drive, like a beacon of hope, there was Kate's camper van, but no one was at home.

A man had walked past. 'Kate?' Jacques had called. 'Do you know Kate?'

He'd nodded. 'They are all at Honeysuckle Lodge, there's a concert on.'

Again, with more directions, Jacques had set off, finding his way through the streets of Sandycove, along Sea Road, down Marine Avenue, towards Honeysuckle Lodge. And leaving Joséphine parked among all the other cars, he'd been met at the door by a woman who seemed to have lost her mind, and then in the room were more of them.

But there was Kate, his darling Kate. She had opened her eyes and was looking over at him. She was crying and he realised she was absolutely terrified. He slid to his knees and in a moment had her in his arms. How could he not have known? Why hadn't she told him? What had he done or said to make her feel as though she couldn't trust him? He kissed her. 'I love you,' he said. 'I'm sorry for leaving you. But I'm here now, and all I want is you.'

She nodded, her eyes closed again, and then, from outside, they could hear a siren.

'AMBULANCE!' came a voice from the hall. In a matter of moments, they had Kate in a wheelchair, which they were able to manoeuvre out of the house, past the van and into the ambulance.

Jacques had hold of her hand and the ambulance crew didn't question if he was going to the hospital, he was bundled in along with them. And they were gone.

In the ambulance, tears were falling from Kate's eyes.

'Everything will be all right,' said Jacques, not sure if it would be. All he knew was he loved Kate and he loved this baby and would give anything to save them. And for a moment, he thought about those people he'd been working with in Greece. They too would do anything to save their families and just then he had a minuscule understanding of their plight and their pain.

'I should have told you,' said Kate. 'I thought you wouldn't want to know...'

'What?' Jacques was confused. 'Of course I would want to know.'

'But you don't want children...'

'That was then,' he said. 'Everything has changed. Everything.' He shook his head. 'I can't believe I was so stupid.' He had tears in his eyes. 'Nothing else matters. I will do anything for you.'

'I've missed you so much...'

'Me too,' he said. 'I should never have gone.' And he took her hand and held it all the way to hospital.

51

LOLA

Back at the house, Lola stood at the window, twisting her hair around her fingers, the way Kate used to do. She looked so worried.

'I remember giving birth to Kate,' Lola reminisced. 'I was terrified. And then they give you this baby to take home and all I wanted to do was to give her back. If I could go back in time, I'd go back and I would hold her and kiss her and not be terrified. I would tell her that I was there, and that I would always be there, and we were going to do it together. All of it.'

Patsy took her hand. 'You've been a wonderful mother,' she said.

Lola shook her head. 'I haven't,' she said, tearfully. 'Not remotely.'

'You showed her that life was for living,' said Patsy. 'You gave her a model of a mother who was adventurous, talented, successful, fun, loving, interesting...' She smiled at Lola. 'They are all good qualities for a mother to have, don't you think?'

Lola shrugged, miserably.

'I'm going to call again,' said Flora, picking up her phone.

'Right, okay...' Flora wasn't saying much, just nodding. 'I see, right. I see. And we can come in at visiting hours.' Lola and Patsy clutched each other's hands. 'And the baby...?' said Flora. 'Under observation... of course, of course. Right. Well, thank you, thank you so much.' She put down the phone. 'The baby was delivered by emergency caesarean section half an hour ago. Tiny, four pounds in weight, and is in the neonatal unit.'

'And Kate? How is Kate?' asked Lola.

'Very tired. She's in the recovery room now.'

'And what is it?' asked Lola.

'It's a girl,' said Flora. 'A beautiful girl. Just like her mother.'

'And her glamorous grandmother,' said Patsy. 'Right, we need to pack a hospital bag... what does she need?'

'I'll do it,' said Lola. 'One thing I know is how to pack a bag.'

52

FLORA

Lola, Patsy and Flora went into the hospital as soon as they were allowed, which was early the following morning. They found Kate was sitting up in bed, looking tired and pale, Flora thought, but surprisingly well. Jacques was sitting beside the bed, holding Kate's hand. He stood up when they all walked in.

'Ladies,' he said, smiling at them, 'we haven't been introduced. Lola, I presume?'

She nodded, holding out a hand, but he kissed her on both cheeks and then another.

'*Enchanté*,' he said.

Lola turned back to grin at Flora and Patsy. 'And these are our good friends,' she said. 'Our very, *very* best friends, Patsy and Flora Fox.'

He kissed them as well and also blessed them with another '*enchanté*', which for some reason made them all laugh, much to Jacques' confusion.

'Have you seen her?' Kate asked.

'Not yet,' said Lola, 'we wanted to see you first. How are you?' She sat on the edge of the bed, taking Kate's hand. They were so alike, really, Kate just a younger version of Lola, the same way of frowning when concentrating, the same smile as though the sun had come out. Lola had her arm around Kate. 'Budge up,' she said, 'this is what is known as motherly affection.'

Kate wriggled away, laughing. 'Get off! I don't think we said anything about public displays of affection.'

The two of them giggled together, the same laugh, Flora noticed, the same way of squeezing their eyes shut. Flora and Patsy exchanged a smile.

'The baby,' said Kate, suddenly. 'Will you go and see the baby? Let me know how she is. They won't let me walk and they wouldn't let me use a wheelchair.'

'One moment...' Lola disappeared from the room.

'We thought you were in Greece,' said Flora to Jacques. 'How did you get here?'

'Car,' he said. 'Boat. And I just guessed she might be in Sandy-cove and when I got here, I kept asking did anyone know her, and it didn't take me long to find her.' He smiled at Kate.

'He's a journalist,' she said, proudly. 'Investigator.'

Lola returned, pushing a wheelchair. 'You don't get to sing a duet with Elton John without knowing how to charm people.' She paused and flicked the wheelchair around so it was beside the bed. 'Also, the man guarding the wheelchairs is an Islandian.'

'An *Islandian*?' asked Flora.

'A superfan,' said Lola, with a vague, dismissive shrug. 'That's what they call themselves. But that's not important right now. Come on, let's go.'

They helped Kate into the wheelchair and Patsy insisted on putting a rug over her lap, and with Lola pushing, off they set, along the interminable corridors, around corners, crossing reception, past the shop, along another long corridor, past the cafeteria, and finally, the neonatal unit, past the nurses' station, and through a large window they could see eight tiny cots.

A nurse was walking past. 'Excuse me,' said Lola, in a charming voice. 'My daughter's baby is in the unit. Is it possible for us to go in?'

The nurse looked at Lola, and then looked at her again, as though she was trying to place her. 'One at a time,' she said.

Obviously, this nurse was no *Islandian*. But Lola didn't seem to mind not being recognised as long as she got to hold her grand-daughter. Kate went first, holding her tiny baby, and then she was passed, very carefully, to Lola. A tear dropped from Lola onto the baby. Flora watched as she said something to Kate, and Kate smiled back, nodding.

'There is nothing like a new baby to bring everyone together,' said Patsy. 'Aren't us mothers lucky with our daughters?'

53

JACQUES

Jacques had forgotten how much the Irish insisted on tea every five minutes, maybe even more regularly. He was also experiencing a sense of disorientation, as though he was an alien who had landed in a strange land and his whole life had changed. Which, of course, it had. He took a moment to try to remember where he was and what on earth had happened. He was in a hospital in Ireland, he was now a father, his brand-new baby was in the neonatal unit and the love of his life had survived a major operation. Life really did change in an instant.

He watched Kate and the baby through the glass. He loved those two people more than he ever thought he could love anyone. It was as though he had finally realised what his life was, and it was to look after them, to be by their side, and care for and mind this beautiful planet... for them, and for his baby's children. And on and on.

They sat in a row outside the unit, drinking their tea. Kate's mother reminded him of someone and then, as she talked about worrying about Kate and something about sewing curtains, he was staring at her. She looked very like the female singer from

The Islanders. He'd been really into them years ago, when he'd been embracing his Irish roots. He leaned towards her. 'You are Lola O'Hare?'

Lola laughed. 'I am. Well, that's just part of who I am. I'm actually Lorraine. Lola is a silly name Paulie gave me.'

'Didn't Kate ever mention it?' said Flora.

Jacques shook his head. 'She said you were a singer, but she never said you were *Lola O'Hare*.' He smiled at her. 'It explains a lot.'

'I hope,' said Lola, 'to be a better grandmother than I was a mother.'

'Stop that,' said Patsy, elbowing her in the ribs, 'we've been through this.'

'Yeah, well...' said Lola. She turned to Jacques. 'Have you talked about names yet?'

He nodded. 'Kate's decided on Paula, named after her uncle apparently. Paula O'Hare-Roux.'

And then Lola began to cry again. 'It's perfect,' she said. 'It's just so perfect.'

54

LOLA

Patsy and Flora had left an hour earlier, but Lola lingered, not wanting to leave but she realised perhaps she should give Jacques and Kate – who made, it had to be said, a very nice couple – some time on their own with their beautiful baby. Lola guessed Paula had inherited the O'Hare stubbornness, which had helped all the women in the family survive. Paula was going to be okay. No, much more than that, Paula was going to be amazing.

On the bus home, she felt her heart was going to burst, feelings of almost overwhelming happiness sluiced through her, making her fear she was going to start sobbing uncontrollably. Instead, she put on her celebrity disguise of sunglasses and headscarf and kept her head down while she thought of little Paula's beautiful face and of Kate's, her incredible daughter. She kept having to wipe her eyes, behind her glasses, hoping no one would notice the strange woman on the bus who was having her own private breakdown.

In Sandycove, she walked the few minutes to her flat, thinking about all the things she needed to buy for Paula. A cashmere blanket, definitely. She'd seen one in the boutique in the village. Baby-gros and little cardigans. And something from her uncle, who would be looking down on her. Paulie would want Paula to have music in her life. When the time came, she would buy her piano lessons and whatever else she wanted. It was as though Lola's life had suddenly revealed another dimension, one she hadn't realised even existed, and she was taking the first steps into this wonderful new world. *I am a grandmother*, she thought. Now she understood why all those women she knew made you look at photographs of their grandkids.

At the doorway of her flat, there was a man sitting on the step. His long legs folded out of the way, cowboy boots sticking out onto the pavement, his tight jeans making him look awkward and uncomfortable. Under his baseball cap, his eyes were closed. Oh my God.

'Richie Taylor,' she said. 'Of all the gin joints and all the small provincial Irish villages in all the world...'

His eyes opened, a smile dawning on his sleepy face. 'Miss Lola O'Hare. Well, fancy meeting you here.'

Now, he was a sight for very sore eyes. He looked tired from his long journey, but if there was a more attractive man on this planet, she was yet to meet him. Or a nicer man, she thought.

'I thought as I was in the neighbourhood, I might drop in,' he went on. 'Pay my respects.'

'I'm so glad you did. Would you like to come in?' Her heart was beating out of her chest as he stood up. He towered over her and he kissed her, just like he had that first time, and she thought she was going to explode all over again. 'I've missed you,' she said, her voice not sounding like her own.

'You know,' he whispered huskily, 'you've never said those kind of sweet words to me.'

'Well, it's true. I missed everything about you. Your guitar playing, your cooking, the way you sing badly in the shower, how good you are with your hands...'

He smiled. 'Now, why don't I show you what I can do with my hands?'

And she shrieked as he scooped her up and carried her to bed.

55

PATSY

Life was no longer frightening, Patsy realised. Being scared, holding yourself back, not forging ahead was often a choice. *I am here*, she thought, *and I am going to live wholeheartedly, I am going to enjoy every moment.* For the first time in her life, Patsy wasn't looking back at everything she had lost, worried about future losses, about other potential crises, she realised that she was just happy to be here, and she wasn't going to waste a moment. The birth of little Paula had been such a beautiful reminder that these precious hours and days we spend on earth should be treasured.

'I'm still here, Jack,' she had said. 'I'm one of the lucky ones.'

She had got herself dressed and eaten her toast for breakfast and looked at the birds on the feeder. *Hello birds*, she had thought. *Thank you for being there.* With the help of her friends, all the sewing had been completed.

Killian had organised a van to come and collect everything – all the folded curtains, the cushions, the chairs upholstered by Valerie – and Patsy walked to the hotel that afternoon to see how it was all coming together.

When she headed into the foyer of the hotel, she almost gasped. The room looked almost exactly like the one Patsy had sketched all those weeks ago. Flora's wallpaper had been beautifully hung on the wall behind the desk, the seating at the windows had been sanded and polished. The book nook, with the little view out on to the side courtyard, was exactly as she imagined. The armchairs, upholstered by Valerie, were already in place, the walls painted a light plaster-coloured pink.

Patsy turned around, taking it all in, savouring the moment. She wasn't going to waste her life looking for the mistakes, picking holes in the design, she was going to see it for the gorgeous room it was. It looked magnificent. There were three days to go until the opening; she and Flora had made it.

'Patsy?'

She turned to see Dermot, smiling at her.

'How lovely to see you,' he said.

'Hello, Dermot...' She found herself smiling back.

'Admiring your handiwork,' he said. 'I have got to say, it looks wonderful... hotels can be such awful places, but this is really lovely. *I'd* even stay here...' He smiled again.

'I'm really pleased,' she admitted. 'I hope Killian is too...'

'Oh, he's cock-a-hoop,' said Dermot. 'Seems unusually enlivened by this project. I think he's met someone. Hasn't mentioned it to me, but I can tell. His *eyes* look happy. Haven't seen that in him in quite a while.'

'Flora too,' said Patsy. 'She's looking happier... a lot happier.' Being creative does that to a person, realised Patsy. You got fixed along the way.

Dermot rocked a little on his sandals, as though wondering what to say next. 'Would you...?' he began, just as Patsy started to speak. 'No, you go on. Please,' he encouraged her.

Life is for living, Patsy reminded herself. *Life doesn't frighten me.*

Bring it on. All of it. Work, creativity, fun, laughter, adventure. Every single drop.

And love. She wanted it all. No more thinking she wasn't good enough, no more hiding away.

She smiled at him. 'Would you have time for a cup of tea? We could go across the road to Alison's café?'

'As long as there is a slice of Victoria sponge going,' he said. 'I saw them earlier and they have real cream in the middle.' He gave her his arm to slip hers into. 'I couldn't think of anything nicer.'

They sat opposite each other in the small nook she had designed a lifetime ago for her interiors course, a pot of tea and two slices of cake in front of them.

'So, anything strange or interesting happen lately?' Dermot was pouring the tea.

Patsy found herself smiling. 'Life is always strange and interesting...'

'If you're lucky,' he said.

'Well, my daughter's ex-husband was arrested for fraud...'

'Good God!'

Patsy found herself laughing. 'Yes, so life has its way of keeping you on your toes.'

'It does indeed. Now, shall I tell you what I've been doing?'

'Please do.'

'I've been researching the best route to the south of France. If we leave next week, it will take two days to drive and we will be in Avignon for a glass of wine by 6 p.m. I have found a lovely little hotel by the bridge. Two rooms. And we drive the Luberon valley. All we have to do is have a good time. You'll be my guest.' He popped some of the cake in his mouth. 'Would you like to come?'

Patsy nodded. 'I would like that very much.' She smiled at him again.

Dermot smiled back. 'Well, then, I will do the booking and I would say this is the kind of strange and interesting I like.'

'Me too,' said Patsy. 'Me too.'

56

FLORA

Edith came with Flora to the Garda station where she had to give a statement regarding everything she knew about Justin.

'You have nothing to worry about,' said Edith, as they stood outside the building. 'In all my various brushes with the long arm of the law, I find when under questioning, just stick to the facts, refuse to be intimidated and never, ever accept a cup of tea if you are offered one.'

'Why ever not?' Flora couldn't imagine what on earth Edith might be suggesting. 'Do they *poison* them?'

'No,' said Edith with a shrug. 'It's just a fact that members of *An Garda Siochana*, our glorious police service, are not known for their tea-making skills. Part of their recruitment tests involves making a cup of tea and if it's too good, they are rejected.'

Flora laughed. 'I almost believed you,' she said, as Edith preened a little. 'Why are you so happy, anyway?'

'Well,' said Edith, 'you remember my pastry-chef lost love? What I hadn't told you was she was back in Sandycove... and after a little... persistence, also known as loitering...'

'Careful,' said Flora. 'You could get arrested for that.'

'Well, we've reconnected. Lots of walking, talking...' Edith played with the scarf around her neck. 'She bought me this.'

'It's beautiful.' Flora was so happy for Edith. In all the years she had known her, this was a whole new lens through which to view her. Edith had developed a happy kind of strut, a bounce in her step, as though she was walking on air.

'And cakes,' she said. 'She has brought back cake into my life. For years, after she had left for Paris, I couldn't touch the things. The thought that she was far away making the blasted things, while I was sobbing my heart out in the Women's Studies department was too depressing. And now she's back, I can eat them again.'

'Wait...' Flora's brain was sifting through the clues. 'It's Sally-Anne? From the bakery?'

Edith was nodding. 'Old school friends, then partners, then exile... and now togetherness.'

If Edith was anyone but Edith, Flora would have hugged her.

'That's wonderful,' she said, instead. 'It's so romantic.'

'What's for you won't go by you,' said Edith. 'Isn't that what they say? And Sally-Anne has been for me and I for her, since we were sixteen. Us girls from Sandycove are able to weather any storms, are we not? It's because we grow up by the sea, we don't wait for fine weather, for blue skies, to crack on.' She looked up at Flora. 'Now, this won't help you make that statement, will it?'

'No, but I feel less nervous,' said Flora.

'Well, let's go in there and you tell them everything. We'll make sure the awful man gets what he deserved.'

Flora nodded, swallowing. To think that she was married to him. To think that she had *loved* him. It was time to move on and build a *much* better life, one on her terms. No more waiting for other people to fulfil their dreams. It was time to get on with her own.

'By the way,' said Flora, 'you mentioned all your run-ins with the law... what have you been doing?'

'Oh,' said Edith, 'mainly protests. Women's rights, that kind of thing. Handcuffing myself to the railings outside of men-only golf clubs. I threw a kumquat at a professor who said that women weren't as academically able as men...'

'A kumquat?'

'It was all I had left in my fruit bowl,' said Edith, matter-of-factly. 'Another time, I lay in front of a politician's car who had refused to support a women's refuge. I had to be carried off by two policemen. They were actually really very nice to me and told me they were completely on my side. We ended up sharing a Chinese takeaway in the cells.' She shrugged. 'The world of the haberdashery was quite the retreat from all my activism.' She smiled at Flora. 'Now, ready to go in and spill the beans on Justin the criminal?'

Inside Sandycove Garda Station, they were asked for their names.

'Flora Fox,' she said. 'Here to give a statement about Justin Moriarty.'

'Edith Waters,' said Edith.

'Flora Fox,' said the man, speaking as he wrote it all down. 'To give statement. And solicitor Edith Waters.'

Edith and Flora gave each other a look, before going into the interview room, where Flora told them everything she knew, handed over the photographs she had taken, recalled dates, even drew the layout of the study and labelled where everything was.

The Garda was impressed. 'Nice drawing,' he said. 'Do it professionally, do you?'

'She does,' said Edith, proudly. 'She's a professional designer.'

'You can tell,' remarked the Garda. 'This is quality work this.

We normally get an indecipherable scribble. This is very helpful indeed.'

Edith gave Flora a nudge and a nod. 'Told you,' she said. 'Now, these Garda know what they are talking about. Renowned for their refined taste, artistic sensibilities and their love of the aesthetic world.'

The Garda was taking it all in. 'We do our best, Ms Waters,' he said. 'I mean, we have to know about everything.' He smiled. 'Now, would you both like a cup of tea before you go?'

Edith and Flora burst out laughing. 'No, but thank you,' said Edith, primly. 'We must be on our way.'

57

PATSY

The whole village had been invited to the hotel opening. Outside, tables had been set up with icy glasses of champagne and black velvets. The window boxes were festooned with tumbling pink flowers. Everyone gathered in front of the ribbon which had been strung across the front door.

Patsy hadn't slept very well, her mind active with a million checklists. Were the curtains hanging perfectly? Did the colours work as a whole? Was there space to move around? Did it work as a hotel reception, a meeting area, a place to relax?

Over the last three days, she and Flora, along with Dermot and Jacques, and Lola and Richie had worked to finish the reception. The curtains draped perfectly, lightly skimming the floor, the cushions on the banquettes inside the bar were plumped, the rugs were positioned exactly, the books on the shelves were artfully placed and Flora's wallpaper was pasted to the wall. It looked magnificent and truly breathtaking.

Now, Patsy and Flora stood arm in arm.

'We make a good team, don't we, Mum?' said Flora.

'The very best,' said Patsy, giving her a squeeze.

'Well, if it isn't the most talented designers in Ireland...' They turned to see Killian behind them. 'I've been admiring everything all day,' he went on. 'And I love it. Totally Sandycovian, don't you know?'

Patsy and Flora laughed.

There was the sound of a glass being tapped. Killian was standing in the doorway of the hotel. 'Ladies, gentlemen, *Sandyco-vians*... welcome to the opening of your new hotel... a place where I hope you will gather for food and drink, which you will see as an extension of your own homes. I have to thank Patsy Fox for her incredible work on the reception area. Patsy has very kindly agreed to work as a consultant for the rest of the hotel and the bedrooms and bar area will replicate Patsy's designs throughout the hotel. Also...' He turned to Flora. 'We were lucky enough to be able to use the bespoke designs of Flora Fox. She created a brand-new design which you'll all be able to see now...'

He gave Flora the quickest wink, Patsy noticed. She turned to look at Flora who was smiling up at him. Her daughter did not look like a woman whose soon-to-be ex-husband was facing a fraud charge. In fact, she looked happier than she had looked in years.

Lola was standing with that tall, good-looking American man, his arms draped around her shoulders, his chin on the top of her head. You couldn't take your eyes off her, thought Patsy. Charisma. Star power. She had it in buckets.

Dermot stepped into the space beside her. 'Sorry I'm late,' he said. 'I just had to pick something up.' He handed her a paper bag. 'A guidebook to Provence...' He smiled.

She found herself smiling back. Forget fear, forget all the things she had lost in life. She had the world's most amazing daughter, she lived in a wonderful community, and she was about to embark on a trip with a really lovely man.

'I'm ready,' she said.

58

LOLA

At the opening of the hotel, Lola's swimming friends were talking about currents, tides and swells. Nora spoke once of being pulled out of the inner harbour, as though she was being tugged by an invisible rope. Catríona told a story about being nudged by a seal as though it wanted to be stroked like a dog and Brenda recalled once being spun around in a small whirlpool which had formed.

'Some would say,' said Nora, 'that was a portal to the underworld...'

Brenda laughed. 'I felt like I was being sucked down a plug-hole,' she said. 'Maybe the underworld is just a giant drain.'

Lola watched as, across the room, Doodle Matthews talked to Richie. 'So, the mandolin is basically a guitar?' she was saying, her head on one side, smiling up at him.

Richie was showing her the different strings on his instrument, how the curved back gave a resonance to the sound. 'Once I found the mandolin,' he was saying, 'there was no going back. It's like finding the right person, your soulmate...' He lifted his head, and found Lola, fixing her with a look that rooted her to the spot.

She returned his look, thinking how lucky she was to have found him. How lucky she had been in life, to have Kate, and now Paula. You could make mistakes, she thought, but you were luckiest of all if you could make things right.

And then Richie was walking towards her, his eyes still on hers, as though he wanted to take her to task. But there was something about the way he held his jaw. Not anger. Something else. He looked more determined than she had ever seen him before. He stood in front of her, taking her hand. 'Excuse me!' His voice lifted above everyone else's in the room. 'Excuse me, folks...'

His hand was warm and big, covering hers. Maybe he was going to request another song? She tried to think what she hadn't already performed and what people might want to hear. She looked around for a glass of water, you couldn't lubricate your voice on whiskey and ginger ale.

'Sorry, folks,' went on Richie, 'it's just that I have something to say... something to do, if I could have a moment of your time... because...'

The room was silent, everyone looking over, listening.

'I met this woman a couple of years ago now, and it's safe to say she drove me wild. I think that many of you will understand what I mean when you meet someone and they blow you out of the water...'

Beside Lola, Catríona and Brenda nudged each other.

'That's next,' said Catríona, making Brenda giggle.

'I mean,' said Richie, 'it was like drinking the most incredible glass of bourbon. I'd spent a life drinking good liquor, fine liquor, but then there was this...' He smiled at Lola. 'And it was so fine, so nuanced, so damn interesting, that I was ruined.'

Typical of Richie, to be so kind and complimentary. He was always so generous with how he considered other people, never jealous or petty, just happy for others, never comparing himself with anyone else. You could learn a lot from Richie Taylor. Lola was still trying to think of a song when Richie dropped to one knee. There was a collective gasp from the crowd, a hushed anticipation, delight suddenly palpable.

'In front of all these fine people,' Richie was saying, 'I wonder if you might consider me as a life partner, someone to walk this life alongside you? I promise to be your best friend, to mind you and take care of you. I even promise to get better at making all this Irish tea business. It's an art, I hear, but one I will master. But, most of all, I would just like to love you. All the time... forever, until the end of our days.' He smiled at her, and Lola felt her insides collapse, like a soufflé.

Someone cheered, a few others began clapping and Doodle Matthews was fanning herself, as though she had suddenly broken into a hot flush.

'Lola O'Hare,' said Richie, extricating a small box from the pocket of his slightly too-tight jeans, 'will you marry me?'

Inside was a golden band with three small diamonds in a row. For some reason, she felt like crying as she nodded. 'Yes,' she was saying, as he rose to his feet, taking her in his arms. 'Yes, yes, yes...'

And he kissed her again, that deep kiss that he did so well, his hands on her face, those gentle but strong lips. The crowd had broken into cheering and foot-stamping.

Richie was still looking at her, smiling now. 'I love you, Miss O'Hare,' he said. 'Always have, always will.'

'I love you, Richie Taylor,' she said, smiling back, her heart lifted.

Adrenaline again, thought Lola, *you can't beat it. The good thing about it is that it can be found everywhere, you don't have to be on stage to feel this good.* She looked around for Kate, and there she was, smiling back at her mother. They looked at each other for a moment, saying everything without saying a word, blessing each other, loving each other, the past put to bed, wrongs put right. Things were going to be different, very different indeed. She'd been given another chance.

59

FLORA

Edith and Sally-Anne were standing, both with a black velvet, near the brand-new reception desk, when Flora went over to them.

'Sally-Anne was admiring your beautiful wallpaper and fabric,' said Edith. 'I was telling her I will be selling these in the shop. Now you won't be working for me any more...'

'You're sacking me?'

'No, you'll be working from the shed in the garden...'

'Well, formerly a shed,' said Sally-Anne. 'Now a very nice office space.'

'I've had it done up,' explained Edith. 'I want you to have it as Flora Fox HQ. On one condition...' She wagged a finger in Flora's face. 'I want to see more of your designs. I want to sell them in the shop, and I want your mother to make some ready-made cushions for me to sell, that's if she wants me to.'

Flora was nodding. 'Yes,' she said. 'Absolutely. Yes.' It was as though she had found a new-old self. You were never the same as the *old* you, but could always be a better version. You could never give up on yourself. Always believe. That's when it all went wrong, when you stopped believing.

'Ah,' said Edith, 'here is the man himself. Mr Walsh. He looks like the cat that's got the top of the milk. It's beautiful, Killian... isn't Flora's wallpaper beautiful?'

'It's gorgeous,' he said. 'I can't take my eyes off it. Transforms the space, it really does. And...' He looked at Flora, beaming in that way he seemed to have permanently adopted lately. 'Do you think, Flora, that you could create more wallpaper for my other hotels... and fabric, of course?'

'I think that could be arranged,' said Flora.

'You look happy,' said Edith, peering up at Killian. 'Relief at the end of a project? Or something else?'

He laughed. 'Something else, actually.' He began to blush under the weight of the gaze of Edith and Sally-Anne.

'He's won the lottery,' said Sally-Anne.

'Kind of,' said Killian.

'He's discovered the meaning of life,' suggested Edith.

'Right again,' said Killian, who seemed now almost giddy, and was still blushing.

Flora wondered if the object of his affections was at the opening. She looked around the room for a woman holding a cat on a lead, or someone who looked nice enough to deserve him. She realised that even if she had started to develop feelings for him, she had to focus on herself and her next steps. And she wasn't ready for romance. Her last one had derailed her spectacularly; she couldn't let that happen ever again. Instead, she was going to be happy for him.

'Now, Killian,' said Edith, 'I wanted to talk to you about who you wanted to provide the hotel with cakes... I was thinking of Sally-Anne here...' She slipped her arm through Sally-Anne's, drawing her closer.

Flora drifted away, finding other people to talk to. Everyone from the village seemed to be here, talking, laughing and drinking the free fizz and black velvets with a fervour not seen since The Rolling Stones took over the Chateau Marmont in 1976.

I love this place, she thought. She couldn't think of anywhere else she'd rather be. Now, if Kate could be persuaded to stay, to settle here in Sandycove with Paula and Jacques, then life would be perfect.

Flora stayed later than anyone, wandering and talking, meeting old friends and new friends, including Ailish and Lewis, and some of the women from yoga. She had a feeling of complete safety and security, as though she was back where she belonged, as though she was in the right place, had found the right path again.

Later, much later, Killian found her.

'By the way,' he said, 'Ashanti Elaine is recently returned from a drumming seminar in Ahascragh. She was sorry not to be able to make the opening but she called me earlier and can meet you tomorrow? I can come with you if you like?' Killian went on. 'If you need moral support...'

Flora shook her head. She had to do this on her own. 'I'll be fine,' she said. 'Honestly...'

'Sure?'

'Sure.'

'I was wondering if I could walk you home?' he said. 'I've got something to say.'

Maybe he wanted to give her advice about the divorce, about what she should say to Ashanti Elaine the following day, so she found herself nodding, and they left the hotel together. The sky was still light, and the starlings were singing their hearts out in the trees as they turned on to Sea Road. For a moment, Flora felt a little strange. She wanted to say how much she'd enjoyed meeting him... but she felt awkward. 'Are you happy with everything?' she asked.

'With the hotel or with life? The answer is yes to both. It's been amazing to meet everyone... and the fact Dad seems happy is great. Gets him off my hands...' He smiled at her. 'And you? Are *you* happy... with everything?'

'Definitely.' Whatever was going to happen, she knew she could handle it: Justin's trial, getting a divorce, starting over.

'Look,' he said, 'you know I've been going on dates...'

'And I'm really happy for you...'

He nodded. 'It's... well...' He stopped in the street. 'I've discovered there's one person I would like to ask out... I don't want to make things weird if she doesn't want to be bothered by me. And if she isn't interested, that's absolutely fine, I can take rejection. I'm a grown-up. Mostly. But I've also been alive for long enough to know sometimes you have to seize the moment... because... well... it's just that...'

'You've met someone?'

'Only, she's probably not interested...' He looked at her. 'Are you?'

'Me?'

He nodded. 'I don't want to make things difficult. I like you... more than anyone I have met for years... I mean, I don't want to say "ever", but I think it actually could be... but I'm getting carried away. I've had three glasses of champagne and I'm not a drinker... but... I wanted to say that I like you, and I'm interested, and if you like me and you're interested, then great, and if not, that's great too. Well, not great. But fine. That would be fine. Disappointing. A little dispiriting. But if you don't take a chance, what are you left with?'

Flora had started to laugh, feeling happiness spread through her. 'Well,' she said, 'I'm interested. I mean, I've got a lot to do, to sort out...'

He nodded. 'Of course...' But he was smiling, that beaming smile that made him look even more handsome, and the exact opposite to Justin. His hand brushed hers, and then somehow his hand was around hers and they held hands for the rest of the way. It felt completely normal. More than normal, it felt completely right.

All those bad decisions she had made didn't matter. All that mattered was the one she was making now, and this time she knew she was on the right path. She almost felt as though she was floating.

'By the way,' said Killian. 'I have a very important question...'

'Such as what is my star sign? Libra. My car? I don't have one. Or my job? I'm working on it.'

He shook his head. 'Dog person or cat person?'

'Dogs,' she said, grinning back at him. 'Every single time.'

And they kissed. And she knew she would never have to make herself feel small for someone else ever again.

60

KATE

Paula fitted exactly in her arms. She'd never thought she'd be a mother, and now here she was with a daughter. She kept waiting for the nurses to take Paula away from her, to say that she wasn't doing a good job and someone else would be much better. But they didn't. And Paula was putting on weight – quarter-ounces at a time – and slowly this tiny scrap of a thing was looking stronger and healthier, her skin turning to a healthy pinky glow. Kate spent all day with her in the neonatal unit, expressing milk, changing her, dressing her in tiny white soft Babygros, and falling utterly in love. She'd never felt anything like it. Obviously, she was in love with Jacques, but this was a love she'd never experienced, a furious, beautiful, uncomplicated love.

No one ever tells you, you fall in love with your baby, she thought, as she walked quickly along the long corridors of the hospital to see her, butterflies in her stomach, excitement building. She would see that little face again, feel her little body in her arms.

Jacques was equally smitten. He was staying in the camper van while Kate was in hospital, and he would drive in from

Sandycove every day, bringing food, books, chocolate, whatever he thought Kate would need.

'I can't believe it,' he said, gazing at Paula, when he arrived that afternoon. 'It's a miracle.' He smiled at Kate, as though amazed at how everything had changed.

She nodded. 'It's mind-blowing,' she agreed. And then, 'So, you are *happy* about this?'

'Of course!' He looked puzzled.

'But you said you never wanted to have children.'

'So did you! I would have talked about it if you had wanted them, but you were so sure...'

'That was another lifetime ago...'

'But I love you, I love Paula, I want to look after you, make sure my girls are happy and safe. I thought we could find somewhere to live, just the three of us. Make a home, be happy... what is it? Live happily ever after?'

Kate laughed. 'That's the dream.'

'A nice dream, no? A good one to aim for?'

She nodded. 'A very good one to aim for.' She looked at him. 'So you want to live together? With us?'

'Of course!' He looked shocked that there might be an alternative. 'I want to live with the two of you. Always. I can cook and clean, I can mend cars, and do... what's it called? Doing it yourself?'

Kate nodded. 'DIY.' She was smiling to herself, though.

'I won't give you a moment's regret if we can be together as a family.'

A family. She liked the sound of it. 'There is one person I would like to have a family with and that's you,' she said. Family was taking on an expansive definition. She'd thought she was alone in the world, but along with Paula and Jacques, she also had Lola, now the doting grandmother.

They hadn't decided where to live yet. They *could* go back to Saint-Sauveur, but Kate wanted to stay and Jacques was more than happy to agree. The thought of saying goodbye to Flora and to Patsy, or leaving the Honeysuckle Warblers, was awful.

'Sandycove is a nice place,' Jacques said. 'And if we can find a decent bakery and a cheese shop, then it might be bearable.' He smiled at her. 'France is a ferry away.'

'I want to stay,' said Kate. 'Here, in Sandycove. I want to stay right here.'

'Well, then,' Jacques said, 'that is what we shall do.'

'But first,' she said, 'I need to call someone…' She borrowed Jacque's mobile phone.

'Rosslare Filling Station. Marie speaking.'

'It's Kate… and I just wanted to let you know that I had a healthy little girl. Well, she was premature, but she's doing really well.'

'Well, good God and the saints! I've been worried *sick* about you! You were so pale that day. I watched the news to see if you crashed and then that man turned up and… well, there ye are. A baby! Wait a minute. FRANK! FRANK! SHE'S HAD THE BABY! WHAT DO YOU MEAN WHO? THAT GIRL! THE ONE WITH THE VAN!' She came back to Kate. 'He's away with the fairies that one.'

Kate smiled at Jacques and felt completely happy for perhaps the first time in her life. *This moment*, she thought, *remember this moment and guard this feeling and these people with everything you have.* 'Everything all right with you, Marie?'

'Well now, it couldn't be better, so it could. My eldest is home next week. In from Perth. And my second eldest is joining her in Dubai. Don't ask me how, but they say I'm not to worry. And so we'll have a full house. Frank will be around to keep the station going. WON'T YOU, FRANK!'

'We'll come and see you soon,' said Kate.

'Now, don't leave too long. It's only summer for a bit, and then it's back to the rain and we're all better in the sun, aren't we? Mind yourselves now,' said Marie, and she was gone.

61

FLORA

'We need to place an order,' said Edith, coming in from the back room into the shop.

'I'll do it now,' said Flora.

'You have all the details, do you not?' Edith stood beside Flora. 'I would say thirty metres in both colourways and I think we could offer the wallpaper, don't you?'

'I don't think she does wallpaper,' said Flora. 'I think it's—'

But Edith interrupted. 'She does. I've just seen it on the wall of the hotel. It looks beautiful... I want to sell it in the shop. Ask her if she is doing a range of napkins and tablecloths?' She was smiling at Flora. 'So, you contact the designer... Flora Fox is her name, I think.'

Flora felt tears spring to her eyes. 'I'm not... well, I suppose...'

Edith was nodding. 'I am looking forward to seeing them on the shelves.'

The bell on the door rang as a customer walked in. 'Ah,' said Edith, 'we were just talking about your lovely hotel...'

It was Killian, smiling at them both.

'And I'm very proud of this young lady.' Edith smiled up at

Flora again. 'I've commissioned some for the shop. All she needs now is a good divorce lawyer and she can move on with her life. What did I say, Flora? Is the six weeks up yet?'

'Definitely,' said Flora.

'If it's a divorce lawyer you're after,' said Killian, turning to her again, 'I have the very best in the country. She does it part-time these days. She's a yoga teacher now...'

'Not *Ashanti Elaine*?' Flora asked.

Killian nodded. 'She used to be called Acid-bath Elaine because of how easily she used to be able to dissolve marriages... all that would be left would be the valuable assets spiralling around the plughole...' He gave Flora a look. 'She managed to get me through my divorce... without her, I wouldn't have survived. You need someone on your side. I'll give her a call, if you like.'

'I like the sound of this Acid-bath yoga woman,' said Edith.

Killian nodded. 'That's how I started going to yoga. I was wrung out from my divorce, fifty per cent of my assets gone... and she said I should join her class. Next thing I knew, I was doing a headstand and humming. I hadn't felt more sane in years. And if you are going to have someone fighting your corner, it may as well be a woman who can switch from devastating divorce lawyer to incense-burning hippy within a matter of moments.'

'My kind of superheroine,' said Edith, approvingly.

'I'll call her,' said Killian, looking at Flora. 'If you want me to?'

'She does,' answered Edith. 'And Flora, I will come with you to any meetings or hearings. We will make sure you are protected from that monstrous miscreant, and get what you deserve.'

Killian nodded. 'Me too,' he said, but he was smiling at her. 'But first, she needs feeding. Dinner. The Sea Shack this evening? I am thinking lobster with garlic butter and some hand-cut shoe-string chips, and a very nice white wine and an ice cream sundae for dessert. What do you think?'

Flora was already nodding. 'I think I could find room in my diary.'

'It's a date,' he said. 'And hopefully my last.' They grinned at each other.

'What is it that Virginia Woolf said?' Edith was looking at the two of them. '*One cannot think well, love well, sleep well, if one has not dined well*? Whether it is lobster or cake... eat well and the rest will follow. Now, Flora, why don't you take the afternoon off to come up with a business plan to show me. We need to get you going.'

And that's exactly what Flora did, as well as visiting Kate and Paula and of course Jacques, who took Paula for a walk along the hospital corridors while Kate and Flora talked, returning with whatever food he could find in the cafeteria. He'd procured what was labelled a 'ham baguette' which he examined carefully, as though it was an object he couldn't quite recognise. Kate and Flora watched as he took one chew... and chewed... and chewed. 'I can't swallow it,' he said. 'It's as though it is not actually food.'

Kate and Flora laughed and Kate's hysteria turned into quite worrying crying, causing Flora and Jacques to become concerned for her. Eventually, she managed to get control of herself again. 'It must be all the hormones,' she said.

Abigail arrived with flowers and crocheted booties and shawls from the ladies. 'They are all dying to see Paula,' said Abigail, who then took hundreds of photographs to show them when she returned to Honeysuckle Lodge. 'And,' she went on, 'no pressure, but if you were thinking of staying on at the Lodge and working with the ladies... part-time obviously, more choir and whatever... then we have the little house in the orchard. It's been painted, cleaned, new kitchen and we're waiting for the plumber to come in to check the new shower is working and we're good to go.' She smiled at Kate. 'It's just until you find your feet. And I was thinking, when you are up to it, if you would like to work with the ladies, we can all mind Paula at the same time. I've spoken to them and they are thrilled at the idea.' She looked anxiously at Kate. 'I know the ladies would love it... as would all of us.'

'Yes,' said Kate. 'I'd love it too. Jacques is going to work as a freelance for a while, writing a column for his old paper and whatever else turns up.'

Lola and Richie had arrived then, with more clothes that Lola had bought and a bag for Jacques. 'From the French bakery in the city centre,' she said, handing it over. 'Run by a French woman.' Jacques received it gratefully. 'But we're going to have to try you on Irish soda bread,' went on Lola. 'With butter. See if we can't change your mind. Richie is already sold.'

Richie nodded happily. 'I'm staying just for the bread,' he said, giving Lola a sidelong glance. 'No other reason.'

Kate turned to Flora. 'I have something to ask you,' she said. 'I was hoping you would like to be Paula's godmother? We'd be honoured, wouldn't we, Jacques?'

He nodded. 'Absolutely.' He smiled at her.

'I couldn't think of any role I'd rather do,' said Flora.

62

LOLA

Lola hadn't been to the graveyard since Paulie's funeral, but Kate had insisted they would go. Lola was due to fly back to California to talk with a film producer about her song. Zachary had phoned from Maui with the news. The thought, however, of leaving Kate behind, along with the beautiful Paula, was awful.

'I don't want to go,' said Lola. 'I'm not going...' She felt tearful and had been trying to tell herself that she still had music to make and a life to live. But Kate and Paula, and of course Richie, were all that mattered to her.

Kate was pushing the pram beside her, while Lola tried to organise her thoughts and control the rising emotion. She didn't want to cry, not in front of Kate, and make it all about her, when Kate had only been out of hospital for a week.

'So they like the song, then?' Kate was saying.

'Apparently they do,' said Lola. 'It's going to be the theme of this big new film...' She shrugged. It didn't really matter, she thought. Success was this: walking with her daughter and grand-daughter, talking, being together. This was what made a person happy, that deep, inner contentment. When she fell asleep at night now – with Richie beside her – she thought of Paula's face or something that Kate had said earlier and she held them both close in her mind. She slept deeper than ever.

'Well, it sounds amazing...' said Kate. They were on Sandycove's main street.

'But...' Lola paused.

'But what?'

'I'm going to miss you,' she said.

Kate looked at her. 'I'm going to miss you too.' They held each other's gaze, taking in their faces, how similar they were, how much they had been through, together and apart. 'But your life isn't here, is it?'

'It could be...'

'You're not ready to retire... not yet...'

'No, not yet...' Lola admitted.

'It's not forever,' went on Kate. 'You can come back and see us. We'll come and see you?'

'Will you?'

Kate nodded. 'Of course.' She smiled at her mother. 'I wouldn't miss it. Any of it. I'll even come and see you perform.'

Lola laughed. 'Now, you've lost your mind.'

Kate shrugged. 'I've heard you're very talented...' She slipped her right arm through Lola's, and they both took a handle of the pram. 'Now, are you hungry?'

'I thought we were going to Paulie's grave?'

'I thought we might bring him some chips,' said Kate, giving Lola a look. 'You know how much he liked them.'

Lola laughed suddenly. 'We should,' she said. 'I think he'd like that.'

* * *

They sat on a bench, Paula sleeping in the pram beside them, a paper parcel of salty, hot chips between them. 'Paulie Finnegan, musician, aged sixty,' read Lola. 'Not a bad sixty years.'

'I don't think he would have appreciated the half-dead carnations,' said Kate.

'Probably his mother's handiwork. I wouldn't say she has green fingers. The old wagon.'

'Well, nor do you,' said Kate. 'And she is your mother.'

Lola gave a laugh. 'Well, you can't blame mothers for everything.'

They smiled at each other.

'I'm going to buy a house in Sandycove,' said Lola. 'For me and Richie to stay in when we come back. And if there is anything I can give you, let me know. I have some savings and I would like to buy you a house... what do you think?'

'Thank you,' said Kate. 'That would be amazing. I feel so lucky.'

'What's mine is yours,' said Lola. 'You were there from the beginning.'

'Money would help as I would like to do a teacher training course... there's one starting in September.'

'What kind of teacher?'

'Music,' said Kate. 'Don't know where I got the interest from...' She winked at Lola. 'I'll miss you,' she went on, 'when you go back to LA... but this time I want you to go... because...'

'Because I'm coming back,' said Lola.

'Yes.' Kate took another chip. 'And Paulie, we love you, we miss you, thank you for being there for us, for all those years.'

Lola nodded. 'Best brother...'

'Uncle,' said Kate.

'Best brother and uncle ever. Thank you, Paulie.' She turned back to Kate. 'Thank you for giving me another chance.'

'The feeling's mutual.' Kate smiled back at Lola and Lola felt another tear well up and splash onto her chip. She popped it into her mouth before she lost it completely.

That evening, Lola and Richie went over to the cottage in the grounds of Honeysuckle Lodge, where Kate and her little family were now living. Jacques had made dinner and, with Paula slumbering in her Moses basket, they sat outside by the old orchard.

'How did we end up with two such fine men?' said Lola, smiling across at Richie, who was sitting on the ground, in front of Lola, his back against the bench. She could feel his arm against her leg.

'I was saying the exact same thing to Jacques,' said Richie. He pronounced it 'Jack', which for some reason only made Lola love him more. 'How did we find such beautiful women?'

Kate laughed. 'He's so smooth...'

'Just like wine,' said Lola, taking another sip. 'Is this the last bottle from the Auberts?'

Kate shook her head. 'There's still four to go. And then, we're going to drive back for a visit. Stop off in Rosslare and then back to Saint-Sauveur. We want everyone to meet Paula... and to bring some wine back with us...'

'It's not a bad road all the way to France,' said Jacques. 'My Joséphine did it...'

'His car,' explained Kate to Richie.

'There's just a bit of sea in the middle,' went on Jacques. 'Easily traversed...'

'The world is smaller than it was,' said Lola. 'We're all closer than ever. Leaving isn't the same any more.'

'It's not as bad,' said Kate, who reached out her hand and took Lola's. 'We're together apart.'

'Together apart,' murmured Lola.

'I hear a new song being formed,' said Richie, leaning against her playfully. 'I think the old creative juices are flowing.'

'Talking of juices flowing,' said Lola. 'Jacques, let's have another glass of wine. And then that's me for the evening. Richie and I will leave you three to it.'

'I have a cheeseboard,' said Jacques. 'And they are all *Irish* cheeses.' He raised his eyebrows, as though he could hardly believe it himself.

'You mean the French aren't the only ones who can make cheese?' said Kate.

'I'm learning a lot,' replied Jacques. 'But wine?' He shook his head. 'No. Never.'

'*Vive la fromage*,' said Lola, making Jacques laugh.

'Yes!' he said, delighted. 'Another song, perhaps?'

Lola shook her head. 'I don't think that's got Grammy winner written on it, do you?' She nudged Richie with her leg.

'Oh, I don't know,' Richie said. His hand felt warm on her calf. 'There are many surprises to be found in life. You never know how things can turn out.'

The four of them sat in the fading light, talking of life, love and music, of future visits, holidays and celebrations.

Paulie, thought Lola, *I know you're looking down at us, so just to say we love you, we miss you and thank you.*

Up, Lola, she thought she heard him say, *I'm looking up at you. And I love you too.*

And there was his laugh, just like it always had been, and she smiled to herself.

* * *

LOLA O'HARE COMES HOME FOR NUPTIALS TO MUSICIAN RICHIE TAYLOR

By Shazza Keegan, chief reporter for The Sandycove Newsletter

There was a big party in Sandycove with family and famous pals.

The bride wore silver. The groom wore cowboy boots.

Lola O'Hare and hunky fiancé, Richie Taylor, flew in from Newport Beach for their big day and drove straight to the honeymoon suite in The Sandycove Arms. The rain which had threatened to halt proceedings desisted and the wedding party were blessed with almost Californian sunshine.

For the week leading up to the big event, Sandycove was full of long-haired musicians, walking along by the sea and eating fish and chips before teaming up with locals for long-into-the-night sessions. 'Bluegrass-meets-greengrass,' said one regular. 'It sounded pretty good.'

There were two bridesmaids – Lola's daughter, Kate, and her granddaughter, Paula, who slept the whole day in her Moses basket.

The ceremony took place on the beach in Sandycove, and the groom played the mandolin, as the bride, a vision in a long silver dress, walked from the wedding car – an old French 2CV – towards the gathered guests. The celebrant was a family friend, Dermot Walsh, who had just recently taken humanist instruction so he could officiate. His partner is another pal of the O'Hares, the interior designer, Patsy Fox, mother of another designer, Flora Fox, whose wallpaper you may have read has been used to redecorate Áras An Uachtaráin, the president of Ireland's residence.

There were tears and cheers of joy when the couple said 'we do', but there wasn't a dry eye in the house when the bride's daughter, Kate, sang one of her mother's most famous compositions, 'Where There's You There's Me'.

There was a detour to local nursing home, Honeysuckle Lodge, by the wedding party to see 'old friends' before everyone piled back to The Sandycove Arms, where the dancing and music went on until the early hours. One guest refused to give up the microphone and began her own concert of Islanders' songs, much to the guests' amusement.

'A great day,' said Lola, giving her toast. 'A great day in a wonderful life. Thank you all for coming. And as my friend Patsy says, "It takes courage to continue." So here to all of us, may we have courage. May we all continue!'

63

FLORA

The wedding went brilliantly and afterwards, in the early hours, Flora and Killian went back to the flat above the haberdashery where she now lived. Edith had moved in with Sally-Anne, the two taking up residence in the lovely flat above the bakery, which had a roof garden and the constant delicious aroma of bread and cake. 'I'm in heaven,' admitted Edith.

'I am now the number one Lola O'Hare fan,' said Killian. 'I had no idea I knew so many of her songs.'

'Pity Lola didn't sing them,' said Flora. 'Then you might have loved them even more. Doodle Matthews doesn't quite have the voice.'

'But she has the passion,' laughed Killian. 'And the confidence.'

Killian had moved into the flat the previous month and, so far, living with him had been immensely enjoyable. The last man she had shared a house with had been Justin, and this was entirely different – this was actually fun. Every Sunday morning, they went to yoga with Ashanti Elaine in her guru mode. Acid-bath Elaine had proved herself to be a formidable divorce lawyer, just as Killian had promised, and once Justin's family home was sold to pay off his debts, she managed to siphon off a small payout for Flora, just enough to launch Flora Fox Designs.

Justin was currently being held in Mountjoy Prison, awaiting trial. Robert had engaged some extremely expensive lawyers who were pursuing Justin aggressively. The case, as far as Flora knew from phone calls from Robert, was expanding exponentially, as more of Justin's clients looked back over old accounts.

Flora had walked back up to the old house where the new owners were renovating. The pine kitchen was in a skip outside, the wardrobe doors tucked behind them, the pink bathroom suite piled on top.

A woman had appeared from the front door. 'You can take anything you like,' she said. 'If you're one of those skip-diver people.' She smiled at Flora. 'But who would want a pink bathroom or a pine kitchen these days?'

'I quite liked them,' said Flora, as the woman looked puzzled. 'I mean, I quite like them.'

The woman shrugged. 'Each to their own. I can't believe the previous owners lived with it. It was Justin Moriarty, did you know him? He swindled hundreds of thousands of euro off people and yet lived in a time warp... what a strange man. I saw him on the news. His hair was crazy. It looked as though he'd been electrocuted.' She paused. 'He wouldn't have been, would he?'

'I don't think electrocution is a standard disciplinary procedure in Irish prisons,' said Flora. 'But you never know...'

'And he was wearing these stained jogging bottoms, as though he'd borrowed them from the lost property... and... ugh...' She gave a shudder. 'He had bitten fingernails, as though he'd been chewing his hands off.' She stopped. 'Wait, you didn't know him, did you?'

'Vaguely,' said Flora. 'I don't think I knew him well at all.

There is one thing I wouldn't mind taking from the skip. One of the knobs from the kitchen cupboard doors, if that's okay? It's good to be reminded of knobs in your life and to never make the same mistake ever again.'

She was going to put it pride of place, a warning to herself. From now on, she was moving forwards.

Robert had told her that he and Sandra were back together. 'I've forgiven her,' he'd said. 'She was just feeling unloved and, let's admit it, *that man* knows how to put on the charm.' Robert was refusing to mention Justin's name ever again.

Kate and Jacques had left the caretaker's cottage and bought a sunny two-bedroom house in Sandycove with the help of Lola. Jacque wrote his columns from the small garden shed, and grew tomatoes and made bread. Ailish, Killian's sister, was part of the gang who met up for dinners and long lunches and even bread-making classes run by Jacques. The old camper van was parked outside, ready for their next adventure.

Patsy and Dermot were already on their third holiday. After Provence, they had driven the Romantic Road in Germany, taking in the half-timbered fairy-tale villages along the Rhine, and they had just returned from a trip to Sorrento, where they took a boat to Capri and ate octopus and drank local wine. Patsy returned home with a few more design ideas, which she was thinking of implementing in her latest commission refurbing the local pub, The Island. Her curtain-making business had expanded, and she had to advertise for sewers to help her with the business. Dermot had to invest in a large Dutch bike with a carrier on the front to assist with all the deliveries.

And as for Flora's god-daughter, Paula? She was a delight, always with a smile for Flora, who brought her along the seafront for a walk with Killian on Friday evenings, to give Kate a break.

She and Killian ordered fish and chips from the van and were having more fun than Flora thought possible. Who knew that men who didn't need to go on about their hair all the time or need to be the centre of their existence could be exactly what Flora needed?

64

LOLA

Lola and Richie returned to California, but Lola flew back to Ireland once a month to see Kate, Paula and Jacques, staying in The Sandycove Arms.

Jacques, Kate and Paula had now gone to stay with them in Newport Beach, and the five of them spent the time pushing Paula's pushchair along the boardwalk, eating Richie's famous roast lunches, Lola's trifle. Jacques even managed to find a French bakery which he thought was passable. His soda bread was improving and he now made a loaf every morning for breakfast.

But the real reason they had gone to California was so Kate could accompany Lola to the Oscars, where she had been nominated for Best Song for 'Coming Home'. It had been featured in a small independent film, and Lola said she wasn't going to the ceremony without her.

'I've got a dress already,' said Kate. 'It's the one Elise Aubert gave me... it's perfectly good and it reminds me of an evening from another lifetime... it was for my birthday, with Jacques...'

When the night came, Kate looked magnificent. As always, thought Lola. Admittedly, she didn't look too bad herself, dressed in what could only be described as a space-age toga, and appeared, as Richie said, 'like a moon goddess'.

He and Jacques were on babysitting duties and watched the ceremony from the living room in Newport Beach.

Lola hadn't been this nervous for a long time and as she and Kate walked into the theatre, the photographers shouting, 'This way Lola! Lola!' She kept one arm around Kate's waist as they smiled for the cameras.

'Who's your date for the evening, Lola?' someone called.

'My fabulous daughter, Kate,' she said.

'Are you thinking of Paulie this evening?'

'Always,' she replied, as the two of them glided away, arm in arm.

When it came to Best Song and the nominees were read out, she and Kate held hands.

'And the Oscar goes to...'

Lola was feeling calm, as though she was floating, as though awards didn't matter, they were arbitrary strokes of luck. The only thing that *did* matter was love, and the relationships you built and sustained. She and Kate glanced at each other, smiling.

'...Lola O'Hare! For her song "Coming Home"!'

Lola stood and hugged Kate and then the film's producer and the film's star and anyone else that was close by. She did feel like she was flying, as though someone was lifting her up those steps and to the podium. *Paulie*, she thought. *You're here.*

The speech flowed and she spoke of love, of loss, of friendship, and she told the world 'about a village called Sandycove from where I come. It's a small place, full of interesting people who care about each other, who will lift you up and set you on your feet again. And it's a place where love blossoms and where you will find friends for life. To Patsy and Flora, to the Honeysuckle Warblers, to the sewing army – I will see you all soon. To Paulie, I am so glad you are here with me tonight. And to Richie for coming to find me, and to Jacques for minding Kate. But most of all to Kate and Paula, the centre of my world... Daughters make life beautiful. If you are lucky enough to have a daughter, then you have the opportunity for a life full of sweetness and beauty and everything that makes life worth living. Cherish them and cherish every moment!'

ABOUT THE AUTHOR

Siân O'Gorman was born in Galway on the West Coast of Ireland, grew up in the lovely city of Cardiff, and has found her way back to Ireland and now lives on the east of the country, in the village of Dalkey, just along the coast from Dublin. She works as a radio producer for RTE.

Sign up to Siân O'Gorman's mailing list here for news, competitions and updates on future books.

Follow Siân on social media:

facebook.com/sian.ogorman.7

x.com/msogorman

instagram.com/msogorman

bookbub.com/authors/sian-o-gorman

ALSO BY SIÂN O'GORMAN

Friends Like Us

Always and Forever

Mothers and Daughters

Life After You

Life's What You Make It

The Sandycove Supper Club

The Sandycove Sunset Swimmers

The Girls from Sandycove

LOVE NOTES

LOVE IN EVERY CHAPTER

WHERE ALL YOUR ROMANCE
DREAMS COME TRUE!

THE HOME OF BESTSELLING
ROMANCE AND WOMEN'S
FICTION

 WARNING:
MAY CONTAIN SPICE

SIGN UP TO OUR
NEWSLETTER

https://bit.ly/Lovenotesnews

Boldwood

Boldwood Books is an award-winning fiction publishing company seeking out the best stories from around the world.

Find out more at www.boldwoodbooks.com

Join our reader community for brilliant books, competitions and offers!

Follow us
@BoldwoodBooks
@TheBoldBookClub

Sign up to our weekly
deals newsletter

https://bit.ly/BoldwoodBNewsletter

Made in United States
North Haven, CT
26 January 2024

47933177R00183